# GEE'S

## FIRST CASE

# GEE'S
## FIRST CASE

By

*Jack Mann*

RAMBLE HOUSE

Second Ramble House Edition

©1936 by Jack Mann

ISBN 13: 978-1-60543-422-3

ISBN 10: 1-60543-422-1

Published: Ramble House 2006, 2010
Cover Art: Gavin L. O'Keefe
Preparation: Fender Tucker

# DEDICATION

## TO MADGE

"When thyself with shining foot shalt pass. . .
And in thy joyous errand reach the spot
Where I made one. . . ."

V.

*Oct. 9th.*

# GEE'S
## FIRST CASE

# CHAPTER I

## GEES, A GIRL—AND INSPECTOR TOTT

THE ABERDEEN-LONDON EXPRESS had just finished its noisy trundle over the Forth bridge when the waiter in the restaurant-car picked up his *douceur* from the table for two in the corner, and the clean-shaven, pleasantly-ugly young man who had sorted out the coins looked up almost anxiously, as if wondering whether he had over- or underdone it.

"Thank *you,* sir," said the waiter, in a tone that proved the tip over rather than under. "Everything all right, sir?"

"Except—yes, thanks, except the sauce *tartare.*"

"I'm sorry about that, sir. If you'd only mentioned it before—"

"No use, waiter—no use," the young man interrupted. "It was not the mixing, but the ingredients. Contract stuff, of course. Not your chef's fault at all. Now tell me, is there likely to be much bustle and confusion at Edinburgh?"

"Much—?" The waiter looked rather puzzled. "You mean—you're staying in Edinburgh, sir?"

"Not this time, I fear. No. What I meant was—will people be sitting on suit-cases in the corridor when we pull out from the North British? Shall I have to climb into the baggage rack to get peace?"

"Oh, no, sir—it's not likely to be really crowded. End of May—too early in the year. And the middle of the week at that."

"Thanks very much, waiter." The young man got up, revealing himself as of well over average height, and so lanky that he looked even taller than he was. His hands were unduly large, though well-shaped, and, as he made his way to his own first-class compartment in the train, he revealed the fact that his feet were enormous. But his walk was that of a trained athlete, and the way in which he balanced himself when the heavy train swayed proved him an old hand at the game—and almost certainly at other games as well.

He went straight to the rather ancient-looking suitcase on the rack, lifted it down, and, opening it, took out a long envelope. From this he extracted two slips of paper, and, licking the four corners of each slip separately, stuck one on the left hand window at the side of the coach, and the other on the corridor window on the right—that is, the left and right windows considered in relation to the direction of the train. Then he put the envelope back and restored the suit-case to its place: a man whom he knew had provided him with a dozen of these "RESERVED" labels—for a consideration, of course. They were the authentic things, not forgeries.

Then this young man sat back in the corner of the otherwise empty compartment and watched from the lefthand window while the heavy train slid nicely to its thirteen-minute halt in the North British station.

"All," he quoted to himself gently, "was bustle and confusion."

It was. Three irascible men looked at his label: the second of them, the young man was sure, uttered his profanities aloud; the others were more restrained. A worried-looking woman in a fur coat—for there was an east wind blowing across the city from Leith that day—came along, dragging a bad-tempered looking small boy by the hand, and following her came a chauffeur leading another boy and a small girl. The small girl pointed at the young man alone in his compartment, and shrilled in a fashion that made him shudder:

"Here's one, Mummy!"

"No," said the woman. "That's reserved, darling."

"Darling," the young man decided from the woman's tone, was the sort of formality that goes with—"Not at home," and "Must you go already?" There was, he would have said, no kick in it. Then he shuddered again, for the woman was evidently getting into the next compartment: a porter trailed a barrow of small cases and packages behind the chauffeur, emptied the lot into the compartment, and, returning to his barrow, gazed at something in his hand with regret for murder uncommitted in his eye. The chauffeur stayed, probably to arrange packages, and either through the partition or by way of the corridor the young man heard those children begin their respective plaints, an indistinct chorus that was to annoy him in some measure all the way to London.

He looked at his watch: three minutes more, and so far his labels had kept the pass as nobly as Roland at Roncesvalles. Then, hurrying, a trifle anxious by the look of her, the girl came along the platform. She gave him a look of wrath, and he knew she had seen the label: he half-started up to pull it off the window, but before he could complete the action she had passed, and paused before the next compartment, ignoring him and his solitude.

She was tall, he saw, and she had a classic profile: rather pale as to complexion—not too much make-up, he decided—with black or very dark hair showing from under her dainty little hat, and lovely dark eyes—doe's eyes. But she had gone on: it was too late to remove the label and invite her in, now. And there were signs that departure was imminent: men stood about with flags and things and looked terribly important, or looked at their watches; porters went along the platform with empty barrows, and a gentle hiss of escaping steam sounded from somewhere under the coach. A warning whistle shrilled.

"Any more for the shore?" the young man murmured to himself.

Then, faced toward the engine as he sat, he saw this girl of his dreams almost running back alongside the train, looking into each compartment eagerly as she passed it. Moving at the limit of his agility, he tore that damned label off the window—and saw her get into the next compartment with the woman and three children as the final whistle sounded and the train began to move again.

"Still," he told himself, "if I hadn't put 'em on, that woman in fur would have dragged those three abominations in here on me, so what have you? And it's a long way to London, yet."

The consideration he had accorded to the situation may be judged from the fact that, when he arrived at this conclusion, the eastern sea was visible and North Berwick not far away.

"Judging by the chorus next door," he meditated again, "she's having a thin time. And those eyes were simply marvellous!"

He looked up. She stood in the corridor, gazing in on him: by the way in which her left arm hung down, he concluded that she had brought her little, black morocco dressing-case out from the next compartment on emerging from it. He crossed his compartment and opened the corridor door. She was looking past him, at the left-hand window.

"Can I help you at all?" he asked.

But she nodded at the window. "It had one on too," she said, ignoring his question. "I'm sure it had, at Edinburgh."

"Yes," he confessed, "but I took that off when I saw you coming back. And then you preferred next door."

"If I have to go back to those children, I shall die," she declared. "That woman ought to have taken a special train."

"Do come in here," he begged. "I've got it all to myself, and—and there's the communication cord if you get frightened."

She entered with a smile at him and a slight shake of her dainty little head. He took the morocco dressing-case from her.

"Facing, or back to?" he inquired.

"Which do you prefer?" But she glanced at the seat facing forward, and he took down his own ancient case and put hers up in its place.

"Oh, but you shouldn't!" she protested. "It's your seat."

"But I want it down." He put the case down on the seat, opened it, and took another label out of the envelope. "I don't know where or how we stop on the way," he observed after licking the corners of the label and sticking it on the window where its predecessor had been, "only that we're due in at nine-fifty-five to-night at King's Cross. And there might be other woes travelling like those three next door. Do sit down, please! I only sat there because of the scenery, and I'm not interested in it any more, now."

She seated herself, and he took the corner facing her. "Do you always do that?" she queried, nodding at the label.

"It's practically infallible," he answered indirectly. "Of course, I'd no idea you'd be travelling by this train. If you'll let me know in advance next time, I'll hold it on the end of a stick at the North British and take it down when I see you."

Her forehead wrinkled in perplexity, he saw, and at the sight divined that she was questioning whether she had done right in coming into this compartment. Then the children next door shrilled again.

"I feel sure I've seen you before, somewhere," she said abruptly.

"Holding up the traffic, probably," he answered. "I couldn't have seen you, though, or I should have let it go. On point duty."

"Do you mean you're a policeman?" she demanded sharply, and the perplexity in her expression gave way to a transient fear.

"Well, look at my feet," he counselled. "You see, the Army doesn't want brains, and the Law doesn't want common honesty, and the Church doesn't want anything. So when I suggested the police force to my father as a profession, he agreed there might be something in it."

"And now"—she sounded rather trepidant over it—"you're a detective, I suppose?"

"Worse—far worse." He felt in his breast pocket. "I spent two sad years in the force, but now—" he took out a card and offered it to her—"look at that! Blossoming out—what?"

She took the card, and he estimated that his hand could hold six of hers, easily—she was dainty from head to foot. She read:

---

GEES

CONFIDENTIAL AGENTS

Consult Gees for Everything
From Mumps to Murder!
37, *Little Oakfield Street,*        *Initial Consultation;*
*Haymarket, W.*        *Two Guineas.*

---

She frowned heavily over the card, and offered it back to him.

"Keep it," he urged. "You might need to consult me."

So she put the card in her handbag. "You are a representative of that firm, you mean?" she asked.

"No—I'm it," he assured her.

She took the card out again and looked at it. "But—it's them, surely?" she inquired. "Gees—plural."

"They, you mean," he corrected her. "No—they are me—I mean, I'm they—that is, it. Gees. It. Me—I mean I."

She reflected. "It sounds—well, irreverent," she observed.

"No, only half. There isn't any plural," he assured her. "Gees—it stands for Gregory George Gordon Green—me. I, I should say."

"Do have an aspirin!" she begged suddenly.

"Do I look like a dope fiend? No, really, it is my name."

"They are, you mean," she corrected him. "But they must have chloroformed you to make you take it."

"No—they chloroformed the vicar."

"Oh, this is awful! What vicar?"

"The one who christened me. They had to operate twice to remove his stutter. My father managed to say it all right at the font, and wasn't a bit affected afterward. At least, so they told me later."

"And you really were a policeman?"

"Not then. When I grew up. Two years of it. But—well, I ought to have gone into the army. There's too much discipline in the police force for anyone like me. It's put me agin the law."

"How do you mean that?"

"Well, you know—all this organisation and—take lottery tickets. Though it's getting almost difficult to take them. The law! Damn the law! And people go in for crime as if it were an amateur affair. They don't realise what an organisation there is against them, built up and systematised as it is. Crime ought to be organised—people ought to train for it properly if they mean to go in for it. Burglars' colleges, night schools for forgers—proper equipment and all that sort of thing. It's no use trying to conduct a big industry in a casual, haphazard sort of way, when you've got that intensive, systematised police opposition to face. All these untrained people, each working alone! What they need is a co-operative system, and proper training."

"It sounds almost sensible, as you say it," she reflected.

"It *is* sensible!" he insisted. "I was in the police force long enough to know what the ordinary and generally altogether untrained criminal is up against. Crime doesn't pay—an old truth, but true only because crime isn't properly run—isn't systematised."

"And this—this confidential agency you talk about?"

"Oh, that! Well, you see, I've only just started it. Must do something, you know. I've got an office and a secretary, and went all the way to Aberdeen in the hope of getting a case. But it wasn't. When I got there, they said my fees were too high."

"How disappointing for you!" she said sympathetically.

"But I might have known," he pointed out. "Aberdeen."

For awhile they sat silent: a ticket-inspector came into the compartment and, with his little punch, relieved each of them of a fraction of the weight they had to carry to the end of the journey. He had gone his way when, looking toward the corridor, Gees saw an unobtrusive sort of man, in a lounge suit of the fifty-shilling vintage, pass the compartment slowly and make such an elaborate business of not looking in as to render it certain that he was. Gees waited hopefully, and sure enough the man returned along the corridor after a brief while, and took a good, hearty look at the pair in the compartment in passing.

"New to his job," Gees observed. The girl had been looking out of the window abstractedly, and had not seen the man pass at all.

"What was that?" she asked, turning her beautiful dark eyes his way.

"A man should know his job," Gees amended, and hoped she had not fully comprehended his original observation. "Like me, for instance. I do a couple of years study at police work, make myself thoroughly conversant with it, and then launch out as a whole police force on my own. In my little office—initial consultation, two guineas. Now what could be fairer than that?"

"I don't know," she said vaguely and abstractedly, and resumed her survey of the landscape to the east. As they were now approaching the grimy industrial vicinity of Newcastle-on-Tyne, Gees felt sure she must have something on her mind: nobody, he knew, would wilfully scrutinise that outlook with the idea of imprinting it on the memory.

But he left her alone, for the time being. That individual who had walked along the corridor and back was, he knew, what he would have termed a disfrocked rozzer: in plain English, a policeman who had only recently been put on plain-clothes work. This was quite probably his first plain-clothes job, and, by the way he had looked in here, he was making an awful hash of it. He might not be specially interested in the occupants of this compartment, but, on the other hand, it appeared that he had them under observation to some extent.

Reviewing his sins, Gees came to the conclusion that the man could not be detailed to watch him: that rather flamboyant card announcing the existence and purpose of the confidential agency was not yet a month old, and though anything of the kind, as Gees knew from his experiences with the force, was highly unpopular—and all the more so since he was stealing police thunder to a certain extent, having walked out after absorbing as much of procedure and methods as he could—they could have nothing on him yet to justify putting a man on to watch him. Besides, knowing as one Inspector Tott knew that Gees was not nearly such a fool as he looked, they would have put on a more efficient type of man than this, had they wanted to watch him.

Unseen by the girl, he gave her an unbiased scrutiny—that is to say, though he admired her type, he put admiration in the background for the purposes of his survey. Clever—yes, the forehead indicated it: extremely self-possessed—yes, as he had already seen: attractive enough to be very dangerous to the average man: a trifle unscrupulous, for she had appeared to approve his views regarding the necessity of organising crime in order to render it profitable: quite a woman of the world, in spite of her apparent youth, as she had proved by her manner in entering his compartment. Altogether, he decided, the really charming type of girl one always hopes to meet, and always misses meeting. But, in order to prove that rule, his luck was in.

If that fat-headed loon in the corridor were really watching her, what was her little game? No decoy for an ordinary crook enterprise, Gees felt sure, for she was far too expensively attired and too good style in herself for that. Political? But the political game, in spite of assertions in thrillers to the contrary, is not aided by that type, for she was innocent of Mata Hari allure or suggestiveness. He was deliberating over other possibilities when she turned her head and nearly caught him studying her: she did not quite catch him at it.

"Are you one of the Shropshire Greens?" she asked abruptly.

"No, just a Green Green," he answered. "You know— family supplied the name, and Providence weighed in with the nature."

"I once met a man on the boat who talked so much about the Shropshire Greens," she explained. "Forgive the question."

"Oh, easily," he assured her. "Did you say *the* boat, though?"

"A cross-channel boat," she explained again, but managed to convey by her tone that she did not like the question. Gees divined that her admission of having been abroad was involuntary, and already regretted. Yet everybody went abroad nowadays: there could be nothing in it.

"I didn't know there were any special Shropshire Greens," he observed, with a view to putting her at her ease again.

"Lots," she said ironically. "Village greens, you know."

"But I'm a town Green," he countered promptly.

"Like the one at Paddington—green no longer," she suggested.

"I've never known my name to be so really productive before," he remarked. "It appears to have lasted us all the way from North Berwick, and we haven't really started on derivations and ways of spelling it. And now I think of it—did we stop at Berwick?"

"Oh, don't be so appalling!" she urged impatiently.

"But I really didn't notice!" he assured her. "Can you wonder at it? I was engrossed in talking to you, and nobody came in on us."

She glanced at his label still on the window. "No," she assented. "Nobody. I expect you have a *Bradshaw* in that nice new office of yours. Consult it when you get there, and find out if we stopped."

"I'll ask my secretary to look it up the instant I get in to-morrow morning," he promised. "It shall be a first duty. Meanwhile, do we tea? I feel that tea is one of the fondest things I'm of, at this moment. Will you come along to the restaurant car with me?"

She shook her head ever so slightly and smiled at him. "It's very nice of you, but couldn't we have just a pot in here? I had a very good lunch, and don't wish for anything to eat."

She was keeping out of sight of that fifty-shilling-suit rozzer, he reflected, as he pressed a bell-push. No, though, she had not seen the man. Perhaps she disliked walking along swaying corridors. He ordered a pot of China tea for two when the attendant appeared in answer to his ring, and, when it arrived, marked the way in which she filled the cups just to the right height and no further. A practised traveller, evidently, used to trains—and boats.

"You live in London?" he inquired, after a sip at his cup.

"Oh, look!" She pointed through the window with her free hand. "An aeroplane! Flying in our direction, too."

"Service plane," he announced, after a glance through the window. "A de Havilland Fighter—no, it's a Fairey. Nice buses to handle."

"You fly, then?" she inquired.

"I've done a bit—got my ticket and all that. You see, supposing I got an inquiry in at my office about flying— someone wanted to steal a plane or crash his rich uncle? I have to be in a position to advise."

She gazed ahead through the window. "It's nearly out of sight, now," she remarked. "Did you ever meet Schroder?"

"That Russian chap with a German name who put up those records last year," he observed. "Can't say that I have. Do you know him?"

"I read about him," she answered evasively—he felt sure it was an evasion. "Richthofen was killed in the War, wasn't he?"

"I believe so—yes. And you said you do live in London?"

"No." The framing of the question, as he realised as soon as he had uttered it, invited her inconclusive answer.

"But I do want to see you again!" he pleaded.

She smiled. "Neither did I say I did not live in London," she said.

"Then my luck is in! You do!" He made it an accusation.

"Sometimes. I've been—away—and I don't expect to be there long this time. This is—" she hesitated—"just a visit, say."

"Couldn't you manage to come and consult me about something while you're there? I'd waive the fee for the initial consultation. I only put it on to keep away the people who might think I'm a sort of workhouse infirmary. The something-for-nothingers."

"I don't know. I must think about it," she said demurely.

"The address is on the card—it's the third floor. I chose the furniture myself, and it was delivered in plain vans."

A little frown of perplexity indicated that the final slogan meant nothing to her. She spoke perfect colloquial English with no trace of accent of any kind, but, coupling up her query regarding the famous Russian ace with this ignorance of a catchword nearly everyone used, he began to question—was she English? Her Parisian *ensemble,* her delicately pale complexion—was she, or was she a foreigner fully conversant (apart from that one slip) with English life and ways?

A little later, an attendant entered the compartment and removed the tea-tray: after he had gone, the girl spoke hesitatingly:

"I wonder if you'd mind if I put my feet up and rest for a little while? I've had such an exhausting day—"

"Why, certainly!" he hurried to assure her. "Just a second—if you'll move out of the corner, along the seat a bit."

Rising, he reached down his suit-case and dust-coat from the rack. He placed the suit-case in the corner in which she had been sitting, made a loose roll of the coat, and put it on top of the case.

"Head rest," he explained. "Try it and see if it's right."

She lifted her feet on to the seat, smoothed down her skirt, and lay down with her head on the coat. "Just nice," she said.

"Excellent! Shall I get a table booked in the restaurant-car and waken you in time for dinner?"

"How nice of you! If I find it possible to sleep, that is."

He composed himself in his corner opposite her, and, seeing that she closed her eyes, let his own gaze travel along her as she lay. Little hands—dainty little hands: equally little feet—

"What are you thinking about?"

She had opened her eyes again, he saw.

"What tiny, beautiful hands and feet you've got—and my own tremendous far ends," he explained. "If we could only shake 'em up together a bit, now—"

But she started up. "That's a brutal insult!" she exclaimed.

"Please, I didn't mean it to be," he pleaded humbly. "I didn't mean anything insulting. Only that—that Providence had blessed you with lovely feet and hands, and been cruelly lavish to me. Do forgive me, please, so I can forgive myself."

She composed herself on the seat again. "The apology is accepted, for this once only," she said coldly.

As she closed her eyes again, he did not reply. With that sharply uttered reproof, she had given herself away as not English—the pronunciation of the word "brutal" had betrayed her. Gees had once heard Hillaire Belloc lecture, and now he noted in her trick of saying the word just such a variation from fully English speech, as he had heard in some words uttered by the great author. No, not English.

She was really asleep, he decided. An exhausting day— what had she been doing before boarding this train at Edinburgh? She looked perfectly healthy, not one who would become exhausted over a trifle.

He sat brooding, and the great express rushed southward.

They dined together at the corner table for two at which Gees had lunched. The evening was serene and luminous—when they went down by Peterborough, he saw the smoke rising straight into the air from the tall brickworks' chimneys. And, when they returned to their compartment and heard again the horrid sounds of youth from next door, Gees looked at his suit-case in the rack. Yes, it had been moved in his absence, and probably thoroughly overhauled, for he had not locked it. He thanked the fifty-shilling-suit rozzer for the attention, mentally, and wished him luck. There was nothing questionable in the case.

Then they went thunderously through the tunnels beyond which King's Cross awaited them. Gees took down the morocco suit-case and put it on the seat beside the girl.

"Thank you," she said. "Now I want to ask you—when I get out, let me go away alone. Don't go with me."

"But I was hoping to see you all the way?" he protested.

She shook her head. "No, let me go alone."

"May I see you again?"

"I don't know. If so, I have your address."

"And I don't even know your name!"

"That is true." But she did not tell him the name.

Her eyes were soft, lovely. "May I kiss you?" he asked.

"If you do, I shall instantly pull this cord, and give you in charge as soon as the train stops."

She meant it, he knew. Her eyes were still lovely, but no longer soft in expression. She was fully determined about it.

"I apologise—again," he said.

"You ask every girl that, of course," she asserted.

"On my word, only one other, at a first meeting. The one who is now my secretary. And she wouldn't, either."

"So you made her your secretary, in the hope that she would relent?"

"On the contrary," he dissented, "because I knew she wouldn't. You can't have that sort of thing in your office."

"Neither am I cheap," she said cuttingly, and took up her case. For the train was slowing alongside the platform, then. "And I go my way alone from here. Thank you for all you've done—and more for what you have not tried to do. For the present—good-bye."

Then there was just a hope, he reflected, as he let her precede him out to the platform, that she meant to see him again. Just a hope!

He saw the woman with three children, looking as if it were the last day and she knew the worst, but he had no pity for her—let her find a porter for herself! Then, at the exit from the platform, he saw something else that drew all his attention.

The fifty-shilling-suit rozzer, probably getting out from the front coach, preceded the girl past the end of the platform, and made a little signal that Gees, through his police experience, recognised, to one of two men standing together and looking along the platform as if they had come to meet somebody. When the girl passed out, the rozzer, in view of the two men, made another barely noticeable signal, and at that one of the two—Detective-Sergeant Johns, Gees knew—left his companion and followed her.

So fifty-shilling had been keeping watch on her, and now Johns was taking up the trail! But evidently they had nothing on her, or, with three of them available, an arrest would have been effected there and then. Suspect, for some reason, but no case proved against her.

Well, he himself had been asked not to follow her, and perhaps it would be as well to comply with the request, on the whole. So cogitating, he passed out from the platform, and a voice arrested him—that of the well set-up, alert-looking man (he might have been a prosperous young business man, but Gees knew he was not) who had been waiting with Detective-Sergeant Johns:

"I say, Green?"

"Utterly incorrect, Tott," Gees retorted, turning on him.

"What do you mean, man?" the other demanded sternly.

"Oh, you can't scare me now," Gees told him serenely. "If I'm merely Green you're merely Tott, not Inspector Tott, to me. And I mean it's utterly incorrect to address me with 'I say,' when evidently you don't say. You haven't said. Besides, it's uncooked."

"What on earth are you talking about, man?" Inspector Tott snapped.

"Uncooked—not done. I thought you knew that one. It's really not polite to address a man as 'I say,' even if you did have him in uniform and make him salute once—"

"Oh, don't waste my time! Look here, I'm going to give you one word of warning, my lad, and it's the last."

"Say not so, Tott," *Gees* urged, with undiminished serenity.

"That silly business of yours—that silly office and pretty secretary," Tott pursued without heeding the persiflage. "We couldn't quite make out what you were up to with it, but now I see the sort of company you keep I have an idea. I warn you, watch your step. You've been one of us and know what we can do and can't do."

"You don't approve of my company, eh?" Gees asked interestedly.

"Oh, don't try to come it over me! You know perfectly well that wherever that woman goes she takes trouble with her—and you so careful not to be seen leaving the train with her, after the two of you had had a compartment to yourselves all the way down! This is my final warning to you—watch your step!"

"About a thirty-three inch pace, except when I'm in a hurry," Gees retorted gibingly. "And a fairly light tread, in spite of my big feet. Good night, Tott—don't dream about me."

He turned away and sought a taxi.

"Bees in the bonnet—bats in the belfry," he murmured to himself. "What a lovely recreation alliteration is!"

# CHAPTER II

# FATHER

HAVING paid off his taxi at the top of the Haymarket, Gees walked to Little Oakfield Street, which involved little more than a hundred yards of exercise, and let himself in at number 37 after assuring himself in ways that his police experience had taught him that he had not been followed. If Tott had put the fifty-shilling man or anyone else on to follow him, the sleuth had given it up when it came to the utter seclusion of this street. For, though London roared about its pleasures less than a hundred yards away, Little Oakfield Street was entirely deserted at this hour of ten-thirty, or thereabouts.

Gees walked up to the third floor—the building was old, and there was no lift—and took out another key before a door which bore a nice new brass plate, on which was engraved:

GEES
CONFIDENTIAL AGENCY
HOURS: 10 to 5
SATURDAYS: 10 to 12.30

He entered, closed the door, and went into the first room on the right of the corridor—his secretary's room. The flat consisted of four rooms and a bath: two of these apartments, both on the right of the central corridor, were devoted to office work—if ever any work should materialise. The rest, on the other side of the corridor, formed his home, and when he had told the girl in the train that the furniture had been delivered in plain vans, he had spoken the truth. In ten days the next instalment was due on the hire-purchase account: father would have to stump up again.

He put his suit-case down on the floor of the secretary's room and gazed at the "IN" tray on her desk. Empty, of course. The tray labelled "OUT" was similarly innocent of contents. Then, opening an unlocked drawer in the desk, Gees took out a large Letts diary on the front of which was pasted a square of paper inscribed—"DAY

BOOK." He opened it, and turned to the date of his departure for Aberdeen, three days previously. From there he read to the last entry, easily:

May 23rd. Arrived 10 a.m. G. to Aberdeen. Left 5.10 p.m.

"Thank God she doesn't charge overtime!" Gees murmured piously. He read on:

May 24th. Arrived 10 a.m. Left 5.5 p.m.

"Didn't even wash," Gees commented again. "If she did, there's no record of it. When she got home, probably. Poor girl—a thin time of it." Again he read:

May 25th. Arrived 10 a.m. 12.30 p.m., Rev. Ambrose Smith called. Codderlewbar Vicarage, Wilts. Scandal in village concerning self and schoolmistress. Urgently in need of advice, but declined to pay consultation fee. Informed him G. expected back to-morrow. Promised to call again then. Left 5.0 p.m.

"Will he call again?" Gees remarked to himself as he put the book back. "Will he hell!" he added, as he slammed the drawer closed. "But it looks as if those 'Personal' ads are going to fetch them."

He took up his suit-case, and, entering one of the rooms on the other side of the corridor, gazed at the neatly turned-down bed awaiting him, and then espied an envelope on the dressing-table, stood up against the mirror so as to catch his eye. He dumped the case on the floor at the foot of the bed, took up the envelope, and withdrew the single sheet of paper it contained and read:

"General Green wants you to ring him instantly on your return. He rang up three times to-day. E.M.B."

The initials were those of his very pretty secretary, Eve Madeleine Brandon. He put the note down on the dressing-table, threw his hat on the bed, and scratched his head reflectively.

"Bless her little heart!" he mused. "Put it where I couldn't miss it, of course. But do I go and see him to-night, or do I leave it till the morning, after the day I've had?

"Oh, may as well go and get it over!"

With that decision, he retrieved his hat from the bed, ascertained that eleven o'clock was still a thing of the future—though not the very far future—and, going to the room which constituted his own office, took off the telephone receiver and dialled a number. A woman's voice answered the call, a voice he knew.

"Oh, Symonds? Mr. Gordon speaking. Is my father in?"

"Yes, sir. He's asked about you several times to-day."

"Tell him I'll be round in ten minutes or less. That's all, Symonds—good-bye." And he replaced the receiver, retrieved his hat, and went down the stairs and out again.

It was less than ten minutes walk to Dawgeley Square, where General Green occupied one of the few houses that have not yet been pulled down to make room for those slums of the rich, the modern blocks of flats which rise like glorified workhouses all over Mayfair. Symonds, the elderly, efficient-looking woman who had answered the telephone, admitted Gees to the house: her rather sympathetic expression denoted that obtaining his next instalment on the hire-purchase furniture in Little Oakfield Street might give him some difficulty.

"He's in the smoking-room, sir," she said solemnly.

Thither he went. A man tall as himself, but not nearly so lanky, rose from an armchair and put down the book he had been reading.

"At last!" he said, inhospitably.

"Sorry, Father. I've been to Aberdeen about a case."

"About a case? What case?"

"Oh, it doesn't matter. I didn't get it. Fees too high."

"Of course you didn't get it!" The elder man spoke with slow, barely repressed bitterness, and kept his voice low and well under control. "You'll never get anything—except ridicule." He reached out and turned a morning paper on an occasional table beside his son. "Yesterday," he said, "an old friend drew my attention to this—look at it!—in the 'Personal column' there. One of those who know your nickname, unfortunately. I couldn't tell him it was not you."

Gees dutifully looked down at the paper, and saw the amplified contents of his card—such a card as he had given the girl.

"There was no reason why you should, Father," he said.

"It's disgraceful! Thank God you didn't put your real name on it, or everybody would have known about it. I tell you, sir, I won't have it! I consented to your going into the police force, hoping to see you an assistant commissioner, with the brains you have and the education I've given you. But you fling that career away—and now this! This infernal nonsense! What good have you ever been? What have you ever done? What do you expect such poppycock foolery as this to do for you? Look at it! 'Mumps to Murder!' Was there ever such blasted nonsense?"

"But I believe in alliteration, Father," Gees protested gently.

"I made inquiries about you to-day—never mind how. You've got a girl in that flat in Little Oakfield Street who might have done well in the front row of the chorus, even if she can't act. If you want to keep a mistress there, for heaven's sake keep her! But don't advertise yourself as the biggest ass in London, for it's not necessary. Confidential agent! Who the devil would put any confidence in you, an ex-policeman who fired himself when he got tired of being one? Now look here, Gordon! Keep that girl on in the flat if you like, but stop these disgraceful advertisements, at once."

"You're making totally unjustifiable aspersions on a lady's character, Father," Gees pointed out gently. "And besides—"

"Oh, blast the lady's character!" his father exclaimed with heat.

"No, that's just what I don't want done," Gees expostulated. "You see, she's my secretary, in a perfectly virtuous way."

"Well, cut her out, then, if you're getting nothing out of it. I was going to point out to you—the Shropshire estate needs a man like you to manage it—we should get half as much again if you went down there and took charge, instead of leaving it to an agent. Why not cut out this infernal nonsense, go down there, and take over?"

"Because it really doesn't appeal to me, Father," Gees pleaded ever so gently. "The charms of country life don't get me. I'd much rather give my agency a fair trial—"

"Blast your agency! Of all the preposterous, impossible, insane ideas ever born of a softened brain—"

"But it isn't. I haven't had time to—"

"You've no time at all to withdraw those ludicrous advertisements," the general interrupted sharply. "It's got to be done at once."

"And supposing it isn't done?" Gees asked.

His father felt in his pocket, took out a shilling, and dropped it on the newspaper. "The conventional thing," he said. "Yours, in that case. You inherit two hundred a year from your mother that I can't touch, and from me you inherit this, if you persist in this—this insanity. The Shropshire estate can go to your cousin."

"Lucky little Bill—he never expected it," Gees observed, and took up the coin. "Father, I know a nice little pub round in Shepherd's Market. Let's go and blue this, and I'll toss you who pays for the other half-pint. I've got a thirst, and you must have one too, after saying all that. Shall we?"

The general gazed at his son, and his fierce eyes softened.

"Damn you, boy, you've got your mother's ways! But about this, mind you, I'm adamant. Give up the folly, and I'll say no more. Persist in it, and that shilling is the last from me."

"Still I'd like to buy you a beer with it, Father," Gees persisted.

"You mean you won't abandon this folly?"

"You've got a will—I've got a will," Gees retorted. "You've got the money—I've got the agency. We're keeping what we've got, each of us. And what could be fairer than that?"

"And the shilling, if I understand you rightly, represents a pint and a half of beer," General Green said quietly. "Well, boy, don't get drunk on it. There's the door—good night."

"Good night, Father."

He went out and back to his own flat. It was, he knew, a Rubicon that he had crossed, for his father meant every word of that warning, and the symbol of the shilling was final, ultimate decision. But Eve Brandon would have to look for another post if he closed down the office, the girl of the train might call vainly, and, worst of all, he would be owning himself beaten, giving up before he had fairly begun.

"Poor old father!" he said to himself as he undressed. "He'll grieve an awful lot, I know, but he'd only have thought me a weak-kneed pup if I'd given in. And I'm not giving in!"

Thinking it over as he ate the good breakfast his charwoman brought in to him—he took no other meals in the flat—he renewed his determination to carry on with the business. Those advertisements had already brought one inquiry—and from as far away as Wiltshire!—and though he felt fairly certain that the distressed vicar of Codderlewbar would not make a second call, the office might be crowded with other applicants for confidential advice—at two guineas apiece—by the end of the day. Father, of course, was a bit old-fashioned: military point of view, too. But one simply had to be progressive and up-to-date and all that sort of thing in these times—or give it up and go mud-dodging in Shropshire. Ugh!

And she had asked if he were one of the Shropshire Greens!

He poured his final cup of coffee as an accompaniment to the after-breakfast cigarette—the best cigarette of the day—and knew, from the sound of a typewriter cover being removed in the room across the corridor, that Eve Madeleine was settling to do nothing for the day, because there was nothing to do. He always thought of her as Eve Madeleine, and always called her "Miss Brandon" when speaking to her. Some day, he feared, he would get the two sets mixed, and call her "Miss Madeleine," or "Eve Brandon." Then, either there would be trouble, or he would look a bigger fool than usual.

When he had first seen her full name on her insurance card, he had longed to ask her if she really belonged to the Smith family, but had refrained. Ever since she had proved her fitness for secretary-ship by declining to be kissed, they had got on well together, but Gees knew he must never take liberties, either with her name or anything else.

He drank the last of the coffee and crossed the corridor to her room, the one nearest the outer door. She sat at her desk, and, lowering the novel she had been reading, looked up.

"Morning, Miss Brandon."

"Good morning, Mr. Green."

As always happened when he first saw her at the beginning of the day, he felt that he had chosen his secretary wisely. She was tall, but not over tall; her features were piquantly irregular, her eyes a good, normal shade of blue, and her hair brown with reddish lights in it; her chief attraction consisted in expressiveness, both of eyes and lips, though—as Gees knew—she could present a perfect poker face at need. As, for instance, when he had asked if he might kiss her, and discovered that he might not.

"Have we got a *Bradshaw* on the premises?" he asked her.

"An *A.B.C.,*" she answered, "but not a *Bradshaw.*"

"Well, she said a *Bradshaw*. There's no urgency about it—she's not likely to turn up here in an indecent hurry. Get one when you go out to lunch, and find out for me if the 2.5 from Edinburgh stops at Berwick. That's all about that. I went through the day book when I got back last night. That parson won't come back, I fear."

"I came to the same conclusion," she said.

"No. Now I wonder—ought I to go out and lasso a few two-guineaers and drag 'em in? But then, I'd probably rope the wrong ones, not being a Tex McLeod. I think we'll intensify the advertising campaign. Something's got to be done—Oh, thanks for putting that note where I couldn't miss it, Miss Brandon. My father threw me out on the cold world last night, and even carried the melodrama to the point of handing me the conventional bob. I'm having it framed, since he wouldn't come round the corner and mop it with me. But it means that something undoubtedly has to be done—somebody, I mean."

He advanced into the room and seated himself on the corner of her desk. "If not," he added, "the plain vans will come for the furniture, and you and I will have to sit on the floor till the landlord comes and throws us out because the rent isn't paid. Don't get worried yet, though—the next instalment isn't even due for another ten days, and quarter-day is years distant. Now to business."

"You mean the Aberdeen affair?" she asked hopefully.

He shook his head. "Aberdeen is off. But business, all the same. Miss Brandon, do you recall the legend of Saint Anthony?"

"Tempted by the devil, you mean?"

"Just that. It happened to me yesterday, and my devil was a dream. Not a cold pork and pickles dream, but the one that makes you angry over waking up. She travelled alone with me all the way from Edinburgh to King's Cross— near enough, that is—and she must have been a devil, because Tott was waiting for her when she got out."

"Tott?" she echoed questioningly.

"Ah! I see I must explain. Detective-Inspector Tott. Not a divisional man, but special—with a roving commission. He had to make an arrest in the division I was in—when I was in it—and I was detailed to go with him. I happened to be useful, so he got rather friendly with me—you know, in the way that the managing director gets friendly with the office boy. I mean, he knows me when he sees me. He saw me at King's Cross last night and gave me a final warning. At least, he said it was that. He told me my devil took trouble with her wherever she went, and he didn't like either me or you."

"Didn't like me?" she asked, and sounded rather perturbed.

"Don't get alarmed—I'll protect you. My office and my pretty secretary, was what he said. I will say for him that he's got good taste. But to business. Do you know why the woman took her dog when she went to market?"

She gazed at him doubtfully, and shook her head.

"Because two heads are better than one," he explained. "It's so simple—like the plain van people. Now let's put our two heads together about my devil—I'm not being suggestive, and only mean that figuratively. Discuss her, and see if we get anywhere."

"Yes, I see," she assented. "She travelled with you all the way?"

"Not quite. I'll explain that first. She got in the next compartment, but didn't like imps, although she was a devil. There were three in that compartment, and I don't blame her a bit. She came into the corridor and asked if she might join me, and was I angry? I nearly embraced her on the spot—but that part comes at the end of the story, the reason why I didn't. She got in, and we got really pally. That is to say, I told her all about myself, and some of it was true. I gave her our business card, and after tea she said she'd had an exhausting day and went to sleep—genuinely went to sleep, too—till dinner time. She didn't look as if she'd had a thick night saying good-bye to friends, so why was she exhausted?"

"Was that—the train journey, I mean—the last stage of a longer journey for her?" she suggested.

"Ass! Fathead! Not you, Miss Brandon—me. Of course that was it! Didn't I say two heads are better than one? She'd landed at Leith and caught that train—and the boats that decant passengers at Leith are not altogether luxury liners. Also you couldn't call the sea off the Scottish coast exactly restful yesterday morning—the train runs along the coast on the way down from Aberdeen, you know, and I saw the spray flying up over the rocks. You've hit it, and they considered her important enough to put a disfrocked rozzer on the trail."

"A what?" she inquired in a puzzled way.

"A plain clothes man, then," he explained. "But he was a bad specimen. He wasn't—well, he hadn't the requisite *savoir faire* for the job. Best they had in stock, I expect. Anyhow, he was on the train to keep an eye on her, and he must have got through to London to have Tott waiting at King's Cross with Detective-Sergeant Johns, who is Tott's right hand, as I happen to know. Johns took up the trail from King's Cross—went off after her when the disfrocked rozzer gave Tott the signal that she was the one. Am I making it all plain?"

"Quite plain, thanks," she assured him.

"I want you to know all about it, because I think she'll look me up here—she's got our card. To carry on, now. The rozzer must have got through, I think—you can wire or telephone or something from those trains, I believe, even if it didn't stop at Berwick—and I give you my solemn word, Miss Brandon, that I was so busy talking to my devil that I don't know whether it did or no, but think it didn't. Hence the *Bradshaw* when you go out to lunch, to make sure."

"I could trace it in the A.B.C.," she offered.

"No hurry—let's get on with the tale. We talked, mainly about me. But now—I hadn't any of Saint Anthony's luck. Not only was my devil not out to tempt, but she wouldn't even be tempted. When I made the first advance—in quite a nice way, of course—she threatened to run me in, and meant it. I could see she meant it. Which rules out the common vamp. She was much too expensive to be an ordinary crook or decoy, and didn't act like one. And I don't think she was political, though I'm not quite sure about that."

"What was she like?" she asked.

"Tall—perhaps an inch taller than you are, but not more. Dark, with one of those pale complexions, and lovely dark eyes. Foreign—but you have to get her goat to make her give it away in her speech. Normally, she talks perfect English—but she didn't know what plain van means, by the way she took it. Also I'm nearly sure she knows Schroder, the Russian airman."

"And her name?" she asked after a thoughtful pause.

"She dodged giving it—beautifully. I hoped Tott might give it me when he told me he didn't like the company I kept, but he didn't, either. And she insisted on going off alone from King's Cross, so I let her. Just as well, perhaps, since Johns trailed her."

Miss Brandon thought it over in silence. Gees took out his cigarette case, and she accepted one from it. He lighted both cigarettes.

"Your interest, Mr. Green?" she asked at last.

"Guineas, of course! Foreign, worth Tott's attention—I put this agency before her with mumps to murder emphasised, and she may think we can help—at whatever it is. Bread cast upon the waters—for heaven's sake don't think I fell in love with her!"

"You don't sound as if you had," she reflected.

"One other reason for telling you. I'm going to keep this agency going till it flourishes if I have to sell out all the capital I possess. And from last night onward we've got Tott and his myrmidons all wrong. We're suspect from henceforth, for once Tott gets an idea about anyone in his head, you can't jimmy it out with a crowbar, even. The police are agin us, dead agin us. And we should worry!"

"Yes." The irony in her voice was patent. "You sound worried."

"So do you!" and he laughed. "When I think of some more, I'll come in and tell you, Miss Brandon—keep you posted on our first case, though it hasn't begun, yet." He got off the corner of the desk. "What are you reading?" he added.

"One of Keeler's." She held the book up.

"Ah! Clever chap, Harry S.K. Always manages to get the human touch, somehow. Well, I won't keep you from it any longer. Don't forget that *Bradshaw* at lunch time—I want something to read myself, in addition to finding out about that train stop—or no. And if any ideas occur to you on what I've told you about our devil, just jot 'em down for me to look over the last thing before I go to bed. They may fructify in my brain during the night. Oh, now I remember, she gave nothing away. Nothing whatever."

"And some of what you told her about yourself was true."

"Quite a lot of it. Also she knew there were Shropshire Greens, but I denied my heritage—before renouncing it last night. I knew what my father thinks of the agency, and didn't want her to know I belonged to him. Now I really will leave you to your book, and get on with the *Times* crossword. Must keep the old brain in trim."

He removed to his own room, next to hers, and settled to the crossword at his desk with terrific concentration. But he kept one ear apart from his task, in the hope that the doorbell would ring.

The hope was still unsatisfied when he went out to lunch. When, on returning to the flat for the afternoon, he let himself in, Miss Brandon looked out from her room.

"It didn't, Mr. Green," she said.

"Thanks so much, Miss Brandon," he answered. "Let me have the *Bradshaw*, please. I've finished the crossword."

# CRAPGER III

## CRRISGIRE—RRD JORRS

BY TEA TIME OF THE FOLLOWING DAY—Miss Brandon made the tea, and Gees always took a second cup—all hope concerning the vicar of Codderlewbar had vanished, and Gees had begun to think his devil had forgotten all about the agency. He took his empty cup into his secretary's room, refused another refill, and, returning to his own desk, settled to composing a rather more lurid advertisement which could be edged through the censorship to which "Personal" columns are subjected in most newspaper offices. For there had been no more inquiries in response to the original announcement of the existence and purpose of the agency, and something had to be done.

Suddenly Gees dropped his pencil and had to grovel for it under his desk. The doorbell had rung!

A minute later, Miss Brandon stood in his doorway.

"A lady to see you, Mr. Green."

"Tut-tut, Miss Brandon!" he reproved her. "There are so many, you know. Which one is this?"

"I'm sorry," she answered, "but she declined to give me her name. I think, by your description, though—" She did not end it.

"Show her in, please, Miss Brandon."

The lady of the train entered the room. Since she had refused to give her name, Miss Brandon could not announce it. The door closed silently, and, differently, but just as tastefully dressed, the lady of the train stood before Gees' desk. He hastened to place a chair for her, and then went back to his own.

"Do sit down, please," he urged. "I'm—I'm delighted. I won't say it's unexpected, because I hoped, you know."

She seated herself beside the desk and opened her bag. "To consult you professionally," she explained without preface. "Do I pay the two guineas now, or at the end of the consultation."

"I told you I should waive it, in your case," he said.

"Very well." She closed the bag again calmly. "Now to explain—"

"First," he interrupted, "since it's professional, I must have your name and address, please. It is essential."

She opened the bag again and took out a card which she placed on the desk. Gees took it up and read:

```
┌──────────────────────────────────┐
│                                  │
│                                  │
│      Miss CHRISTINE LENOIR       │
│                                  │
│                                  │
└──────────────────────────────────┘
```

and he noted that the card had been printed from an engraved plate, not from type. Therefore, it had not been procured specially for this occasion at a shilling-a-hundred-while-you-wait shop. And the name made him long to ask if she were a member of the Smith family, but he restrained the impulse.

"And the address?" he inquired.

"London, for the present," she answered.

"Ah! Pretty comprehensive, what? Well, we'll waive that too, though I insist on it in all other cases. Now what is it, Miss Lenoir? I mean, in what way can I assist you?"

"It was something you said in the train, the day before yesterday," she explained. "You gave me the idea then that I might interest you."

He remembered, and nodded a grave assent. "It is perfectly true that crime in a general way is a failure because of the lack of organisation among criminals," he said.

"But I am not interested in crime," she told him.

"I am, intensely," he countered. "From all angles."

"And I am not," she insisted, rather impatiently.

"Ah, but think of all that mighty field of enterprise!" he urged with soulful fervour. "Think of what might be accomplished in it by one with a master mind! One with vision and breadth of aim!"

"Are you interested in humanity?" she asked.

" 'Madam,' " he quoted Micawber from memory, " 'it was the dream of my youth, and the aspiration of my riper years.' "

"Willing to help humanity?" she persisted.

"Well," he hedged, "for a consideration. If humanity likes to come here in shoals, and put down two guineas a head—"

"Oh, money!" she interrupted scornfully. "Yet—of course. But in return for loyalty—for absolutely loyal service."

"That is understood," he assured her. He had placed her, now, almost with certainty: Tott's interest in her, combined with the revelation she had just made, told him so much that he had no scruple in promising anything she might ask.

She looked him full in the eyes. "The temple of the pentagram," she said. "That is, if you are sincere."

She was sincere, he knew: an idealist—a fanatic, probably.

"And where is it?" he inquired after a pause.

She shook her head. "I will tell you no more," she answered. "If you are sincere you will find it—seek till you find it."

Some train of ideas—he could not have told what it was— recalled Detective-Inspector Tott to his mind. "Will you excuse me a moment?" he asked, and, rising, went to his window, which gave on to Little Oakfield Street, and looked out without touching the gauze curtain. And, as he had suddenly realised would be probable, down in the street Detective-Sergeant Johns stood, looking into a shop window which probably mirrored the doorway of number 37. Gees went back to his desk.

"Madam," he said, "it is as I thought. Humanity is interested in you—one item of it is, I mean. Waiting for you, in fact."

"I know," she answered. "I have been unable to shake him off."

Johns would take some shaking off, as Gees knew: he was in a different class from that of the disfrocked rozzer. And Gees himself, whether there were money in it or no, wanted badly to know more about the temple of the pentagram and the people who— possibly—worshipped there. By throwing Johns off her trail, probably, he could win her confidence: besides, after the way Tott had treated him at King's Cross, it would be a pleasure to get a bit of his own back on Johns.

"I assure you it's quite easy," he said. "That is, if you'll trust me. I have a sort of a grudge against that man myself—not personally, but against the man he represents. May I help you?"

"In what way?" she inquired doubtfully.

"To get rid of him," he assured her confidently. "I'll find that temple all right, and we can renew our discussion there, if you will."

She gave him a long look—a facial analysis, in fact.

"Yes," she said at last. "I will trust you."

Since she would be in no worse case than at present if he failed her, it seemed the best course she could adopt—he decided that she had been wise. He rose, and took his soft felt hat from the stand in the corner. "I'll go with you," he said. "You may trust me implicitly. That man is going to be worried—exceedingly worried. Do you mind if I go down first, just to make sure he *is* worried?"

"But what are you going to do?" she asked doubtfully.

"Take you out another way. I must tell you, though, it will cost you ten shillings—a note for preference, since it is to tip a man. I am waiving my fee, but you must pay necessary expenses."

She took a ten-shilling note from her bag and handed it to him.

"Thanks," he said. "Now if you'll go first—I want just a word with my secretary. I won't keep you a second."

He merely opened the door of Miss Brandon's room, and spoke without entering—without seeing her, in fact, since the door prevented it.

"Miss Brandon, if anyone should call before I get back, I have not been in since lunch. And, most particularly, nobody has called."

"Very good, Mr. Green."

He let Miss Lenoir out from the flat, then, and went with her down the stairs to the ground floor. There, with the outer door open, he saw Sergeant Johns still interested in the contents of the window across the road—the shop was devoted to men's underwear—and still more interested in the mirror at the back of the window. But the entrance hall of number 37, Gees knew, was far too gloomy for the mirror to reflect him or his companion. He beckoned her still farther into the gloom, and they went down bare stone stairs to the basement of the building, and along a passage till they came to an iron-sheathed or iron door. Gees rapped on it with the handle of a penknife, waited, and presently the door slid aside on rollers and a shirt-sleeved, sackcloth-aproned boy faced the pair.

"Tell Mr. Barnes I want the street, Percy," Gees said, and drew his companion through the doorway, on which the boy rolled the door back into its place and preceded them to where lights shone in the gloom of this long, iron-pillared cellar.

There was a vinous, heavy reek in the air, and, when they reached the lighted area, Gees paused beside one of the men at work there. Wine-bottling from a pipe of port was in progress. One man drew the port from the great cask by means of two big, handled, copper cans, which he thrust alternately into the flow from the tap for filling, and emptied into a bigger copper receptacle on the stand near which Gees had halted. From this tank six copper pipes led down, terminating over a white enamelled trough, and under the end of the trough was another copper can to catch any waste that might be spilled. The man before the stand was placing bottles under the ends of the six pipes and removing them as they filled; occasionally, when a bottle had been overfilled, he splashed a spoonful or two into the can at the end of the trough, but for the most part he placed the full bottles almost without looking at them on a shelf on his left, and took empty ones to replace them from a trolley standing on his right. Then there was another man at a corking machine who took the filled bottles from the shelf and drove the corks, and yet another with a pot of molten wax over a burner, who dipped each corked bottle in his pot and impressed it with a seal. Percy and another boy acted as feeders to these men where necessary.

"Fascinating business, this," Gees observed to the girl. "I've watched them at it for half an hour at a time. Out of a whole cask like that, they won't spill more than a couple of pints."

"Just showing the lady round, sir?" the man at the stand asked.

"No, Barnes," Gees answered, and put down the ten-shilling note on the stand, "we want the street."

"Righto, sir. Coming back?"

"No. Also, we haven't been here."

"Righto, sir—we'll see to that, George?" he lifted up his voice. "Lift!"

The man with the pot of wax stopped work and came forward.

"Thanks so much, Barnes," Gees said. "Follow George, Miss Lenoir, and now you'll be able to tell your friends that you've been through the cellars of one of the biggest firms of wine merchants in London."

George led them among the iron pillars, past rows and rows of mighty casks, and lines and lines of bins in which bottles of wine lay ageing, until they came to a square little well projecting beyond the wall of the cellar, with daylight showing in it. George clicked a catch and pulled back a folding grille, and the three of them passed on to a square of iron flooring; he moved a handle, and the flooring went upward. Gees and the girl stepped off the iron on to street paving, and the lift with George on it went down again.

"Now, Miss Lenoir," Gees said, "you're nowhere near Little Oakfield Street, as you see. Straight along there will take you to Lower Regent Street, and Piccadilly Circus will be only a minute away."

"And you?" she asked, gazing at him.

"Oh, I'm going back to the office—the other way," he answered.

She went on gazing at him, and he could not read her expression.

"There will be a service in the temple of the pentagram at eight to-morrow evening," she said. "If you go to King's Road, you will find it easily. That's in return for what you have done for me."

"Delighted," he said, taking off his hat. "Good afternoon."

He watched her until she turned the corner and disappeared on her way to Piccadilly Circus, and observed that she did not look back; he noted, too her grace of movement—not as a matter for admiration, but because he might have need to recognise her from a back view at some time. For, though he had waived his initial fee and charged only expenses, he knew quite definitely that he had taken up this case.

On the way back to the Haymarket and Little Oakfield Street, he reviewed his data. He had divined her aim, and felt sure she was not alone in it: her mention of a "temple of the pentagram," whatever that might be, pointed to associates, for one did not conduct services in a temple alone. It sounded like a game that children might play, yet there was enough of earnest in it to draw Tott's attention to her, and Tott, as Gees knew, would not exert himself over anything unless it had real significance. And now, throwing Johns off her trail like this fitted in admirably with the part Gees himself meant to play in the case—as he saw it then. He had given her confidence in himself by the move, to a certain extent, and the game he was playing and meant to play with Johns would leave the worthy sergeant guessing, and would cause Tott to regard Gees with no more disfavour than at present. Tott suspected him already: he could do no more than that.

Thus reflecting, Gees came to number 37, Little Oakfield Street, and divined without looking at the man in front of the outfitter's window that the bait had been taken. He heard—

"I say, Green?" Just behind him.

It was the gambit Tott had offered at King's Cross. Gees took the pawn instantly.

"Wrong, Sergeant." He faced about and spoke blandly. "You say you say, but you don't say. Besides, it's a rude form of address."

"I mean—look here, I want a talk to you."

"Initial fee for consultation, two guineas," Gees responded sweetly. "Pay, and talk—or don't pay, and shut up. Good-bye."

"Half a minute!" Johns had an inspiration. If he could catch the woman who had gone into this building less than half an hour before, locate her in Gees' flat, Tott would not grudge two guineas on an expense sheet for such definite proof that Gees was allied with her. "Does that mean consultation up in your rooms?"

"In my office," Gees assented. "But, knowing you, it's cash down, Sergeant. And please remember I'm Mister Green, now."

"All right—I'll pay now." Johns took out a wallet from which he extracted two one-pound notes, and added to them two shillings from his trouser pocket. "What do I get, though?" he asked cautiously.

"Oh, anything within reason," Gees answered lightly. "Up to half an hour for a full statement of your case, if you wish."

"Righto. Lead the way." And Johns, confident (as Gees knew) of finding the lady, handed over the money.

"I'll give you a receipt when we get in the office," Gees promised.

He led the way up and into the corridor of the flat. Outside the door of the secretary's room he paused.

"Miss Brandon, has anyone called while I've been out?"

"Nobody, Mr. Green."

Gees led on to the door of his own office, and saw as he ushered his visitor in that the latter looked slightly dashed, as if he rather regretted that two guineas. Throwing his hat on to his desk, Gees turned and faced the man.

"Now, Sergeant, what do you want?" he asked.

"A look all over this place—every room," Johns answered bluntly.

"The pleasure is mine—but if you pay two guineas every time you inspect a furnished flat, the great Tott will surely put you on the carpet on pay day—that is, unless this is private and not to be charged to expenses. Now what would you like to see first?"

"All of it," Johns retorted, as bluntly as before.

"This room? The scheme of decoration is my own idea."

Johns looked round. There was scarcely a place in which a cat could hide. Of course, Gees had come in after the woman had entered, and did not yet know himself that she was waiting here for him.

"I've seen enough of this," he said. "Now that room where you spoke to a Miss Brandon outside the door."

"Certainly," Gees responded happily, and conducted him thither. And Johns saw Miss Brandon sitting at her desk, and bowed to her.

"Excuse me, miss. When did Mr. Green go out of here?"

"He went out for lunch," she answered. "I haven't seen him since, until now. You have not been in, have you, Mr. Green?"

"Not since I went out to lunch," Green answered, standing well inside the room to give colour to the Jesuitical assertion.

"Now the other rooms, then, whatever they are," Johns said rather glumly, turning to Gees again.

In turn they visited the bathroom, the sitting-room, and bedroom, on the other side of the corridor, and all the time Gees was careful to leave the doors open, thus giving his visitor every opportunity of seeing if anyone attempted to steal out from the flat. But, naturally, nobody did anything of the sort. In the bedroom, Johns turned on his host with extreme discontent visible in his expression.

"Is this all there is?" he demanded.

"All," Gees answered solemnly. "Your money's worth."

Johns strode to the wardrobe, opened it, and looked inside. Then, closing it again, he looked under the bed, and even punched the bed itself, though it was flat enough already. He went and looked into the corridor, but nobody could have gone out without his hearing.

"She came up here, I know," he said incautiously.

"Oho!" Gees exclaimed interestedly. "A lady in it, is there? Oh, Sergeant—Sergeant! I'm shocked at you!"

"My trouble is that she's not in it!" Johns declared angrily.

Gees followed him to the secretary's room, and saw him face Miss Brandon with angry determination visible in his face.

"You say, miss, that nobody has called to see Mr. Green?" he demanded. "Nobody since you saw him before he went out?"

"I have already said so," she answered quietly.

"And you say he hasn't been back in here since lunch?"

"He has already told you so," she said, as quietly as before.

He turned on Gees. "Look here, Green—"

"*Mister* Green!" The interruption was sharp, commanding.

"Mister—" But on the word Johns paused. He glanced at Miss Brandon, sitting there all grave and interested, and knew he could not express one tenth of his feelings, even if she had not been present.

"Ah, what's the use?"

He turned and went out, not quite foaming at the mouth, and slammed the door. Gees seated himself on the end of Miss Brandon's desk.

"Somebody once called that a wooden oath," he observed, and, taking out his case, lighted cigarettes for them both.

"I know," she assented. "It's very expressive. The slam, I mean, as well as the description."

"Yes." He laughed, quietly. "Now he'll go down into the basement and find the door into the wine cellars. Barnes will tell him nobody has been in there—Miss Lenoir gave him ten shillings to say just that, or I did for her—and poor old Johns will walk up the wall and lay an egg. I'm nearly, but not quite, sorry for him."

"Miss Lenoir?" she questioned. "She gave you her name, then?"

"She gave me that name—Christine Lenoir."

"And who is she—do you know?"

He shook his head. "It may be an alias," he explained. "Even if it isn't, I was only an ordinary divisional man, and Tott is special—given special cases of not exactly criminal significance. The name may be quite well-known to him and still unknown to me."

"You couldn't forget such a name if you'd heard it," she remarked.

"True—Oh, true! Now, Miss Brandon, since we've started being busy and raked in two guineas to-day, take your little book and make marks in it while I dictate as much as I can remember of a conversation while it's fresh in my mind. We ought to have everything on record, for I foresee we're going to be exceedingly busy for awhile."

She got the book and pencil out, and he dictated a fairly detailed record of the afternoon's events: his memory was sufficiently good to permit of most of the conversation he had had with Miss Lenoir going in, and, at the end, he stood up.

"One copy only of that, Miss Brandon, and destroy your notes as soon as you've typed and checked it over. Bring it in to me."

She brought it into his office eventually, and waited while he read through the script, pencilling a minor alteration here and there.

"Thanks," he said at last. "Nothing else, I think. And it's long past your time for leaving, too."

"I don't mind," she answered. "It's such a blessing to have something to do, instead of idling the day away."

"Well, we may be quite busy over this yet," he said cheerfully.

When she had gone he went to his bedroom and pushed at the heavy wardrobe. It slid easily on castors along by the wall, and revealed that a square of the wallpaper was separate from its surrounding area. Inserting a knife-blade in the crack at one side, Gees pulled open a door and revealed a fairly large safe built into the wall: this he opened with a key from his pocket, and inside it he placed the typed record: there was nothing else whatever in the safe.

"It looks frightfully lonely, but that can't be helped," he observed. Then he closed and locked the safe, swung the hinged panel back into its place, and rolled the wardrobe into position in front of it.

Having finished this task, he decided that a visit to King's Road might be a good move, and got his hat and coat.

# CHAPTER IV

## THE PLACE OF MEETING

"WHATEVER IS DOING IN CHELSEA," Gees told himself, "can be learned here. Whatever isn't, can't."

Therefore, he entered the Markham, and called for half a pint of bitter in a tankard. Rita herself served him—Rita with her shining little Burne-Jones head and ways of doing and saying things that keep the saloon bar of the Markham in good order, and, for a moment, he caught a glimpse of Mrs. Andrews, who is mother to half Chelsea's bad boys and knows all the others by sight—one of the greatest-hearted women and at the same time one of the shrewdest the district has ever known. Gees took a sip from his half-pint, and looked round.

When he had told himself that one might find out anything that happened to be doing in Chelsea by going into the Markham, he meant one who knew the ropes—one who would not be lost in such an assemblage as he saw here on the Friday evening. For there were all sorts: artists, would-be artists who would never do anything, a stray commercial traveller enjoying the noise, a peddler of buttons and braces and matches taking a rest, two white-faced boys who might have been anything—but were not—five or six girls and women whom Gees knew well enough to call them by their first names—and respected them none the less for that, since they were not of the sell-myself class—and certain nondescript hangers-on to the regular community of the Markham.

"It looks as if I might," he told himself, "but quite possibly nobody here knows the place. Anyhow, it's good beer."

He applied himself to making converse with a man whom he knew slightly, one who was doing good service in a hospital not far away. Also, as he knew, one who knew most things, if not everything.

"Temple of the pentagram," the other man echoed the name, and shook his head. "Nowhere near my street—but then, I'm the other side of Fulham Road. No, I never heard of it. But here's George and

Dorothy—George knows everything, and Dorothy can tell you the rest."

George nodded at Gees, who turned from greeting Dorothy.

"What are you on?" George inquired. "You can see for yourself nobody in here has got mumps, and Mrs. Andrews won't have murders on the premises. She's got a phobia against that sort of thing."

"I'm after a place, George," Gees told him. "Not the sort of place you get paid for taking, but one with walls and a roof. It's in the vicinity of Kings Road, and that's all I know. Except that it's called the temple of the pentagram, or something of the sort."

"Umph! What do they do there? What's the cult?"

"Search me. When I've been there, I'll be able to tell you."

"George?" Dorothy put in, "I wonder if it's that five-sided, ramshackle old place not far from the embankment? You know—it's in—what's the name of the alley or court or gardens or whatever it is? Turn down by the Commercial and go along Radnor Street, and turn right and then left and—I forget exactly, but you know the place I mean."

"Of course!" George agreed. "It used to be called the pentacle, though—some kind of gang used to hold mysteries there till the police broke them up. I dunno what their cult was—"

"Oh, you can find every cult on earth in Chelsea," Dorothy interjected, "from spiritualists to sadists. But that appears to be the nearest to your vague description, Gees."

"And where do you say it is, Dorothy?" Gees asked.

"I didn't. There's a hopeless muddle of little bits of streets, down there toward the embankment. But if you go down Radnor Street—"

"Leave it to me, Dorothy," George interposed. "Gees, have you got a pencil and piece of paper on you?"

Gees produced an envelope of which the back would serve, and a pencil, and George took a chair at one of the small, circular tables and began drawing, explaining as the pencil moved on the paper.

"That's Radnor Street—here's King's Road. You go down and turn so, then so, and then so. That little square represents a coal yard. Then you go so, and so, and it's along there—I'll make a dot. On the left. It's crowded into that shape by the other buildings—five-sided. But it's been empty for years, to my knowledge."

A tall, dark woman came and nodded at Gees, and then looked down at the drawing in a casual way. Gees knew her as a writer on one of the leading London dailies; a splendid Alsatian followed her and, with a look up at her as if asking permission to rest, flopped down by the table, sighed, and laid his head on his paws.

"How's the agency, Gees?" she inquired. "Had any mumps, yet?"

"Lots," he answered. "Can I buy you a mumps and soda?"

"Got one, thanks. What's George doing—a geography lesson, or is it a match puzzle? I've got a box of matches, George."

"Don't let Dorothy hear it," he answered, "or you'll lose it before you go out of here. I've never known an automatic lighter use as many matches as hers, and she's only had it since we were married. This isn't geography—it's town-planning. There you are, Gees"—he handed back the envelope and pencil—"that dot is your place, and that's how you get to it, both ways. You're less likely to lose yourself if you come at it from the embankment, I think."

"Dot representing what?" the dog's owner asked.

"Pentacle," George answered briefly. "He's calling it the temple of the pentagram, though. That old closed-up place —you know."

"But it's not closed up any more," she contradicted. "It's open again as a Communist Sunday School, and they hold meetings, too."

"It *looks* closed up," George objected. "Did the last time I saw it, anyhow, and that couldn't have been more than a month ago."

"Well, you don't expect communists to buy paint, do you?" she asked. "Nose paint in tankards, perhaps, but not the other sort."

George stood up and looked into Gees' tankard. "Dorothy's got a chicken in the oven," he announced, "so we can't stay. One for the road, Gees? You'll have another, Joyce?"

He went to the bar and ordered four more drinks. As he returned with the last two and handed Gees his tankard, the door opened, and a man entered. At the sight, the breath hissed between Gees' teeth.

"Skin off your nose, George," he toasted, and drank.

The Alsatian lifted its head to gaze at the newcomer, as if it scented possible trouble. Gees saw him go to the bar and obtain a glass of beer—strangers in the Markham get tankards only by asking specially for them. And, taking no notice of anyone else, the man lowered two-thirds of the contents of his glass before putting it down on the counter, after which he proceeded to light a cigarette.

He was the fifty-shilling-suit rozzer of the train journey, and Gees neglected the talk going on between his companions while he considered ways and means of getting even with Inspector Tott for putting such a man as this on his trail. Going to inspect the temple of the pentagram this evening, he felt, was utterly out of the question, now. But George's envelope map gave him its location, and the service, according to Christine Lenoir, was to be held to-morrow night.

George and Dorothy departed, in the interests of roast chicken: Gees patted the Alsatian, and then, putting down his tankard, bade its owner good night, for he saw fifty-shilling head toward the door. He followed, and saw the man standing at the edge of the pavement, trying to look meditatively unconscious of everyone, and not succeeding.

"I want you"—Gees paused beside the man and spoke in a low tone—"to take a message to Inspector Tott for me."

The other man started visibly as he heard the name, and stared at Gees incredulously. "You—what?" he asked.

"Want you to take a message to Inspector Tott," Gees repeated. "Tell him—first doorway on the left in Sidney Street, opposite the Chelsea Palace. At ten-thirty to-night, I'd say. He'll probably get what he seems to want. Can you remember that, or shall I repeat it?"

"Here, who are you?" the man demanded suspiciously.

"Name of Green—say Mister Green, when you give the inspector the message. He ought to have it at once, too, if he's to have time to make the necessary arrangements. He'll know my name, you'll find."

"Are you *ordering* me to go and give him this message?"

"Far from it—don't get any idea of that sort into your head. Take it or leave it—just as you like. I'm in no position to give you orders, but I think he ought to have the message."

"I see-e." The other's suspicions appeared to vanish at Gees' tone of friendly urgency. "Then you know why I'm here, of course?"

"I don't know anything—I'm not saying any more than I have said already," Gees answered darkly. "But I think— I'm not sure—I think he can get what he seems to want if he turns up there at about ten-thirty tonight. First doorway on the left, in Sidney Street, opposite the Chelsea Palace. Can you remember it all right?"

"I've got it. I'll hop on a bus right away."

Gees watched while the man hopped on an eastbound number 11, and then walked westward as far as Sidney Street to make certain that he had got it right—for he did not want Tott to make any mistake. He saw the first doorway—or gateway—on the left, and read part of the legend on the board beside it:

LONDON COUNTY COUNCIL
PUBLIC ASSISTANCE DEPARTMENT
SIDNEY STREET RELIEF STATION

He turned away, and retraced his steps toward the Gamecock Club, of which he was a member. As he entered the gateway leading to the club premises, he nodded his head repeatedly.

"Yes," he told himself, "he seems to want relief, so he'd better apply there. I'll larn him to put men like that on to trailing me!"

Entering the club, he dined comfortably and cheaply, and, later, spent quite a pleasant evening with two artist acquaintances, for he knew that, if he went back to Little Oakfield Street before midnight, Tott would be after him. And, although Johns had paid two guineas for an initial consultation, Gees did not intend the fee to include Tott's statement of the case for himself and against the confidential agency.

Miss Brandon had uncovered her typewriter, the following morning, and had exchanged greetings with the principal of the agency and settled to the perusal of another novel, when she heard the doorbell ring. A tall man, youngish-looking at a first glance, but not so young when one gave him a more detailed survey, faced her when she opened the door, and she saw hostility in his gaze.

"I want to see Mr. Green," he said without preface.

"Come in," she bade, and showed him into her own room. "May I have your name, please?"

"Inspector Tott, tell him."

She left him in her room while she went to acquaint Gees with this demand. But Gees spoke first.

"Show him in, Miss Brandon. I ought to have told you I expected him this morning, of course. Take your receiver out and listen in to us when you get back to your room. Take us down—all of it. After he's gone, one copy and destroy the notes, the same as yesterday."

He had, at the end of his desk, a built-in, concealed microphone: from it a wire ran down the leg of the desk, invisibly, and thence under the oilcloth and rugs, through the wall, and up the leg of Miss Brandon's desk to terminate in a good pair of headphones. It was a device of which Gees was no little proud, and he had his desk and visitors' chair so placed that anyone seated in the chair was directly facing the microphone, but, of course, could not see it.

He stood up as Tott entered. "Morning, Inspector," he said pleasantly. "Do sit down and have a cigarette. What can I do for you?"

"I don't want to sit down, and I don't want any of your cigarettes either," Tott answered implacably. "I'm here to warn you, Green—"

"Mister Green, Inspector," Gees interrupted. "If you come into my office, extend me the courtesy I show you. I am not calling you merely 'Tott,' and I won't have you call me merely 'Green.' And if that's your attitude, two guineas, please, cash down!"

"The trick you worked on Johns, eh? Oh, no, you don't—"

"Sit down—or get out of the office!" Gees interjected sharply. "I'm not going to have you standing over me to hector me."

He pointed to the comfortable armchair at the end of the desk, and after a brief pause Tott seated himself in it with visible reluctance. Gees crowed inwardly, for he had scored the first point.

"Now what do you want?" he asked.

"You," Tott retorted angrily, "and I've a good mind to have you here and now, too, for obtaining money under false pretences."

"Oh, no, you don't!" Gees told him. "Try to frighten people who haven't served in the force with a tale like that, but don't bring it here. You know as well as I know that Johns agreed to pay two guineas for his initial consultation, just as you know that it's my fixed charge—and I'll send you in an account for this visit, too! And Johns had his money's worth. He wanted to inspect my flat, and he inspected it. It's true he inquired what was the use as he went out, but I couldn't tell him, because he hadn't told me why—"

"Oh, cut out this fooling!" Tott interrupted. "You know perfectly well what he was after, and if you swear till you're black in the face that you didn't take that woman out through the wine cellars, I won't believe you, any more than I believe the men working down there. They know you, and take your money, probably."

"Of course they know me! That firm has supplied my father with wine ever since he set up housekeeping in Dawgeley Square—go and ask to see his account with them, if you like. I've known Barnes down in those cellars since I was a child. And as for swearing anything till I'm black in the face, I refuse to do anything of the sort. It would take too long—you can see I'm not naturally apoplectic."

"Are you going to tell me you didn't throw Johns off that woman's trail? Because, if you are—"

"Off what woman's trail?" Gees interrupted again.

"Oh, come off it! You know perfectly well what woman!"

"I ask you, Inspector—what woman are you talking about?"

"Christine Lenoir, of course—the one you travelled with."

"Oh, that's her name, is it?" He affected intense satisfaction. "She didn't tell me on that journey from Edinburgh to King's Cross."

"No," Tott grunted, "because you knew it already!"

"I give you my word of honour, Inspector, I had never seen her before in my life, and I didn't know her name."

"Well, I suppose I've got to believe you. Christine Lenoir, and you—" he grew wrathful again—"you threw Johns off the trail when I most particularly wanted him to keep on it—"

"You can't support that accusation, Inspector. Johns heard beyond all question that I didn't come in here after lunch till I came in with him, and when we came in there was nobody in the whole place except my secretary. So how I ever got into touch with this woman to throw him off her trail is a problem you'll have to solve—I won't attempt it. Who and what is she—the name doesn't sound English?"

"You know she's not English!"

"I don't know anything, I keep on telling you. But if she's a foreigner, surely she registered on arrival and you can trace her when you want her. Why come worrying me like this over it?"

"Of course we can trace her, as far as where she lives is concerned! She booked a room at Oddenino's and registered at Vine Street. But that's no use to me. I want to trace what contacts she makes, not merely know where she's living, as you know perfectly well."

"I don't. But if you like to engage my services, I'll forego the initial two-guinea fee and take the case up seriously—"

"I'll see you seven miles on the far side of hell first!" Tott interrupted vindictively. "After last night, too!"

"Last night—Oh, yes! Inspector, if you put a fat-headed oaf like that man on to trailing me when I go to see my friends, you obviously need relief. I told him to go to you and tell you where it could be had—and you sound as if you'd been after it."

"Been after it? Heaven and earth! Haven't I? And that oaf, as you call him, went back into uniform this morning. I can stand fools, and have to stand them—but not damned fools. And you—do you think you're the universe, or what? Do you think I'd waste men by putting them on to watch *you?* He wasn't trailing you at all!"

"Good Lord!" and Gees laughed softly. "I'm sorry, Inspector."

"Yes—you look it, don't you? He knew her by sight, or I would never have used him. Both he and Johns were looking for her, trying to pick up the trail you broke yesterday afternoon, and she—"

"What?" Gees asked, as the sentence remained incomplete.

"Didn't go anywhere near Oddenino's last night at all," Tott ended his statement. "There's no harm in telling you, since you probably know it already, and if you don't it makes no difference." He stood up. "That's all, except for what I really came to tell you. Which is that after playing a trick like the one you played on me last night, I'll get you, Green, if it takes me years to do it."

"Mister Green, Inspector—I insist on it. And do I look frightened by your threat, or do I look frightened? You get me? I wish you'd try this false pretences stunt of yours for a start, and hear the laugh that goes up in court when I take the witness stand. Inspector, you're a very efficient officer, or you wouldn't hold the position you do, but I know you for one who may let a grudge get the better of his reasoning faculties, if you're not careful. Don't let it happen in my case. I'm willing to work in with you——"

"*You* work in with me?" Tott broke in stormily. "Give away everything to the Lenoir woman, is what you mean, if I'm fool enough to trust you! Not on your life, *Mister* Green! After last night, and after the way you tricked Johns by getting that woman away, it's plain war between you and me—and you're going to lose. Your best course would be to shut down this fool office and take to pig-farming. If you'll do that, I'll leave you alone. If not, look out for yourself."

"I can, and I intend to do just that," Gees answered quietly. "This office stays open, and thanks for your plain statement of intent. I know exactly how we stand, and I'm *not* going to lose! You forget I know all the tricks of your trade by experience, when you make a threat like that. I do, and I'll match you trick for trick. That's all from my side, Inspector. Don't slam the door on your way out, and ask Johns to shut it more gently if he should call on me again—he made a terrific row going out yesterday. Can you find your way, or shall I come to the door with you?"

Without a word Tott turned and went out, and Gees noted that he closed the outer door of the flat very gently indeed.

"Thanks, Miss Brandon"—Gees took the sheets of typescript. "I'd better just run through it before I lock it away. Now make out an account to Inspector Horace Tott—you've got his address, I think. Initial consultation, two guineas. Stamp it as a letter—don't send it unsealed. That's all for now, thanks."

# CHAPTER V

## THE GREAT PANJANDRUM

IT BEING SATURDAY, Miss Brandon put the cover on her typewriter at one o'clock and became Eve Madeleine to Gees until Monday morning: that is to say, she went home, wherever that might be. Gees went out a little later, and crossed Piccadilly Circus with a view to lunching at Oddenino's, but suddenly remembered Tott's having told him that Christine Lenoir was staying there: the place was therefore barred to him, for, if any of Tott's watchers caught him in it, the inspector himself would instantly conclude that the pair were meeting there to plot mischief. So, a little annoyed over it—for he liked Oddenino's as a feeding place—Gees walked on and on, and came to rest and food at last at Bertorelli's, on the north side of Oxford Street. He got rid of a good deal of the afternoon by looking into shop windows, and resolved to sell out a thousand pounds of his small capital, unless his luck changed by the end of the following week. For it did not appear probable, then, that he would make any money out of this case of Christine Lenoir, and the plain vans people had to be paid if he wished to keep his nice furniture. With the optimism that a man of his type does not lose till the late thirties, he told himself that the luck would change in time, but quite probably not in time for that next never-never instalment. And shop windows were attractive, too, especially those of second-hand booksellers.

Toward evening, he took a bus to the King's Road and proceeded to the Gamecock, where he dined as on the preceding night, but earlier. Then, walking to the Embankment, he made sure that he was not being followed, and by eight o'clock, steering by George's envelope-map, he reached the dingy, ramshackle, five-sided building that he sought, and saw plastered on the wall beside the doorway a hand-scrawled poster announcing that there would be a meeting for "Initiates and Comrades of the Pentagram" at 8 p.m., that the speaker was "Initiate-Comrade Leonid Denghisovski," and that all were welcome.

He entered, and saw at the far side, faced toward the door, a rostrum on which stood a jug of water and a glass, while on the wall behind it a large pentagram recently painted in vivid scarlet rendered the peeling, dingy distemper of its background still more depressing. Beside the rostrum stood an old cottage piano, and all the foreground was occupied with rows of bentwood chairs of the cheapest kind.

As audience, there were a dozen or so of rough-looking youngsters and two middle-aged females of the charwoman class, one of them apparently not too sober. At the piano sat a man who reminded Gees of Sir Henry Wood, except that his face lacked the fine intellectuality which characterises that of the great conductor: he was not exactly a caricature of his original, but a poor edition. A little beyond the end of the instrument Christine Lenoir was seated facing toward the meagre audience, and, standing at the rostrum, was a man of medium height, with a chest of great depth and breadth, and almost abnormally long arms: he appeared to possess enormous physical strength. His clean-shaven face had the pallor of one long deprived of sunlight: his nose was a beak, and even before he began to speak there was a smouldering fierceness in his dark eyes, widely-set as they were under thick, black brows. He had, too, a ring of black hair above which the bald dome of his skull rose pinkishly, and at the very top there was a small pink knob, either of flesh or bone, a startling excrescence that made the man look utterly sinister, and even repulsive.

For some moments Gees could not place the incident or circumstance to which this strange being belonged in some way, and then he recollected that great father of laughter, Francois Rabelais.

Here stood the Great Panjandrum, with the little round button atop. And surely those two shoddy females facing him were Loblollies! And—

But in a deep, resonant voice the Great Panjandrum spoke:

"Comrades, to open our meeting we will sing the Marsellaise."

The man at the piano struck up that maddening, unforgettable melody with which Rouget de Lisle put heart into a nation, and, following the example set by Christine Lenoir, the audience stood to sing. Her voice and that of the man at the rostrum led them, and where they did not know the words they Ummed and Arred. They sang: even the two females screeched, and Christine's voice soared clear and sweet:

*"Aux armes, citoyens!"*

At the end they all sat again, except the man at the rostrum—evidently Initiate-Comrade Denghisovski, for he began his address.

He called them comrades: he told them of the chains that enslaved them, of the tyrants who battened on their blood and ground them down. He described how, if only they would unite to throw off their shackles, they might win such glorious freedom as that of the workers in Russia, where the solidarity of the proletariat was no dream, but a living, pulsing reality. And so on, and so on, the old, old platitudes that ring out daily at Lunatics' Corner by Marble Arch. And then he told them that a day of freedom was about to dawn for them, that comrades all over England had determined on the end of slavery for the workers, and were about to bring freedom to all their sweated, suffering brothers and sisters. He repeated himself, he mixed his metaphors badly, but he spoke with a fierce earnestness that proved him an enthusiast, while the man at the piano nodded and shook his head till his mop of lank black hair was all rumpled, rather like that of his great and almost leonine prototype. His English was only just so much accented as to prove him of foreign origin, and his vocabulary, Gees noted, was good. And, as he worked himself up to fierceness, the little round button atop grew pinker, as did the bald area of scalp round it, rendering his pallid face more strikingly colourless.

He ended his exordium with a fierce denunciation of blood-sucking capitalists, and an assertion that capitalism must be overthrown before liberty could be attained, and then for a minute sat down to drink a glass of water. Then again he rose.

"Comrades, let us pray."

Again Christine Lenoir stood, and the audience followed suit. The panjandrum prayed, as strange a prayer as Gees had ever heard.

"O, mighty hammer, token of the labours of mankind: O, mightier sickle, symbol of man's reward as he reaps the fruits of earth! Shine on us the radiance that lights a world in travail of a new birth—the birth of freedom and the death of capitalism. Light our way to the establishment of the solidarity of the proletariat and the utter overthrow of the capitalist system. Shine on our comrades in Chelsea and inspirit them: give the holy zeal that can free the workers of this country to our comrades in Elswick, Tyneside and Tees-side, South Wales, the industrial districts of the Clyde—in Birmingham and Wolverhampton, in Shields and Sheffield, and wherever the struggle for freedom of the proletariat is being waged—wherever the battle is set in array. Give light to the people that they may utterly confound the tyrants who now rule over them, and in the imminent day when the battle shall be joined, give us light to batter and hew our capitalist enemies until they are utterly destroyed."

"So be it," said the man at the piano, in a thin, squeaky voice.

"Now, comrades, to close our meeting," said the panjandrum—as Gees decided to call him since his real name was so difficult—"we will sing the 'Red Flag.' "

Led again by Christine and the panjandrum, and accompanied by the piano, they stood and bore witness that the people's flag is red with blood, but not many of them appeared very disturbed about it, Gees noted. Since he did not know the words, he merely moved his lips occasionally, and, while the dreary melody lasted, he thought and thought over that fantastic prayer, especially over the place-names that the panjandrum had listed in it.

*Every one of those places was a site of a key industry!* Inspector Tott's interest in Christine Lenoir was no longer a thing at which to wonder. So far, evidently, he could do nothing, for probably there had been no real grounds on which she could be refused admission to the country (or, equally probably, the authorities had admitted her in order to trace these associates of hers and render them harmless) and a meeting like this did not contravene the law. Wilder assertions than those of the panjandrum are made every day at Lunatics' Corner, and the police listen and pass on, merely keeping order in the crowd.

The panjandrum spoke a benediction:

"Comrades, may the radiance of the hammer and sickle light you on your ways, now and evermore."

"So be it," said the man at the piano.

Christine took up a bundle of booklets that had lain beside her chair, and went quickly to the door. The audience filed out, and to each she gave a booklet, on the cover of which, printed in red and in large type, were the words—"RUSSIA'S EXAMPLE: FREEDOM." The less sober of the two women observed that Russia seemed a nice place, from what she'd 'eard about it. Gees, approaching the door, held out his hand for a booklet, but the girl shook her head.

"After," she said. "Wait."

He counted out the others—fourteen in all. Christine closed the door and turned to him again.

"Will you come and be introduced?" she asked.

He went with her to the piano, where the speaker had joined the pianist. The pair stared at him, rudely.

"Initiates," Christine said, "this is Comrade Green. I have told you how he helped me yesterday. Comrade Green, this"—she indicated the speaker—"is Initiate-Comrade Denghisovski, and this"—she glanced at the pianist—"is Initiate-Comrade Nikolai Smirilov, sometime Prince Smirilov in Ukrania, but now a leader in the cause."

"Comrade, we welcome you," said the panjandrum, "and for the help you gave Comrade Lenoir, we thank you."

An imp in Gees' brain insisted that the panjandrum ought to have called her "Comradess," but he realised that it was a clumsy feminine.

"Comrade," he said solemnly, "it was a very small thing to do, and it gave me great pleasure to do it." He might have added that it had induced Detective-Sergeant Johns to part with two guineas, but refrained. If these people heard that, they might ask for a subscription to their cause, and though he intended to stand in with them and learn all he could of their real activities, he did not intend to part with any money. Rather, if possible, he would get some out of them.

"You are with us, comrade?" Smirilov asked.

"Heart and hands," Gees assured him. And, in a physical sense, it was perfectly true: he had no compunction over deceiving them.

"He did not say 'soul,' you note," Smirilov observed to the panjandrum—as Gees now insisted to himself that he would consider the other man. "He is not of those who are poisoned by the opiate of the masses, religion. They only use that word."

"He is with us," Christine said, and smiled at him.

"I am with you," Gees said again.

Inwardly, he began to characterise the talk as fat-headed tomfoolery, but hoped it would lead on to some knowledge of what action was intended in those key-industry places.

"You comprehend our aim?" the panjandrum asked.

"Not entirely," Gees answered. "Freedom, of course."

"Freedom, by revolution," the panjandrum said solemnly.

Gees shook his head. "You'll find it difficult in this country, I'm afraid," he remarked. "The bulk of the people are—" he was about to say "content," but realised that the word might not please these people—"too sluggish and apathetic," he ended.

"Comrade," the panjandrum asked, with the air of a schoolmaster, "what was the cause of the French Revolution?"

"You can search me," Gees answered, and saw that all three of his hearers frowned momentarily at the levity. "I'm not strong on history, I mean. I believe it was—yes, the Jacquerie, they called it."

"Wrong," said the panjandrum. "It was hunger, and the rage of the hungry who saw their tyrants fed and opulent."

"Well, that's your trouble, in this country," Gees said. "There are not enough hungry people to revolve—to revolute, that is."

"But we shall make them hungry," the panjandrum told him.

"You mean—bring wages down, somehow?"

"A simpler way—a much simpler way. Paralyse the key industries of the country—bring starvation to the masses. Then—*then* see if they will be sluggish or apathetic, when they cry for bread and see their tyrants full-fed and surfeited with luxuries!"

"Umm-m!" Gees reflected aloud. "It sounds a tall order, to me."

"We know our strength," the panjandrum said. "We know, too, the weakness of our enemies—their fatuous contempt for us. It is unwise to despise your enemy. Hate him—yes. But do not underestimate him. In that is the folly of the capitalists, and by it we will overthrow and destroy them. Soon. The time is near at hand."

He might have been lecturing again, Gees thought. His dark eyes glowed with fanatic zeal. Suddenly he bent forward, staring.

"*Are* you with us?" he demanded intensely.

"Heart and hands, with you," Gees answered as before.

To his utter amazement, Christine Lenoir suddenly seized his right hand, and kissed it before he realised what she was about to do. They were all mad, evidently—and dangerously mad, at that.

"He *is*!" she exclaimed as she let go his hand. "Oh, if you had seen him yesterday, you would believe! We may trust him."

Without one shadow of compunction he repeated: "You may trust me."

"We will make him an initiate," said the panjandrum solemnly.

"Comrade," Smirilov intervened, "neither Schlatzenbaum nor Schroder is here. All should be here for an initiation."

"Here are three of us," the panjandrum pointed out. "Comrade Lenoir, although a travelling inspector, can be witness to the initiation. We three can witness to those two, when they come back."

If they wanted him to sign anything, Gees reflected, initiation was off. He did not care what he said or promised verbally, but he meant to put nothing in writing. But, to his relief, the ceremony as explained by the panjandrum was merely oral, and exceedingly brief.

"Comrade," he said, "all that we ask of you in order to regard you as initiate is that you shall swear by all you hold most holy to be loyal to our cause and to keep our secrets. No more than that."

Gees reflected a moment, and had an inspiration. He lifted his right hand above his head and spoke.

"I swear by the holy hammer and holier sickle to be loyal to this cause, and to keep such of its secrets as may be committed to my charge. May the radiance of the holy hammer and holier sickle change to lightning and blast me if I fail to keep my oath!"

The panjandrum grasped his left hand, and Christine his right as he let it fall. "Comrade-Initiate Green," said the panjandrum, "it is the most binding oath of all—you are one with us in our cause. And know that if you even so much as attempt to betray us, you bring death to yourself. No matter how or where you try to hide, we will find you and kill you. But we trust you—we know that no man dare break such an oath, and we believe you are loyal to the cause."

Gees knew he was, but did not specify what cause— certainly not theirs! Since they were fools enough to believe him capable of helping to bring starvation to the people of Britain, let them keep it up by all means, until he had discovered their means of organisation. As for the oath, he regarded it as most unholy twaddle, but useful for the time being. Like all fanatics, these people were very childish.

"I am certainly loyal to the cause," he said.

The panjandrum looked at a fat gold watch which he took from his pocket. "For to-night, it is enough," he said. "I must go, too. You can be very useful to us, Comrade Green, for Comrade Lenoir has told us that you are fully familiar with police organisation and ways. We need such a one. And in addition, I foresee you as destined for a special mission here in Chelsea, when the day comes. But first you must be told our plans—part of our plans. Comrade Lenoir?"

"Yes," she said, comprehending the request without further explanation. "We will not keep you, comrade—nor you, Comrade Smirilov. I can tell him, and—we meet at Kestwell to-morrow?"

"To-morrow," he assented. "Good night, comrades."

He took his hat from behind the rostrum and went. Smirilov squeaked a good night and followed him out, and Gees and Christine faced each other. There was admiration in her gaze at him.

"I felt we should win you, even in the train," she said.

"What was that about your being a travelling inspector?" he asked. "Forgive the question, but I want to know all I can."

"Certainly. Appointed by the Left of the Comintern. Denghisovski is chief of the revolutionary organisation in this country—I put it to you quite plainly, comrade, now that you are a sworn initiate—he is the chief. I am merely here to report progress, and to make certain that our funds are not being wasted. For revolution is not cheap, in a country like this. The standard of living is so high."

He wanted to roar with laughter at the confession, but kept a grave face. They were determined to organise discontent, but found the task difficult because they had first to create the means of discontent—the people as a whole were too satisfied to feel it.

"And Tott is after you," he suggested thoughtfully.

"But can do nothing, because I am not active," she pointed out. "These others, the staff of the revolution, they must be careful, but since I merely report their activities he cannot touch me."

"I see." But he questioned inwardly whether she were justified in considering herself thus inviolable. If Tott found cause enough against the others to arrest them, he would contrive some means of roping her in too. He already had his eye on her.

She moved toward the door. "Shall we go?" she suggested.

"Together, you mean?" he asked in reply.

"Why not? I have much to tell you, now."

"Right. I know, let's go down to the Clarendon at Hammersmith. We can talk, there, and we're bound to be seen, wherever we go."

He would take the risk, he decided. Nothing had been said or done to-night that could incriminate him, and neither Tott nor any of his men could prove his intimacy with the revolutionaries prior to this meeting. And he wanted to know—everything!

"Yes," she assented. "I don't know it, but will trust myself to your discretion. Let me first tell the woman who has charge of this place to lock up for the night."

They went out, and she called at a cottage near-by and spoke to a woman who acted as caretaker for the building. Then Gees led the way toward the Embankment: so far, he had seen nothing of Johns or anyone else who might belong to Tott's army of sleuths.

"We'll get a taxi," he said, "and cut out the Clarendon. The Castle at Richmond strikes me as being a better place."

# CHAPTER VI

## WAYS AND MEANS—AND THEN CHRISTINE

THE MAY EVENING WAS KIND, and, since the meeting in the temple of the pentagram had taken less than an hour, and Gees' initiation had been a fairly rapid affair, there was still some daylight left when he seated himself opposite Christine at one of the tables on the Castle lawn at Richmond. There was a band, but fortunately it was inside the restaurant; there were occasional gramophones in boats that passed on the river, but—again fortunately—they were distant. There were also gnats, not distant, and altogether it was a perfect evening and therefore abnormal for the time of year.

"Rather an ideal hiding place," Gees observed indolently.

"Ideal," Christine assented, and watched the ice he had ordered for her as it slowly turned to slush, "but not a hiding place."

"If you don't want to be seen, go where you can be seen easily," he remarked, and made the ice in his glass tinkle against the side. "Do you mind telling me what and where is Kestwell, Miss Lenoir?"

"It is a building estate," she answered. "Comrade Denghisovski bought it, and has not developed it. He has boards up announcing that plots of land are for sale, but they don't get sold. He sees to that."

"Keeps it as a hide-out, eh?" he suggested.

"No," she dissented. "The only safe hiding, as you remarked just now, is that of openness. When Denghisovski and Smirilov go to Kestwell to-morrow, they will go quite openly, as I shall go. And, I hope, as you will go. Schroder and Schlatzenbaum will be back to-morrow, and they will be at Kestwell. You must meet them, now."

"Kestwell being where?" he inquired, after thinking over such a meeting. She appeared to be hurrying him, he felt.

"About three miles beyond Leatherhead," she answered. "There are two hundred acres of vacant building land, and an old farm-house with outbuildings. The land behind the house forms a good landing ground for Schroder, as you will probably see to-morrow."

"If I go," he observed.

"Of course you will go. You are one of us, now."

He remembered, then, the panjandrum's threat of death. By her tone, it appeared that she too meant business.

"Don't you think you have bitten off rather a big piece with the idea of revolution in this country, Miss Lenoir?" he asked.

"Our teeth are good," she answered, thus proving that she understood the idiomatic slang—as she did not that of plain vans.

"As—for instance, now?" he suggested, and offered her a cigarette which she refused. He took one for himself and lighted it.

"How do you mean that?" she asked.

"The forces of law and order are also fairly well equipped, speaking in a dental sense," he pointed out gravely.

"I see. Law and order—yes. But when we have destroyed order, there will be no law. As, without law, there can be no order."

"Then you mean definitely to destroy order?" he asked.

"To bring about starvation, riot, revolution—death to the tyrant capitalists and the extinction of their system," she answered composedly. "To strike simultaneous blows at the power stations of the key industries. We do not believe in war as the capitalists know it: our war is more deadly, for we use the people who have been their tools and slaves against them, and a whole people roused to action against its rulers is more deadly than an army as the capitalists know it."

Never had he known a situation so grotesque: this lovely, dainty, apparently cultured woman sat here talking calmly of ruining a nation, and—what was still less credible, though true—evidently expected him to approve the madness she was preaching.

"And when is all this to happen?" he asked.

"It must be in not more than a month from this present time," she answered with purposeful deliberateness. "I know this country lives very largely on imported food, but still the harvest is of some importance too. The blow must fall before any of the harvest is gathered in, to ensure that starvation will ensue quickly among the masses."

"But isn't that destroying the very people you want to set free?" he queried. "Excuse the question, Miss Lenoir. I merely want to get it all clear. And if you starve them to death—"

"Not to death," she interrupted. "To rage that means death to their tyrants, the capitalists who drain the life-blood of the masses for their own pleasures. And we do not plan to set the masses free—the workers of the world can never be free. We tell them of freedom, promise it, and hold it out always as a hope, but they must be governed under our system just as much as now, though not—not by capitalism. In that is the great evil that torments the world—until we have destroyed it. Ultimate freedom for us, the leaders of mankind, but for the great masses of the workers—no."

Madness oh madness! The overthrow of a tried, established order, and the setting up of one which denied the possibility of freedom. He brooded over it, and incautiously let his distaste for such an idea manifest itself in his expression. She observed it.

"You are one of us, now," she reminded him coldly.

"Yes, I have sworn the oath," he said. "Don't fear for me— I'll carry it through and be in at the end. In fact, I'll surprise you."

He smiled as he said it, and she smiled back at him.

"I think it quite probable that you will, comrade," she said.

"And now—the means of it—the method?" he suggested.

"Yes. Denghisovski intended me to tell you, if we found as we have found that you are with us, on our side. The method—the simplest of all, purchase. We work on the principle that every man has his price, and where necessary we pay the price. For our plans we do not need the intellectuals—a worker can place a bomb and light a fuse as well as an intellectual. Smirilov and Schlatzenbaum have been at work quite a long time—their permits for staying in the country will both expire at the end of June, and will not be renewed, which is another reason why the blow must be struck within a month. One blow—not just a series that gives capitalism time to organise resistance, but one great blow falling on as many power stations as we can buy men to destroy them. Overthrow, practically, in a day."

"Which means a good deal of money," he observed.

"Not so much as you would think. Denghisovski is the owner and director of an importing firm in Whitechapel, and he has got a credit through your government—I see irony, there. He accumulated a mere twenty-thousand pounds in one-pound notes, and up to the present has spent less than six thousand. Such men as will join and serve us are cheap. To them, twenty pounds is a large sum, and fifty a small fortune. And the bulk of the money, the rewards, will not be paid until the work is done—none of them have yet realised that we shall destroy the value of capitalist currency, and their paper notes will be useless. Nor do we intend that they shall realise it."

Poor devils, Gees thought. If they were enslaved now, what would they be under such cynical taskmasters as these?

"Those meetings—like to-night," he said, half-questioningly.

"They are not futile, if that is what you were thinking," she said gravely. "Each one of those young men—boys, if you like—takes away some of the doctrine we wish to spread among their kind. They go among their fellows and help us to preach discontent, and we tell them nothing of our chief aim, nothing of what I now tell you. They will lounge about the streets, unemployed, and in bars where they drink, and preach our gospel. At the same time such meetings are cover for our real work. If Denghisovski and Smirilov and I met merely to discuss our plans, your Inspector Tott would be suspicious of us, but if we meet as is permitted in this country of free speech, to preach our doctrine, he knows his law will not let him act against us. Those two women who were there to-night—we are not sure of them, but some one of the young men will tell us if they were spying. We pay well for any such information, as they all know."

"And Schroder—you mentioned him in the train, I remember."

"Schroder is here with a Volodskanya Gnomon aeroplane—he took Schlatzenbaum to the north in it yesterday. He had to give an undertaking to take no aerial photographs in this country before they would let him fly where he would in it. Your government is very kind—to everyone but its own people. And when the day comes, Schroder will paralyse railway communications. The Gnomon is very fast, and in a day he can wreck not less than ten important junctions."

"Bombing, you mean?" Gees asked. She was being amazingly frank, but then, the penalty of treachery was death, they had told him.

"Just little bombs, weighing not quite three pounds each," she explained. "But the destructive force of each of them is equal to that of one hundred pounds of ordinary high explosive—we have good chemists to serve us. Such bombs, with time fuses, will do our work in the power stations. You, comrade, will put the Battersea and Lots Road power stations out of action, when the day comes. Denghisovski decided that should be your part for the day, if we won you to us."

"The honour is more than I had expected," he told her gravely.

"London is most important of all," she said, "and by killing those two sources of power we reduce it to chaos. Smirilov will attend to the docks—it is easy to get workers for us there, and he has already bought men to interrupt food supplies. Once that is done, riot follows easily, and then Denghisovski issues orders and takes control. And the two power stations are your task."

"You've got entry for me?" he asked.

She shook her head. "We ask work of you," she said. "With your knowledge of police methods—lie, promise, buy traitors to the capitalists—do what you will, but find some means of entry within three weeks from to-day. Tell Schroder how many bombs you will need to wreck the dynamos, and he will supply them in time for the day."

"But supposing I find it impossible to gain entry?"

"When Denghisovski made you initiate, he told you the penalty of failure, comrade—death. Inevitable death. You must not fail."

The look she gave him with the admonition indicated a personal reason for her not wishing him to fail. He inclined his head in assent.

"The pentagram—is that a real society?" he asked.

"Only in so far as that it forms a symbol for our adherents," she answered. "You see, we know religion only as a poison for the minds of the workers, but they are so much like children that they must have some symbol—from the earliest development of mankind the idea of a secret society has been attractive. We give them that idea: there are passwords, formulas—all childs' play. I can give you a booklet—or if you wish, you can get one from Inspector Tott. I know he has one. It merely proves to him what visionary fools we are, prevents him from regarding us as really dangerous. He is a clever man, one to be watched as he watches us. You will find that man of his, Detective-Sergeant Johns, knows all about your coming here with me tonight."

"We were not followed," he asserted emphatically.

She smiled. "Johns is a very clever man, as is Inspector Tott," she said. "I do not know if we were followed or no, but I am quite sure Johns knows by this time that we are here together, and will report just how long you and I sat talking at this table."

He thought it over. She might be right, of course, but if she had seen Johns anywhere, then his own powers of observation must be more limited than he had thought them, for he had been certain that nobody had trailed them here from the temple of the pentagram.

"And so Battersea and Lots Road are my job," he observed.

"Come to Kestwell to-morrow, and Denghisovski will give you your instructions there," she said. "Come quite openly, by car or how you will. Tott knows now that you are allied with us, regards you as a visionary fanatic, as he regards all of us, and thinks he is preventing us from being dangerous by letting us—what is the phrase?—yes, by letting us put out a lot of hot air. Such meetings as the one you saw to-night confirm him in that view. It is a free country."

"For the present, that is," Gees observed.

She gave him another smile, one of approval this time. "I knew you would be with us," she said, "heart and hand, as you told us in the temple. Yes, for the present—but before this summer ends it will be ours—capitalism's greatest stronghold will be destroyed. Comrade, I have told you enough for to-night. There is to-morrow at Kestwell. And"—she gazed full at him—"even a travelling in-spector is sometimes human. Also, I am a woman, as you realised in the train."

"I realise it now, Christine," he said softly.

She wanted to play the oldest game in the world, he knew, the game that cost Mother Eve her Eden in the beginning of all things. In the train, he had acquitted her of what he termed Mata Hari allure, but she had it now. It left him utterly cold: he would play the game up to a point if she wished it, but calculatingly, an actor all the time. And he knew, with Denghisovski's warning in his mind, that whether he played this game with her or kept on at the sinister game of revolution in England, he was sporting with death. Tott might see these people as visionary fanatics, and in one way might be right in so regarding them, but, admitted as he was now to their inner councils, Gees knew that they were in earnest, and deadly dan-gerous.

"And you"—her voice had grown caressing—"big hands, big feet, and so big a heart—*hein?* You know, comrade, there to a woman is one of the greatest evils of your capitalist system in England. A woman may not tell a man if she finds him attractive. It is immodest, wrong—she must wait for him to speak. We are wiser—we know that a woman has just as much right to speak her heart as a man, to take him and discard him at will as the capitalists take and discard their women. Is it not better so? Should such as I am not be free?"

"Free as the air, my dear," he assured her. "And you're very lovely, you know. The man who would discard you hasn't been born, yet. You're quite right—all this sham modesty is the merest bunk. Let's have crudity, by all means—speak our minds. Workers of the world, unite— especially when they're opposite sexes and feel an affinity for each other. Good word, that—affinity."

"One finds it so seldom," she observed sadly. "But you— you think our thoughts and speak in our ways. We know that love be-tween man and woman is in reality a brutal thing—one must strip away the sentiment with which capitalist poets and idealists have cloaked it. Man in a state of nature stunned his woman and bore her away, and to this day woman asks that of the man of her choice. Force, fierceness, conquest—love! In nature there is no sentiment, no modesty."

"For instance, take a walk round the Zoo," he remarked quite gravely.

"I do not know your Zoo—only the *Jardin des Plantes* in Paris," she answered. "But it is the same—you are right."

With that she gave him yet another key to the reason for this fantastic yet dangerous folly on which she and her associates were bent. They had, evidently, no sense of humour at all: they were so terribly, damnably in earnest over their project that they could not see it in its real proportions, could not see that they were aiming at the destruction of a system that, whatever its faults, had been tried and proved through centuries as workable, in order to establish another of which the defects were glaringly apparent before it was put into operation. They were out to do evil for the sake of utterly problematic good to a lesser proportion of humanity than found good in their present lot—and could not see their own absurdity.

But, Gees reflected, he must not underrate them. Denghisovski had remarked the folly of underestimating one's opponents. So far, there had been nothing but talk, but the nature of it proved that it was far removed from the hot air of the average agitator. These pentagrammists or whatever they called themselves were in dangerous earnest over their plans, and apparently cleverer than most of their kind.

"I generally manage to be right," he remarked calmly.

"You have had much experience of women?" she asked.

"Well, you know, there are women and women. You, now, I should say you're unique. But I wouldn't class myself with Saint Anthony, exactly, if you understand what that means."

He recollected that when he had had a passing inclination to submit to the temptation with which the saint had been assailed, she had not merely denied him the opportunity, but had threatened to run him in. And now, it appeared, she meant to run him down.

"I understand," she said, and smiled provocatively. "Comrade, it grows late, and though Johns or somebody will know we have been here, perhaps it would be unwise for us to go back together. I shall see you at Kestwell to-morrow, and there may be—opportunities."

It was flagrant man-chasing, he reflected as he beckoned to a waiter: on the whole, the capitalist system of relationship between men and women had more kick to it—this was too blatant altogether. He paid for their refreshments when the waiter came to the table, and asked the man to summon him a taxi. Then they went out to the entrance.

When he put her in the taxi and bade the driver take her to Oddenino's, she gave him her tiny hand and smiled at him.

"We shall not always travel separately, dear comrade," she said.

(There was, though neither could foresee it then, to come a day when that prophecy would recur to both their minds.)

"Who can say how soon, Christine?" he answered, and pressed the hand he held as if reluctant to release it.

"When the day comes," she said softly. "One in aim, one in heart. And to-morrow we meet again. I am so glad to have won you to us."

"Not more glad than I am. Good night, Christine."

She went away, and he walked off after the taxi had gone, intending to go to the station and get an electric train to Waterloo. There was no hurry about getting back to his flat, and, until he had sold out some capital, the fewer taxis he took the better.

It being a Saturday night, and a summery night at that, Richmond main streets were full of people. Gees turned left from the Castle forecourt to go to the station, and even as he turned saw, across the road, a middle-aged, slatternly-looking woman, apparently not too sober. In just such a state, in fact, as she had appeared to be when she and another had listened to the panjandrum in the temple of the pentagram, two hours or less earlier.

Inspector Tott, Gees realised, was a very clever man.

# CHAPTER VII

## RESTWELL

WAKENING EARLY THE NEXT MORNING, Gees realised that the day was Sunday, and that therefore he had nothing to do—or rather, that he could get up at what hour he liked, since Eve Madeleine would not be coming in to help him to do nothing. But then he remembered the preceding day and evening, and got out of bed to find and read over the copious notes he had made before going to bed of the meeting in the pentagram temple and his subsequent talk to Christine Lenoir at Richmond. For, being now thoroughly interested in this as yet profitless case, he intended to dictate a full account of every stage of it to Miss Brandon—to make a daily diary of it, in fact.

The notes, he found, recalled points of talk and happenings that were already beginning to fade from his mind: it was evidently a good idea, this of recording impressions while they were quite fresh. He made a few additions to his screed, and then lay thinking awhile. Yes, here was another good idea: if he went to Tott with what he had learned, ridicule would be his portion, he knew; a talk with Tony Briggs, a schooldays friend of his who was now in the Foreign Office, was distinctly indicated. Tony might be able to reduce the nightmare these people seemed about to produce to a mere nausea such as is due to indigestion, or might regard it as Gees himself felt he must, now. If old Tony were in London this week-end—

Gees sprang out of bed again, went to the telephone in his office, dialled, and waited. The calling signal gave place to a voice:

"Damn you, who's that at this unearthly hour?"

"Just on ten, Tony," Gees answered. "I expect my charlady in with the offal at any minute, now. Want to see you, old lad. Urgent."

"You urge yourself back to bed for another hour or two! If you come round here before twelve, I'll murder you!"

"I haven't had a bath yet either. Twelve it is, Tony. Look for me then. Cheerio." And he hung up and went back to bed—and breakfast in it, when his charlady eventually arrived to provide the meal.

Twelve o'clock was striking when he rang the bell of a flat in a block just off St. James's Street, and Tony Briggs, a perfect fashion-plate of a man in summerish light-grey, with all accessories perfectly harmonised in his colour scheme, himself opened the door.

"Very much on time, aren't you?" he inquired sourly.

"Morning, Tony—how very swish you look," Gees responded cheerfully. "As to time, they teach you in the police force to be very exact about it, and bad habits are hard to lose." He followed Briggs to an exceedingly untidy lounge type of room, and flicked ash off the arm of a chair with his handkerchief before seating himself on it—on the handkerchief, which he placed on the chair arm. "Yours are, I mean," he proceeded. "Why the hell can't you do something to this room, instead of turning yourself out like a shopwalker bridegroom? You need waking up, my lad! Tony, I'm rather up a tree, and want your help in sawing it down."

"Then stop slandering my flat, or get out," Tony ordered.

"Well, it's your flat, thank God! Ever heard of a woman—a peach of a woman, as far as looks go—named Christine Lenoir?"

"Who hasn't?" Tony asked in reply, interest evident in his tone.

"Me, till she gave me her card," Gees told him. "Travelling inspector for the Left of the Comintern—I think that's it."

"Was that on the card?" Tony asked innocently.

"Oh, yes—in large capitals on both sides! Don't be an ass, man! I got it at a meeting last night, from a friend of hers named Denghisovski, but he's the original Great Panjandrum, really. The little round button is most nauseously atop. Or maybe Smirilov said it, or perhaps she did herself. One of them did—they were all there."

"You have got a nice lot of friends, Gees! We know all three of 'em, of course. An inspector-chap—I expect you know him, man by the name of Tott—he's keeping an eye on the gang for us."

"Do I know Tott—or do I know Tott?" Gees said wistfully. "You mean you trust this lot and their doings to him?"

"If you know him, laddie—and you give me a faint suspicion that you do—you'll know they can't get far without his discerning eye taking a squint in that direction. We get such a lot of that sort of thing nowadays—people all going to blow the world up, hot air merchants of all breeds, and especially the Communist breed. You see, what makes the Communists so hopping mad is that the country has got over the worst of its depression, and things are on the up-grade. And that's hell for revolutionaries. They had their big chance in the coal strike of '21, and missed it. They won't get it again."

"You think that lot is safe with Tott, then?"

"Would he let them run loose if they were not? It happens to impinge on my department, this branch of inactivity, so I know a bit about that crowd. Denghisovski, Whitechapel importer—been drawing fairly heavily on a trade credit these last few months, and Tott hasn't yet found out if the money has been exported to the man's spiritual home, or what has been done with it. Schlatzenbaum, tailor by trade, and he'll be out of the country in six weeks, for we won't renew his permit. Don't like him, in fact. Then there's Smirilov, a renegade aristocrat, and if I began to tell you the things he did in the Odessa massacres, you'd be sick on this floor, so I won't. But he'd hate it if he knew how many of his friends he's tipped off to us. We've deported nine or ten of them, and I think six are doing penal servitude, but he doesn't know yet that we caught them through their association with him. So you see he's a useful member of society. Then there's the flying man, Schroder—he got here only recently and gave an undertaking not to photograph things, so we let him trundle his—what's the thing? Oh, yes! Volodskanya Gnomon 250 h.p. monoplane. We let him wander about in it and talk to people in different places, and those people go on the books. When he stops being useful in that way, he'll have to go home. Can't have too much of that sort of thing, you know. Am I being really interesting and helpful?"

"You're a jewel, Tony! I'll dust this room for you, if you like."

"Leave the blasted room alone, can't you? Then, of course, there is the fair Christine. Y'know, Gees, those people never trust each other. You spy on me, I spy on you, and somebody else spies on and is spied on by both of us. Mutual mistrust society—even the man in the street can get a pat on the back if he hares off to the secret police and tells 'em his next-door neighbour hoards bread tickets in the gramophone, or something of the sort. They take the neighbour down cellar and blow his brains out. Christine is a sort of super-spy, recognised as such. She's over here to see that this crowd don't go to sleep on their job, and we don't mind, bless her heart! Probably there are others in with the gang, and if so, she'll lead Tott to them before she goes home again. Quite a good-looking bird, I believe, though I've only seen photographs, so far. Want any more?"

"You know they've got a plot to smash—"

"My dear chap, haven't they always got a plot to smash something? What the devil would they do if they hadn't? It's their permanent mission in life, and if you could look through some of our files, you would see that the Great War was a mere skirmish compared to the things that haven't happened to the dear old country these last fifteen years or so. Let 'em plot! More plots, more convicts doing time. Tott knows just as much as you could tell him, and after that he really comes down to what he does know, and that's a whole bibful. In the words of the dear old nineteenth-century model of propriety, we are not amused. We are even thirsty after all this talking—what abaht it?"

"Too early for alcohol—I've not long had breakfast," Gees said.

"Damn your suspicious mind, man! Who said anything about alcohol? I've got some genuine Trinidad limes in the meat safe."

"Then lose a few," Gees advised. "It sounds good to me."

They had a long lime squash apiece, and Gees found that Tony, having said all he meant to say, wanted to drop the subject. So they discussed the Derby, the mouldiness of politicians, and a few other things, and then Gees went off to lunch at the Windsor, just outside Victoria station. After that, he ascertained that the train he wanted to catch went from Waterloo instead of from Victoria to Leatherhead; he missed it, and caught the next.

The Sabbath afternoon was more like that of a July day than of one falling toward the end of May, and Gees sighed with pleasure at sight of the annual miracle, foliage of late spring, as he descended from the electric train at Leatherhead station—he was the only passenger to alight there. In the station yard he found one mouldy four-wheeled cab— an authentic growler, in fact—and the driver, on being wakened, appeared to resent the idea of taking somebody somewhere. The horse remained asleep until requested to get a move on.

Yes, the driver had heard of a place called Kestwell— Kestwell Farm, he believed it was, and he thought it was somewhere over Cobham way. A railway official coming on duty confirmed the man's thoughts: you went up Potton Hill and took that lane on the left, and there was a board up. They were going to build there, but hadn't started yet.

Gees got into the cab after the driver had told him it would be four shillin's. The horse was wakened, and they set off along second-rate roads which were reasonably quiet, since the average Sunday motorist prefers to herd in gaggles along the main roads, and dump his picnic basket where he can get a seasoning of dust and petrol fumes on his food. Eventually the driver said "Cubberyer" to his steed, and bore heavily on the near rein: the cab reeled unhappily into a lane of scarcely two-vehicle width, and Gees saw late primroses down among the hawthorn stems of the hedges on either side. And even in the shade of the cab, with both windows down, he knew the day was warm.

The son of Nimshi bore heavily on both reins and said—"Whoa!" and Gees got out and paid him, for the board was in sight beyond a gateway in the right-hand hedge: there was no gate, and only one post remained, evidently from a remote antiquity. Gees read on the board:

## RIPE FOR DEVELOPMENT

### THE KESTWELL ESTATE

UNEQUALLED VIEWS IN ALL DIRECTIONS
GUARANTEED GRAVEL SUBSOIL
BUILDING PLOTS FOR SALE

*For Particulars Apply to the Sole Agents:*
SKINYER, NEATE & QUICK,
Solicitors,
1, FLATTACRE STREET, E.C.6.

The cab turned about, and to Gees' disappointment did not turn over: had it done so, the man could not have righted it alone, and it would have been there when he wanted to go back. But, he reflected, as he turned toward the gateway, one cannot have everything in life.

He saw about thirty yards of gravelled drive, grass-tufted and ridged, rather than rutted, by the traffic of many vehicles in time past. At the far end was a redbrick farmhouse, with discoloured stone pillars serving the two purposes of supporting the porch roof and proving the place of Georgian build: it was two-storeyed, and there was one low-set, casement window on each side of the open doorway, and similar windows above. Before it was a big chestnut tree, under which a litter of fallen blossoms showed like snow at this distance. At the back were outbuildings; byres, stables, and an old, red-brick barn, and beyond them a great stretch of open meadow land sloped up toward a high, untrimmed hawthorn hedge, a very forest of a hedge, starred with blossom and utterly hiding all that lay beyond. Under the chestnut tree stood a big saloon car of American make, unattended, and there was no sign of life about the place, apart from birds and bees.

The afternoon was undoubtedly warm, but, Gees reflected, Derby day was near at hand: he could remember only one Derby day that had not been chilly and miserable, and that had not been one that he had chosen to attend the historic meeting. The weather and himself generally managed to be at cross-purposes, though to-day was an exception. A slight raspiness of the throat told him it was near on tea time, and he went hopefully along the grass-tufted drive toward the house.

When he reached the open door, he found that it was innocent of either knocker or bell-knob in the lintel. He took out the pocket knife he always carried, a nickel-handled thing which boasted a screwdriver, corkscrew, and pair of scissors in addition to two ex-cellent blades, and played: "Father's pants will soon fit Willie," in a flat monotone on the panel of the door, thus breaking at least four paint-blisters. Nothing happened, and he played it again. Steps sounded from somewhere at the back of the house, and a small, dark man appeared, attired in cord riding breeches with field boots, a chessboard-patterned sports jacket, and a not-too-clean shirt open at the neck. He came to the door, and, Gees noted, kept his right hand in the pocket of his sports jacket: if the bulge of that pocket were not lying, the man's fingers were closed round the butt of an automatic pistol.

"What do you want?" he demanded suspiciously. He nearly said—"Vat do you vant?" but it was not quite that. He had blackish, peering eyes deeply set, and a nose that bespoke a small-holding in Palestine, and Gees hated him on sight, and wanted to tell him that he was a liar before he made any statement at all. He looked like one.

"My name is Green," Gees said. "I have been asked to call here."

"Ah! Comrade!" the little man exclaimed, his expression changing to one of welcoming pleasure. He did not quite exclaim: "Ach! Kamerard!" but nearly achieved it. "Come through. We had thought they had caught you for something, and I myself thought it was a spy of that devil Tott, till you tell me." His hand came out from his pocket, and Gees noted that the bulge remained in it. The hand was far from clean, but he offered it freely, and shaking it became an inevitability. "We are out at the back—you will like some tea, *hein?"*

"Certainly," Gees assented, "but I don't know your name, yet."

"I am Ivan Schroder, der—(he certainly lapsed from 'the' to 'der')—great Schroder. And my Gnomon is behind the trees at the back—you must see my Gnomon! Come through, comrade."

Entering, and shuddering slightly at the contact of that dirty, fishily clammy hand, Gees followed the little man along the central passage of the house, and noted that it was bare of furniture of any kind. They passed two doors, leading evidently into the rooms of which the windows gave on to the front of the place, and then two more before they went down two brick steps into an unfurnished scullery— there was a stone sink, and a plunger-pump over it, and the flooring was of dampish white bricks, while the ceiling was low, as had been that of the central passage. A gloomy house, and silent, with mould on the wallpaper and an air of having been long deserted.

They passed through the scullery, through a small, brick-floored and walled courtyard at the back, and came out to openness and sunlight. The outbuildings were all to the left of the house, echeloned away toward a thickly-grown copse or shrubbery on the big stretch of meadow land, and to the right, on the grass and beside a fairly large pond, Gees saw a small table, innocent of any cover, with a tea equipage on it, and bent-wood chairs surrounding it, these last occupied by Denghisovski, bigger than ever in a pale, double breasted flannel jacket and very loose trousers: Smirilov, Sunday-dressed in black lounge jacket and striped trousers, Christine Lenoir looking very lovely in summerish black-and-white with the hat of a *maquerelle,* and a fourth person, obviously as big a liar as Schroder by the look of him, in a suit of such vast check that it would have taken three to show the pattern fully. Schroder called out as he led the way:

"He has come!" (He did not quite make "Gome" of the last word.)

The panjandrum stood up, and the little round button atop appeared to deepen its hue with pleasure. "We had given you up," he said, and gave Gees a handshake which evidenced his enormous strength—not that he made the pressure painful, but Gees knew the strength was there. "Comrade, we are glad, for we need you. For your part, on the day."

"And here I am," Gees said pleasantly, and, dropping his hat on the grass, he smiled at Christine. The panjandrum's handgrip had told him quite plainly that he was flirting with death, so he had to make the flirtation seem a real allegiance. "I thought the train went from Victoria, but it was Waterloo. That's why I'm late—I missed it, and had to wait for the next. I'm terribly sorry—comrade."

He thought to add the last word, as evidence of loyalty.

"You have yet to know Comrade Schlatzenbaum," the panjandrum said, and the man in the check suit stood up. "Comrade Green, Comrade Schlatzenbaum. Who will destroy Lots Road and Battersea on the day."

They were quite sure of him, evidently. Schlatzenbaum curved his nasty, pudgy figure in an exaggerated bow of greeting.

"Kamerad, you are velcome," he said throatily.

"I am honoured to meet you," Gees told him gravely.

At that he bowed again, to such an extent that he must have creased his stomach. Christine lifted a brown earthenware teapot.

"Tea, comrade?" she asked. "We are just having it. I made it."

"Then it is impossible to refuse," he answered gallantly. "Besides—" more practically—"I'm simply yearning for some. No milk, thanks. I see you have lemon there. And no sugar, either."

"We feared you might have been caught," the panjandrum observed, as Gees took his cup from Christine and smiled his thanks.

"Not even followed, to the best of my knowledge," he answered.

"I warn you, on that score, do not underestimate the forces against us," the panjandrum said solemnly. "They are very clever."

"Tott is very clever," Gees agreed, and remembered the woman in the street at Richmond, the night before.

"Ach!" said the panjandrum, still more solemnly. "I myself will kill that Tott when the day comes. I will kill him very slowly. But we are not here to talk of our pleasures, comrade. This"—he waved his hand in a way that included the farmhouse and outbuildings, the thick copse beyond the buildings, and the meadow land stretching away toward the mighty hawthorn hedge—"it is to become the seat of the central government of Soviet Britain. How do you see it?"

"Very nice indeed," Gees said, and sipped his tea. Over the rim of the cup he saw Christine eyeing him rather hungrily, as if she looked forward to something intimate beyond these business interchanges: he remembered how —according to Tony Briggs—all these people were card-indexed and harmless. But were they, in reality? Was it just a game in which he played, perilously, in a way against Tott—or was it a very grim danger to the country he loved, and for the sake of which he would second Tott's efforts with all his brain and heart?

"So near London as to be well situated," the panjandrum said, "yet so remote, until the day comes, that it is inconspicuous. We cannot hope to establish a headquarters in London itself. When you, comrade, have played your part with the power stations, and Comrade Smirilov has done his work in and about the docks, London will be hopelessly disorganised, a seat of mad panic. And we must have quiet and order to consummate the revolution—there will be much to be done."

"Obviously," Gees agreed, and took another sip. It was good tea.

"When things have settled down again, we intend that you shall organise a secret police on the lines of the Cheka," the panjandrum announced. "Your staff will be drawn from the workers, for they are the least scrupulous and most ruthless. There will be dregs of capitalism left—I foresee mass executions, for the destruction of the rabid intellectuals who are useless to us. We must have the workers in hand, devoid of all leaders but ourselves, and in this country you have a great body of people—you call them the upper middle class. They must cease to exist—we have no use for them. It will be your task."

"It will be my task," Gees agreed, and thought of Tony Briggs and his Trinidad limes. Marvellous limes—long might Tony live to provide them on Sunday mornings! As good as this tea, in fact. He handed his cup to Christine, who refilled it and passed it back.

"But that is of the future," the panjandrum said. "First, there is the business of creating discontent—the great discontent that shall stir the workers and produce the revolution. Comrade Lenoir, she tells me, has told you of your part with the power stations. Have you thought—have you planned the way in to the stations?"

"It should be fairly easy, given the funds," Gees said cautiously. "I was thinking over it most of the night." Which was altogether untrue, for he had slept peacefully on going to bed the night before.

"You mean, it involves bribery?" the panjandrum asked interestedly.

"I think fifty would do it," Gees said, with an air of grave reflection. He had an idea of making these people trap themselves.

"Say a hundred," the panjandrum said magnificently. "Schroder, give our comrade a hundred before he leaves us. Comrade Lenoir will know that it is well expended, and there must be no stinting over such an important point of our attack. You may need it all, Comrade Green."

"Just one moment," Gees urged. "Comrade Lenoir told me last night that your main fund is in one-pound notes. Supposing Tott or any of his people managed to catch me on my way back with a hundred one-pound notes on me? That would finish my usefulness, wouldn't it, since any explanation I might give them would be distrusted? I think —let some one of you come to my office to-morrow morning with the money, and if you, Comrade Denghisovski, can manage to make it, we can discuss details. That office of mine is as secret as the grave."

The panjandrum thought it over, and nodded.

"It is very wise," he said. "I will bring the notes to you to-morrow, and we will go thoroughly into the business of destroying the power stations then. Yes. Comrade, you are quite right. We must not underestimate this man Tott. He is capable of finding a pretext for arresting you on your way back, and discovering that you hold our money. If you were foreign, it would be different, and he would not molest you. But you are British, and we must take no risks. I will come to your office at eleven to-morrow with the money."

Inwardly, Gees shook hands with himself and patted himself on the back. Revolutionaries, he decided, were born fools, and their trust in a man they had no business to trust was simply marvellous. But then he saw Christine's hungry, happy gaze at him, and knew that she had guaranteed his loyalty. And what could be fairer than that?

# CHAPTER VIII

## CHRISTINE—AND A PICNIC PARTY

FOR a time, seated round the tea table, the members of the party talked generally of their activities. Schlatzenbaum told of workers in the north, men he had suborned in readiness for "the day," and Denghisovski announced that he would bring the first car-load of bombs to Kestwell by Tuesday, but to Gees' disappointment did not say where he would procure them. When all was in readiness, Schroder would distribute the infernal ammunition by means of the Gnomon: three days, he estimated, would be enough for the whole task, and they counted it safest to store all the bombs at Kestwell until just before they were required for use. The bribed workers were to be trusted as little as possible: they were not made acquainted with each other, and Schlatzenbaum, wherever he could, had secured the services of alternative men, so that if one failed the other could act.

"Come and see my Gnomon, Comrade Green," Schroder invited when the conversation slackened, and with a nod Gees rose to accept the invitation. He went with the little man toward the copse he had noted, and, rounding it, saw the monoplane about a hundred yards beyond, headed as it had alighted toward the house. Schroder spoke of it with the joyful pride of a child exhibiting a new toy.

"See the wing-spread, comrade. She is very fast, my Gnomon, yet she has a low landing speed. And in the air, one sets the controls and throttle, and she flies herself. Easy—so easy. You also can fly, Comrade Lenoir has told me."

"A little," Gees' answered. "Enough to qualify for a pilot's licence." He was not going to own to two hundred flying hours, or the fact that he could handle practically any machine.

They looked into the cockpit, and Schroder pointed.

"The button there—the black knob," he said. "It is a Zaleszca two-stage starting dynamo. No propeller swinging and calling for contact, with my Gnomon. And you see she seats two in comfort—she is the perfect air-taxi. All the upholstery is pneumatic, and here, you see"—he stepped up and, reaching inside, canted the hinged driving seat forward—"is our safe deposit. Comrade Leonid makes me the treasurer, and in that innocent-looking brown paper parcel are twelve thousand one-pound notes. For I am to distribute them to our workers on the day—just before they become quite useless."

"What about carrying the bombs?" Gees asked.

"In rear—there is a padded compartment, as for baggage, in the fuselage. And for my own work with the bombs—the brackets there"—again he pointed—"are for the bomb-sights and release gear. It is all ready in a box under the back seat of the car, since I may not fit it until the day. Ah, she is lovely, my Gnomon!"

Lovely, Gees thought, as was Christine who joined them then, with a deadly, terrible loveliness. She laid her hand on his arm.

"He is so proud of it, comrade," she said. "Could you fly it?"

"I think so," Gees answered. "The controls look not unlike those of a Fairey machine I flew once—when I qualified for my licence."

"Ah, but she is much easier to handle than any Fairey type!" Schroder exclaimed. "Comrade, I know! You shall come north with me on Tuesday, to Sunderland. I go there to give money to a man, one of our men. We can go and be back here in the afternoon, for she is very fast, my Gnomon. You shall see what she is like in the air."

"Yes," Christine said. "You shall go with him, comrade. And some day soon you too shall have a Gnomon and be my pilot. Comrade Ivan, leave him to me, now, our future Cheka chief. I will talk to him."

With her hand on Gees' arm she impelled him away from the machine and turned toward the house. They walked slowly across the grass: the other three were still seated at the table, and Smirilov, talking, gesticulated vehemently with a cigarette between his fingers.

"Your board says there are magnificent views in all directions," Gees remarked for the sake of saying something. "Where are they?"

"Ah, the big hedge prevents," she answered. "But come with me into the house, and I will show you. Besides, we shall be alone."

She led him through the scullery and up a bare, dusty back staircase. At the top she opened the door of one of the back rooms, and Gees followed her in: they went to the window and looked out.

Beyond the hawthorn hedge he saw the crest of Leith hill under the westering sun, and thought of the many people happily picnicking there, ignorant that such plotters as these people were so little way beyond their sight. And with an inner sight he discerned far more than that one hill-top: Oxford and its dreaming spires, Cheltenham nestled under the Cotswolds, Dartmoor heather-clad and purpling in the sun, the beauty of the Peak country—from point to point of England his thoughts sprang, and with that inner sight he dwelt on its loveliness in which so many, so very many of its people were happy, and at peace. If this woman and these men had their way, that peace would give place to starvation and riot, mass executions—

"If any act of mine should ever mar the peace of this land I love in any way, may the God Whom these people deny mar me!"

He did not speak the prayer, but it shaped itself in his mind, oath and prayer in one. Again Christine laid her hand on his arm.

"What is it, comrade? What are you thinking?"

He turned and, facing her, realised her loveliness—her hateful, evil loveliness! Reaching out, he put both hands on her shoulders, and knew as he looked into her dark eyes how it is that men commit murders. He wanted to strangle her, to fling her down, senseless, and stamp that beautiful face to unrecognisability with his feet, and with the longing the grip of his hands tightened unconsciously—or perhaps half-consciously—until she gave a little moan of pain, and at that he knew his own folly and released his hold.

"Forgive me, Christine," he said contritely.

"Ah, but I loved it!" she whispered. "That fierceness in your eyes, and the pain of your hold on me—I loved it! Not—not the tender sentiment of a capitalist lover, but the brute strength that holds and rends—your strength, comrade! I loved it."

She meant it fully, he knew. He knew, too, that he had been mad in that moment of murderous rage against her, but she was mad all the time. They were all mad, these plotters—Leonid Denghisovski with his lust for slow killing, Schlatzenbaum with his pudginess and evil face, Smirilov whose sickening cruelties in Odessa Tony Briggs knew, Schroder who looked forward to fitting his bomb-sights and sowing death over England, and this woman who would report on them—betray them without ruth to others over her if they failed from their deadliness. With her parted lips and eyes alight with happiness because he had given her physical pain, surely she was maddest of them all!

"But there will be bruises," he said.

"There will be bruises," she echoed, as if she spoke of dear caresses. "When I undress, I shall see the black marks on the white flesh in my mirror, and I shall be very happy. For love—your love for me—made them. Now I know we may trust you fully, know it utterly, for the love you have proved to me will keep you loyal to us."

Yes, quite mad. He wanted to laugh at her, and at the same time found himself pitying her. She ought to be put away in a cell somewhere, kept under restraint. Or destroyed, painlessly.

"Leonid sees us—he is beckoning to me," she said, standing faced as she was toward the window. "Let us go down."

With immense relief Gees realised that she would not ask him to kiss her, this time: had she asked it, he would have had to comply, he knew, but it would have been like kissing a cobra. He followed her out from the room and down the staircase. They rejoined the others.

"It grows late," the panjandrum said gravely. "Comrade Green, I will come to you with the hundred pounds at eleven to-morrow. We are going back in my car, but perhaps it would be unwise if we took you."

"It would be very unwise, I think," Gees agreed. "As far as I know, Tott has no idea that I came here this afternoon, and it's just as well that he shouldn't get a report of my having been with you, though he knows by now that I have identified myself with you—"

"Wise, wise comrade!" the panjandrum interrupted, with pleasure in his voice. "I see you do not underestimate the enemy."

"I'm not quite such a fool as that," Gees told him. "Well, since I've got to walk to Leatherhead, I'll get away. Probably you'll pass me on the road, since you're going too."

"There is nothing here—except the materials for making tea," the panjandrum observed. "It is unlikely that anyone will discover them, for we keep them under a loose board in one of the front rooms. I tell you if you should come here at any time and like to make tea. You will find the spirit stove—everything—if you lift the board at the left side of the fireplace in the front room on the right as you go out. Until to-morrow morning, comrade."

Having bidden the four men good-bye, Gees went off, and Christine accompanied him to the front of the house. There she put her hands in his and looked up at him, tenderly.

"My bruises—my beautiful bruises," she said. "The marks of your dear hands. What a wonderful lover you will be!"

"You haven't any idea, yet," he said vaguely.

"Go away—go away now!" she exclaimed suddenly. "Else, I may make you stay, and for the present the cause must come first."

He turned and went along the drive, and rendered reverent thanks to all the gods he knew for having escaped kissing her. Never in his life had he loathed anyone as he loathed this woman.

She watched him until he went out from the gateway, and then went back to the four men behind the house. Schlatzenbaum shook his head at her as she approached them, and there was doubt in his gaze.

"I do not like that man, comrade," he said. "I do not trust him."

"Do we altogether trust you?" she retorted.

"Can we trust anyone?" Denghisovski put in.

"We can trust that man," Christine said. "When I went with him into the house, he proved to me how fiercely he wants to be my lover. He is mine, terribly and wonderfully mine, and for me he will do anything. And when he talked to me on the way to London it was of crime, of organising crime to defeat the police. He is such a one as chance will not send to us again, one who even before I knew him told me he was against law. That is, with us. We may trust him."

(As Gees had felt, she had no sense of humour whatever.)

"The responsibility rests with you, comrade," Schlatzenbaum said darkly. "As I said, I do not like the man."

She looked him full in the face. "In a little time, comrade," she told him, and her normally sweet voice was cold and harsh, "this England will be ours, and he will help us to win it. Do not let your likes and dislikes become too apparent, unless you wish to feel a pistol muzzle against your head in some English cellar."

"And if it should prove that we cannot trust him," Denghisovski said drawlingly, "there is always death, remember."

"Not only for him, but for any one of you," Christine observed.

"True, comrade." Denghisovski stood up and stretched his long arms while he yawned. "Comrade Nikolai, will you put the tea things away? Ivan, what will you do—do you go with us? For there is the money in your Gnomon, and if you do, we must take it back."

Schroder shook his head. "I have my sleeping-bag and all I need," he answered. "I will sleep in the Gnomon and be ready for to-morrow."

"And you will take Comrade Green to Sunderland on Tuesday?"

"If he will go—I offered it," Schroder said.

"If?" Denghisovski echoed, rather terribly. "There are no ifs. To-morrow, when I see him, I will order him to go."

"I have already told him, comrade," Christine said. "He will go."

"One handles a lover with such ease," Smirilov observed thoughtfully, stacking the teacups on the tray. "Especially when one is like Comrade Lenoir, able to command any man as her lover."

"Have no fear, Comrade Nikolai," Christine said cuttingly. "I shall never seek to command you in that capacity. Leonid, I will sit with you while you drive. The others can go in the back of the car."

Denghisovski bowed at her. "Dear comrade," he answered, "you may command me in any capacity you like."

"I know it, Leonid," she said coolly. "In the capacity of chief of the revolution in England—and no other."

Smirilov, having loaded the tray, went off with it toward the house. Denghisovski, his hands in his pockets, stood looking toward the hawthorn hedge for a minute or so. The sun was setting over it.

"It is strange," he said meditatively, "to think how few times more the sun will set like this, before this country is all ours."

"Before Comrade Green is all mine," Christine added very softly.

She turned and went toward the house, and as she went she licked her lips, as might a tiger about to make its kill.

Three miles to Leatherhead, Gees reflected, as he went along the drive toward the lane. With a good companion— Tony Briggs, for instance, he would have enjoyed the tramp, but he hated walking alone. If only that infernal cab had turned over!

But it had not. He went out from the gateway, and saw, parked in another gateway which gave entrance to a field on the other side of the road, a baby Austin saloon car. Behind it a rug was spread on the ground, and on the rug sat a young woman, a fair-haired, pretty young woman with both love and laughter in her eyes as she gazed up at the tiny girl child she held aloft. The child was bubbling laughter down at her, its mother, and standing over them was a man who gave Gees just one glance before reverting to enjoyment of his family's happiness. A tea-basket stood open just beyond the edge of the rug: the little party had evidently made a picnic afternoon of it.

Just here—just outside the boundary of Kestwell Farm. The man had not heard Gees' approach, of course, but he would hear the big American saloon on its way out, and would be able to prevent the occupants of that car from seeing his face. And, when Gees had told Inspector Tott about putting people on to trail him, Tott had retorted to the effect that he, Gees, was not the universe, even if he thought he was. Tott would not care how much Gees knew of his activities—would care still less, now he knew that Gees had allied himself with Denghisovski and Christine Lenoir. It was intensely irritating to Gees to realise that Tott regarded him with contempt.

It was, too, quite natural that a motorist taking a Sunday afternoon jaunt with his wife and baby girl should seek a secluded spot like this for them—and for himself. Especially for himself, this gateway which gave him command of that leading to the farmhouse.

Detective-Sergeant Johns closed the lid of the tea-basket as Gees passed by on the other side of the road and took it toward his car.

"Enough there to keep you busy for some while, Miss Brandon," Gees observed at about a quarter to eleven on the following morning. "One copy and destroy your notes, as before. I want a complete record of everything to go to Tott when I feel the case is advanced enough. And if you feel like making any comments or suggestions, don't hesitate over it, but come to me with them. Tott is watchful, I know, but he doesn't seem to appreciate the seriousness of this."

"That is, as far as you know," she remarked.

"Just so—he may be fully alive to it. But don't start that yet, Miss Brandon—transcribing it, I mean. You see by what you've taken down that Denghisovski is coming here to hand me a hundred pounds in notes and talk over using the money, at eleven o'clock?"

"Yes, I noticed it," she agreed.

"Well, he may be here at any minute, now. Earphones out as soon as you've shown him in to me, and get all he says very carefully. I want the man to damn himself thoroughly, and I'm afraid I won't be able to use any of those notes for the plain van people. They'll be wanted as evidence, probably, later on. Oh, and that reminds me!"

"Yes, Mr. Green?" She reached for her notebook again.

"No—I'm not going to dictate any more, before that knobby devil the panjandrum gets here—did I tell you he's the original Great Panjandrum? No? Well, you'll see the little round button atop for yourself when he takes his hat off. Now what the devil was I going to tell you? Oh, yes, I know. West Bromwich Corporation."

"What about it?" she asked amusedly.

"Nothing to smile about," he said. "Remind me about Friday—yes, Friday morning, unless something happens in the meantime—I must get on to my bank manager and tell him to sell my seven hundred pounds' worth of West Bromwich Corporation stock. Don't forget it, please, for I know I shall, and we mustn't lose our nice furniture."

"I'll remember it for you, Mr. Green."

"Then that's all, till the panjandrum arrives. You'd better be writing when he comes in—don't be typing, for if you do he'll notice the cessation of the clatter when you begin taking him down with the earphones, and quite possibly get suspicious about it. Conspirators are naturally suspicious people, and he's no exception to the rule. Our devil appears to be the only really trusting one."

"Ah, but"—she remembered passages in the notes she had taken down—"a woman under the influence of the passion you described believes only what she wishes to believe. That's the reason."

"Well, you're a woman, so you ought to know, Miss Brandon. I like that comment, and want you to make any others that come to your mind. But now I'll go along to my own room—the panjandrum is about due. You'd better get the day-book out and be making entries in it—let him see it open with a pen in it on your desk, and push the typewriter aside as if you were not using it for the present. I'll go, now."

In his own office room, he arranged the armchair at the end of his desk carefully. The panjandrum, if and when he arrived, must talk straight at the hidden microphone.

# CHAPTER IX

## TWO INTERVIEWS

THE panjandrum, ushered into Gees' room by Miss Brandon, looked round approvingly. The plain van people had done the room well.

"Very comfortable, comrade," he observed after the door had closed. Then he went to the window and looked out. "Not followed," he added. "That is, not into this quiet street. Part of the way, perhaps. Not that it makes any difference. You are one of us, now."

"Oh, quite," Gees told him. "Do sit down, comrade."

The panjandrum took the armchair without moving it, and Gees seated himself in his usual place at his desk. The concealed microphone was angled to take both voices, naturally.

"Thank you," and the panjandrum nestled luxuriously. "Now—I have not much time to-day. About the power stations—what are your plans? We do not wish to waste money, and at the same time it is essential that you should reveal all your actions to us."

"Oh, quite," Gees agreed again, realising that the you-spy-on-me-I-spy-on-you machinery was to operate on him as well as on all the rest of the gang. "Well, comrade, I think Comrade Lenoir has told you by this time of my idea—before I became one of your party, that is—for the organisation of crime. A friend of mine, an electrical engineer, was even more enthusiastic over the scheme than myself, and he is on the staff at Battersea. I have yet to devise a plan for Lots Road."

It was all quite true. In comfortable chairs at his club, Gees and his friend had discussed the folly of modern criminals, and agreed that they would remain a social irritant rather than a formidable danger to civilisation, because they lacked cohesion as a body of people.

"Do you propose that we should trust this man?" the panjandrum inquired doubtfully. "I gather that he belongs to the intelligentsia, and that class is equally dangerous with the capitalists, to us."

Gees smiled. "He has a wife and two children—an expensive wife, I should have said," he explained. "Speaking from the capitalist viewpoint, he has about as much principle as I have myself, and I think he would hand me the pawn ticket for his soul in exchange for fifty pounds. Mind, comrade, I do not intend to go to him and reveal our plans. I understand that we have at least a fortnight in which to arrange everything. I intend to sound him, to proceed step by step in corrupting him, to lend him the money, ostensibly, and *to get* him!"

He felt rather proud of the final, fierce declaration. The panjandrum nodded approval, thoughtfully.

"I begin to feel that Comrade Lenoir is right about you," he said. "Write me the name and address of this man on a piece of paper. When I have memorised it, I will destroy the paper. Keep nothing written, comrade. It has been the downfall of too many, the written word."

"My own idea, entirely," Gees agreed as he reached for a pad and pencil. "Not one written word do I keep, myself."

Which was perfectly true, for the records in the safe behind the wardrobe were all typed. He wrote the name and address of Reginald Parkes, electrical engineer, and handed it over, knowing that he had slandered poor Reggie grossly, and Mrs. Parkes still more. The panjandrum took the screed, read it over, and handed it back.

"Destroy it, comrade," he bade. "A friend of mine, a lady, lives in the flat above his in Prince's Mansions. I need not keep it."

Gees took out his lighter and applied the flame to the paper. It curled down to blackness in a glass ashtray on the desk.

"Do have a cigarette, comrade," he urged, and offered his case.

The panjandrum took one, and Gees made a long arm to give him a light. He settled back in the armchair again, and blew a torpedo-wake of smoke ceilingward while Gees lighted up for himself.

"And concerning Lots Road you have no plan, as yet, comrade?" the panjandrum asked after a thoughtful interval.

"Nothing definite enough to report," Gees answered, contracting his brows as if he were still putting anxious hours to the solution of the problem. "Two or three ideas, but nebulous ones. As soon as I can decide on a means of entry, I will let you know. For Parkes, you see, will take care of Battersea, if all goes well, and I intend to look after Lots Road myself—but I have to get in, first."

The statement was not strictly true. He intended to look after the place, but not by getting in at all. Still, a slight inaccuracy of that sort was a thing he could take in his stride.

"I had better"—the panjandrum felt in his breast pocket—"hand you these now." He took out a rubber-banded wad of notes and put them down on the desk. "One hundred pounds—the serial numbers of the notes are consecutive, but you may count them if you wish."

"Comrade," Gees said, and shook his head solemnly. "Between us initiates of the pentagram there must be perfect trust."

"True, comrade," the panjandrum agreed. "Only so can we accomplish our great aims. But mind, you will be held to account for every one of these notes, so keep a mental record of expenditure."

"You shall have a full accounting," Gees promised—and meant it.

"Now, comrade, concerning to-morrow. You will go to Sunderland with Comrade Ivan—it is a matter of only a few hours, but I wish you to gain some idea of the completeness of our organisation. I would suggest that you meet Ivan at Kestwell—go by car, and consider it an expense to be met out of the hundred pounds. To-day, I take it, you will proceed to deal with your friend the electrical engineer."

"Now I have the money, I shall see if I can get him to lunch with me," Gees agreed. "Also, I think, I ought to see Tott."

The panjandrum leaped up from the chair as suddenly as if a hornets' nest had opened under him. Stupefaction in his expression gave place to murderous, vindictive rage as he glared at Gees still seated.

"By God!" he grated out. "You—you die if you do!"

It was odd that one who denied the existence of a Deity still had the habit of invoking Him in moments of excitement, Gees reflected. He smiled and shook his head at the angry man.

"I think not," he said. "Do sit down again, comrade. Detective-Sergeant Johns was keeping watch on Kestwell yesterday afternoon—I saw him when I came out. He must have seen you and the others leave after I had gone, and if we are not careful Tott may be raiding that place just when it would be most inconvenient for us. So I propose to go to Tott and put him off anything of the kind."

The panjandrum sank into the chair again, and a look of vast relief ousted that of wrath from his face.

"I—I apologise for the mistrust, comrade," he said rather uncertainly. "You see, you are new to us, and this—it appeared as if you meant betrayal, as you said it. But how— what can you tell Tott to divert his suspicions?"

"I thought I'd tell him that you asked me down there yesterday," Gees said with an appearance of the utmost frankness—in reality, he was thoroughly enjoying himself. "You, according to what I shall tell him, mean to turn Kestwell into a Communist college—on the lines of Ruskin College and places of that sort, you know. I shall tell him that the building estate idea only means selling off outlying plots to provide funds for the college, and you got me down to consult me as an English man, likely to know people, about getting a good architect—"

"But why should you go to him to tell him any such thing?" the panjandrum interrupted. "Surely he will see that you are merely trying to fool him, and will investigate the place all the more?"

Again Gees shook his head. "He won't, the way I shall put it," he dissented. "There, I shall tell him, is going to be established a plague spot, a cancer that will eat into the capitalist system. One of the most poisonous centres of disaffection that could possibly be established in the country. What is he going to do about it? If he hasn't the common decency to put a stop to it somehow, I'm going to get questions asked in parliament, raise hell generally, and get him thrown out of his job as a spineless inefficient. At that point, he'll have me thrown out of his office, and reckon that since I'm such a dirty traitor to you I'm no use to him, and meanwhile if you like to establish a hot air factory at Kestwell he can comfortably forget all about it. Then he'll leave the place alone, do you see?"

The panjandrum laughed softly. "Clever, comrade!" he said. "Yes, it is clever. And then we need have no fear that the bombs will be discovered there. Yes, go to Tott to-day by all means, as if you were still hot with wrath at the idea of such a college. Betray the idea to him as you say, and make him think you are traitor all round, not to be trusted by anyone. Ah, I must tell Comrade Lenoir of this!"

"Let me tell her," Gees urged. "Tell her to come to the Castle at Richmond again to-night, at eight o'clock, and I will dine there with her and tell her then. Will you do that for me?"

"With pleasure, comrade. Ah, there is a woman! We should not use women too much in our work, but her I except. At eight to-night, at the Castle at Richmond—yes. And she would go much farther than that to find you at the end of the journey. Yes, a great woman."

"Undoubtedly, comrade," Gees agreed.

"And now, your day will be filled," the panjandrum said, and rose to go. "To find and sound your electrical engineer, to fill Tott's eyes with dust, and to meet Comrade Lenoir—the sweet at the end of the meal, *hein?"*

"Savoury, surely," Gees corrected him.

"Ha! Of a truth, savoury! For you to taste, comrade, I think—we others only get the fragrance from the dish."

Gees thought of the Bisto kids, and shook hands. Then he saw the panjandrum to the door and went into Miss Brandon's room.

"Did you get it all?" he asked rather anxiously.

She nodded. "Nearly every word, I believe," she answered.

"Well, transcribe that interview first, and let me have two copies instead of one. I want to take Tott a copy, as well as adding one to the collection in the safe. Get Reggie Parkes on the 'phone for me—no, though, I'll ring him myself. You've plenty to do there."

He rang Parkes and arranged to lunch at Odone's at Victoria. Then he counted off twenty-five of those one-pound notes and pocketed them: on some pretext or other, he could persuade Parkes to accept a loan of twenty pounds, and quite probably some watcher for the panjandrum would be in the restaurant and see the money pass: if not, it would be doing old Reggie a good turn. And, with Miss Brandon's transcript of the interview with the panjandrum, Gees no longer felt that he need keep all the notes as evidence: the five would pay for lunch and dinner.

He waited for the typescript to take to his interview with Tott, and then went off happily and wealthily to lunch with Reggie. It was wiser, he felt, not to telephone Tott and announce that he wanted an interview. A direct onslaught and shock tactics would be better.

"Y'know, Reggie"—Gees leaned on the table at Odone's and stirred his coffee, feeling almost drowsy after his very good lunch—"I feel a sort of call to go and look over Lots Road power station. An urge, as you might say. I'd like to stand under one of those humming giants and hear the music of the spheres—or are they cylinders?"

"Do you mean it?" Reggie, a cheerful, stoutish little man, asked. "Why not come down and look at our place? We're newer."

"No. My guardian spirit, or karma, or what-have-you, declares for Lots Road. Besides, I can come and irritate you whenever I like. It's the thirst for the unattainable, old lad, and it must be Lots Road. Wednesday, I think—yes, Wednesday afternoon, for preference. What can you do about it for me?"

"Well, I can write to my friend Dodgson—he's on the staff there, you know, and tell him you'd like to be shown round. He'll either go over it with you himself or detail a man to do it."

"Excellent, old lad! Dodgson—yes. Any relation to the woman who wrote Young's *Night Thoughts,* or something of the sort? Never mind his ancestry, though—I'll accept him on your recommendation. And you'll write and tell him I'll be along on Wednesday afternoon?"

"I'll drop him a line as soon as I get back," Reggie promised. "And—you're sure it's all right about this twenty quid? I mean, you won't have to come down on me for it in a hurry?"

"Laddie, I am rolling!" Gees assured him. "In that confidential agency of mine I've struck a vein that will crush at eight ounces to the ton, and the stamps are working night and day. I forgot, though—you're electrical, not mining. Now I will get a bill and hie me back to the daily task, the common round. I have to work damned hard, Reggie—at it all yesterday from the moment I got up till dinner time, while you probably loafed away your Sunday like the other plutocrats. And this afternoon—Oh, this afternoon! But it's worth it, my son, and if I sit here much longer I shall go to sleep. Ho, waiter! Bill!"

Having paid the bill, he shook hands on the doorstep with the grateful Reggie, asked that his dear love might be conveyed to Mrs. Parkes and the two little devils, and caught an eastward-going bus. Some few minutes later he handed a card to a uniformed constable, who handed it to a police clerk, who disappeared with it. In far less time than Gees had anticipated, the man returned.

"This way, sir, please," he said.

Gees followed him to the severely plain and rather gloomy office in which sat Inspector Tott at a desk with papers neatly arranged on it. The inspector looked up almost happily.

"*Mister* Green," he said. "Do sit down, *Mister* Green, though I don't run a microphone myself. And I want to tell you before you say a word that my fee for an initial consultation is two guineas."

"Oh, that's easy," Gees responded, and drew up a chair to the desk. He took from his pocket the two pound notes he had left after paying for lunch, together with some silver, and put down the notes and a two-shilling piece. "I might have made it contra to the account I told my secretary to send in to you, but perhaps that hasn't come through to you yet. Please settle it when it does."

He seated himself, and noted that Tott appeared slightly discon-
certed. The inevitable cigarette case appeared, but Tott shook his
head.

"Nope," he said. "Not just now. What do you want?" He let the
two notes and silver coin lie where Gees had put them down.

"First of all," Gees answered, "to ask you if you'll do me a favour
by congratulating the lady who came to the meeting on Saturday
night. I don't recall ever having seen a more convincing drunk who
wasn't one, except Cicely Courtneidge. But tell her she shouldn't
have let me spot her when I came out from the Castle at Richmond."

"Let me tell you," Tott answered, "that I don't care one hoot who
you spot or don't spot. You're just negligible, to me."

"It should have been 'whom,' not 'who,' Inspector," Gees corrected him blandly. "But that was a mere aside. I expect Johns has
told you I was at a place called Kestwell yesterday afternoon, with
friends?"

"Yes, and you'll go inside with those friends, and do time with
them after, if I have anything to do with it," Tott snapped.

"Oh, say not so," Gees begged. "One of them came to see me this
morning, and we had a surprisingly nice talk. He—"

"Oh, tell me some news!" Tott snapped again, interrupting. "All
you amateur sleuths are alike, except that some are worse than
others. And let me tell you, *Mister* Green, you've done the dirty on
me twice, once by putting Johns off that woman, and then by
sending me haring down to Chelsea on a fool's errand. If you think
you can come here and curry favour with me after that, go and souse
your head in cold water. You can't tell me a thing that I don't
know!"

"For instance," Gees observed, quite unruffled by the exordium,
"bombs. Three pound bombs, each of 'em equivalent to a hundred
pounds of high explosive. I can see that's got under your skin, too.
Now would you mind being a little less uppish while I explain,
please?"

"I'll give you just five minutes, and then have you thrown out,"
Tott promised. "I don't like you, and I don't trust you."

"Suits me admirably. Being thrown out, you may like to know, is
part of my programme for this inter view. I'm here to tell you that
Kestwell is being turned into a Communist college, and if you don't
do something to stop it I'm going to have questions asked about it in
Parliament, and you're going to lose your job—"

"Get out of here, you infernal idiot!" Tott growled.

"That's it, exactly!" Gees assured him. "That's what I told Denghisovski I was going to tell you, to put you off nosing round Kestwell and discovering the bombs they're storing there. Y'see, Inspector, you've got to be put off it, because they're going to start storing the bombs in the farmhouse to-morrow, and they're not to be used for another fortnight at least. And I'm to go to Sunderland to-morrow with Schroder, the flying man, to see what a complete organisation they have up there, and I'm meeting darling Christine at the Castle at Richmond again to-night to tell her how I've fooled you and put you off even looking at Kestwell again, and a friend of mine is to blow up Battersea power station when the time conies—I lent him twenty quid of Denghisovski's money at lunch to-day—and I'm to blow up Lots Road myself. Oh, I am having a time! And of course I put my secretary on the microphone while Denghisovski talked this morning, just as I did for you, because I want a complete record of the whole case, and here's the transcript of her notes."

He put the folded typescript down on the desk before Tott, who took it up, unfolded it, and gazed at the top sheet and then at Gees. After some seconds he shook his head, gravely.

"I don't trust you," he said. "I don't trust anyone who touches that pitch—it makes the hands too dirty."

"Oh, I know how you feel about me," Gees answered, "and I gave you good cause to feel it. But I'm not sorry, for what I did with Johns put me in their inner councils, and fooling you over that relief station convinced them you're my enemy. Read that, though."

"And then find out why Denghisovski and you concocted it for me," Tott suggested. "D'you think I've got all the men in the world to spare while you try to make game of me, *Mister* Green?"

"Make it plain Green, if you like, and don't trust me," Gees advised. "I don't care one hoot in a coal yard, and all I want is for you to get on to those bombs at Kestwell. I don't want paying— Denghisovski is paying me, and he handed me a hundred of the best for a start this morning. You needn't trust me, but the bombs will start accumulating at Kestwell to-morrow. And I want one favour from you."

"Here, take this money," Tott said, and pointed at the notes.

"Right—I'll have enough for Christine's dinner without drawing any more on the panjandrum's funds," Gees assented, and pocketed the notes and coin again. "You can send my account back marked paid *per contra,* and harmony will be established again. But one favour."

"What?" Tott barked, in a way that suggested denial.

"Please get in one large man to take me by the collar and run me out. Tell him he needn't mind if he hurts me a bit, and the bigger the public exhibition he makes of me, the better."

Without replying, Tott jabbed down a bell-push at the end of his desk. Possibly he was remembering the first doorway on the left in Sidney Street, at the moment. A constable appeared.

"Ah, Edwards!" Tott said happily. "Take this man and chuck him out into the street. Land him on his nose, if you can—there'll be no damages for assault. He's asked for it, and he can have it."

Gees felt himself caught up, and made no resistance. The large hand thrust inside his collar almost throttled him until the stud gave way, and the other large hand gripping his wrist threatened to break his arm if he afforded the slightest leverage. He was run along the stone-floored passageways, and just managed to keep his feet until his captor got to the doorway and flung him out. He landed on his hands and knees, and felt his soft hat, flung after him, strike his cheek as he scrambled rather painfully to his feet.

"One new shirt, one new collar, and Peter alone knows what else," he soliloquised. "Never mind, though. The panjandrum has already paid."

# CHAPTER X

# ONE SMALL CHILD

ALTHOUGH the dining-room of the Castle Hotel at Richmond is spaciously planned, and the tables set apart for that intimacy between pairs which sometimes precedes marriage and hardly ever follows it, neither Christine nor Gees spoke of any of the objects of their meeting while at dinner in the room. She accounted for her surname by telling him that her paternal grandfather had been French, and that she was the only daughter of his only son, who had been shot during the revolution by the Czarists—and she, then a small child, had witnessed the shooting. Her mother had brought her to England and had had her educated for the most part in English schools, finishing with two years in Paris to make certain that the girl should be capably tri-lingual. After that, she had proved her value to what she called the Left of the Comintern, and had risen to her present important position of travelling inspector. Gees gathered that she had powers almost of life and death, and, what was more, was capable of using them to the best advantage for her party—and, of course, for herself.

They moved out to the lawn overlooking the river for coffee, and, being beyond the possibility of betraying secrets to eavesdroppers, came to consideration of present facts and plans.

"I want very much to hear all you have to tell me, comrade," Christine opened, "but first, I think, I ought to tell you my news. Very grave news for us, possibly. They have arrested Schlatzenbaum."

"You mean—Tott has got him?" Gees asked, and succeeded in looking badly perturbed over the information.

She shook her head. "No—do not let your expression betray alarm, dear comrade," she counselled. "It is not well to show any watchers who may be here that you are so wholeheartedly of our party, for they will know that I should tell you this. No, not Tott, but his own folly, and it was East End divisional men who took him. It was in a bar, the George and Dragon, in the Commercial Road district. He had been drinking, and quarrelled with a man—I think the man was a spy who forced the quarrel, in reality. But however that may have been, Schlatzenbaum put his hand to his hip pocket, and instantly they were on him. The charge is carrying a loaded firearm without a police permit—they took his automatic pistol when they searched him."

"And that, of course, will mean deportation," Gees observed.

"Imprisonment first," she pointed out. "Three to six months—and in a month or less he will be at liberty again, free to take vengeance on the slaves of the capitalists who did this thing. But it was utter folly; I have warned them all, but now I shall order that no one of them is to carry firearms of any kind until the day."

"It's the best course," he agreed. "They're no use in this country, really. You never get away with a killing, and people know that so well that a mere threat is generally ineffective."

"That is, under the capitalist system," she said significantly. "We shall change it, of course—we leaders, that is. But there—you see, comrade, I understand English life and temperament, which perhaps is the reason for my loving you so intensely—because I understand you and read your thoughts so easily. I know the English."

"I could see that as soon as I met you," Gees lied cheerfully. "You get the sense of humour that makes us what we are."

"Ah! That sense of humour! The poor slaves of the capitalists who were driven to death and sang 'Tipperary' as they marched! Deluded, but laughing to the end. A wonderful people—and think what we shall make of them when we have destroyed their tyrants!"

"Ah, think!" he almost sighed. "What you will make of them!"

"We—for you are one of us," she insisted. "You will head the secret police, and have the right of killing. But I would have said—it is not easy to get others who can comprehend the English temperament as I do. Comrade Leonid—yes, in some measure, yet he too has the innate savagery of the Slav—I know he loves killing for its own sake. And Smirilov. He too enjoys a mass execution, and was one of the most active in the Odessa purgings. But genius there may be madness here, which is why you are so valuable to us. You know the English temperament as my countrymen can never know it. You will see where a certain leniency is a necessity—though I warn you, comrade, you must never be too lenient, never be weak."

"I won't," he promised, and thought what he would do to that Odessa purger if ever the chance came his way. They were thoroughly nasty people, these plotters, and he hoped Tott would go after those bombs.

"I know you will not. And now"—her eyes softened to a personal tenderness—"before you tell me of your day, tell me what I shall call you. I am Christine to you, and the name as you speak it grows new and wonderful even to my hearing. What will you be to me, for I call every one of us 'comrade,' and there must be a special name for you?"

"Well, then, you can call me 'Gregory'," he answered without hesitation. For he hated that name of his like the devil, and took good care that none of his intimates used it even if they knew it.

"Gregory—Grigori—yes, a fitting name for you." He repressed a squirm at the accusation. "Now, Grigori, tell me of your day. Smirilov was there to see you thrown out from the police office, and Comrade Leonid said you wished to tell me of your cleverness with Tott, so the story should wait till I met you. And before that you gave money to a man in a restaurant, Leonid told me. Was it for us?"

He nodded. "One of the Battersea engineers," he said. "He doesn't know yet that he is to destroy the plant there—I am proceeding carefully. Buy him first, then give him his orders."

"And his bombs." She nodded approval. "Grigori, I think you must find another man for Lots Road. For now Schlatzenbaum is immobilised, you will be needed in the north. Your visit to Sunderland to-morrow, I think, will be the first of many. Schroder is to be trusted, but he is not very clever. He is an airman, and not much more."

"Schlatzenbaum was in charge in the north, then?" he asked.

"In some measure. Smirilov organised much of it, but he will be needed to disorganise the London docks, and that is all one man's work until the day. I have cabled Paris for a man to replace Schlatzenbaum here, but he will not know England and the English very well. He has been working for the second French revolution, which is to follow this here, and may not comprehend your conditions in time to be of much use. No. I think you must take charge of the workers in the north."

"Will Schlatzenbaum give anything away?" he asked.

She smiled. "The capitalists may imprison him for his illegal possession of firearms, but he knows quite well that he is not safe even in their prisons if he betrays us in any way. He will not talk."

"And what could be fairer than that?" Gees observed reflectively.

"Now tell me how Tott had you thrown out, dear Grigori," she asked.

"Oh, it was lovely!" he said—and meant it. "You see, his man Johns was down at Kestwell yesterday afternoon, sitting outside the gateway to see who was there, and it struck me that if we were to make the place a safe storehouse for the bombs, Tott had to be put off suspecting its real use. So I went and betrayed you to him—told him the place was going to be turned into a college for Communists, and raved that he'd got to stop it. I told him I'd get questions asked about it in the House of Commons if he didn't, and that I'd see he was thrown out of his job for letting such a hot bed of Communist teaching be established in the country, and, naturally, he had me thrown out. And now he won't bother any more about Kestwell, or about me. He'll think me a traitor to the cause, and won't care what I do, and he'll wait for Communist students to go to the Kestwell college so that he can keep an eye on them when they come out, and we can put bombs in the windows instead of aspidistras, if we like. He won't worry."

She laughed softly. "Oh, I love your English sense of humour!" she exclaimed. "The great inspector, waiting for students at Kestwell, while Comrade Leonid takes bombs there by the car-load!"

"And let's hope it keeps fine for him," Gees observed.

The colloquialism was beyond her, as he had thought it would be. "The weather has been lovely, ever since you and I met on the train," she said gravely. "And now, since Tott merely despises you as a traitor to us and of no use to him, I may meet you where I will—until the day comes when we shall travel always together."

"That's a wonderful thought," he said. "A perfectly marvellous thought, Christine. By the way, how are the bruises?"

"Still there. Black marks, where your fingers pressed."

"I'd like to make some more—lots more. But we ought to be going, I think. How about walking out and seeing if I can spot any of Tott's spies down here? I know a few of them."

"Yes. But first tell me—have you a permit to carry arms?"

He nodded assent. "Two—for a shotgun, and for an automatic."

"Then I want you to take this pistol of mine, for the present. Take the handbag, take the pistol out, and slip it in your pocket, for I have no permit, and we must not run unnecessary risks. I met Leonid at Liverpool Street when he told me of Schlatzenbaum's arrest, and have not been able to hide the pistol since. It is quite small."

Gees took the bag, and, praying to all his gods that Tott would not arrest him for anything on his way home, groped for the pistol, found it, and shoved it down in his trouser pocket under cover of the table. For, he knew, his permit would not save him if he were searched, and Tott, perplexed as to his real intentions, would be only too glad of a pretext for shoving him inside and charging him with anything that would keep him immobilised (as Christine had put it with regard to Schlatzenbaum) for awhile. He felt that he loved the descriptiveness of the word: immobilised burglars, for instance!

"And, since I've got it, we'd better go back separately, as before," he remarked as he handed the bag back. "For if Tott managed to catch me with a loaded pistol on me, and you were with me, he'd take the pair of us. We'll go a bit of the way down toward the station together, because I don't like your leaving me, but we'd better not go all the way. I'll find you a taxi, as before."

He reflected over Schlatzenbaum's arrest as he paid the bill and escorted Christine out from the place. She believed that divisional activity accounted for it, but he felt that he knew better: Tott was uncannily watchful: Schlatzenbaum, probably, had ceased to be useful as a guide to minor plotters—probably Tott knew all the man's connections in the north by this time—and therefore had to go inside as a prelude to being deported. And, thinking it over, Gees could understand Tony Briggs' complacency in connection with these people. They were all taped, card-indexed and cross-indexed to the nth degree, and would be put to hard labour or out of the country at the proper time.

But, in the Volodskanya Gnomon, or somewhere else available, reposed a package containing twelve thousand one-pound notes. Gees himself, after this evening, had only seventy-five similar notes left, and that amount, including office expenses and Miss Brandon's salary, would not carry him much longer than a month. Twelve thousand, if there were any possible means of getting hold of them, would put him on velvet for quite a long time. Little as he liked this rather tepid love-making which seemed to content Christine for the present, he felt that it would be worth while to continue it a bit longer—as long as that package of notes remained available, in fact.

Further, since Schroder appeared to be given charge of the package, and, he, Gees was to accompany Schroder on various trips to the north, it ought to be possible to contrive some way of preventing typed records from feeling lonely in the safe behind the wardrobe.

He gripped Christine's arm in a fashion that must have made another bruise under her sleeve as they went out, and she flashed him a wincing smile in response. They came to the main street and turned downhill toward the station. At the corner, he decided, he would get a taxi and put her in it, and then make his own way to the station.

They walked slowly, and, disengaging his hold on her arm, she took his, a form of intimacy that he hated in public, but endured for the sake of the package in the Gnomon. Just ahead of them was a woman wheeling a perambulator on the pavement, and the small child in the perambulator recalled to Gees' mind the happy little thing he had seen the afternoon before, lifted aloft in Mrs. Johns' hands and cackling laughter down at its mother. Just such another happy little thing.

Events rushed on top of each other with uncanny rapidity when a drunken man came toward the perambulator, staggering up-hill—Gees saw him, and wondered why he had not been taken in charge before he got so far from the scene of his imbibings. He can-noned into the perambulator and overturned it, and as the woman shrieked and the child went flying out into the road a big, six-wheeled lorry came rumbling down the hill—death, pet-rol-driven, and hurrying. But Christine leaped outward, snatched up the child from almost under the radiator as the lorry's brakes screeched under the driver's hand: the girl had no time to return with her burden, if she herself would escape a mangling death, and she went on across to the opposite pavement, missing an up-hill-driven car by another miracle. Gees found that he had the drunkard by the throat and was shaking him savagely, though he had no idea how he had got hold of the man. The mother, as the woman with the perambulator evidently was, was being held up by two other women, and as Christine came back with the child round the front of the now stationary lorry, a policeman grasped Gees' arm.

" 'Ere, let 'im go, sir," he asked solemnly. "I'll look arter 'im. I saw the 'ole thing, an' that lady ought to 'ave a medal."

The lorry driver came forward, and the policeman produced notebook and pencil, and sucked the latter in the approved style, while the inevitable crowd began to gather. Gees saw a light in Christine's soft eyes that was altogether incompatible with what he knew of her.

"It was the bravest thing I have ever seen," he said impulsively. "She risked death twice, and won. And look!"

For Christine gave the child back to its mother, righted the per-ambulator, and, when the shaken woman put her girl in it because she trembled too much to hold her, knelt on the pavement and caressed and soothed the little being until she had it gurgling happily, while the policeman turned to taking the name and address of the lorry driver and car driver who had only just missed killing both Christine and the child. By that time, a fellow-worker of his had arrived, and taken charge of the drunkard who had caused all the trouble.

"Now, miss." The first policeman turned to Christine. "Might I 'ave your name and address, please? And this gentleman's too?" He indicated Gees with the second query.

"Officer, I'd much rather you didn't, please," Christine told him. "You have the lorry driver here, and the driver of the car, and the lady whose child it is—plenty of witnesses. Please don't ask for me or my friend"—and she too indicated Gees—"to give evidence. It was all an accident, and nobody was hurt, you see."

"No, miss, I know, but you might have been killed, an' it was your courage that saved a life as well as your own. You don't ought to—well, I'd take my hat off to you if it wasn't a 'elmet, miss, an' I know what the magistrates'll say when I tell 'em what you done. As this gentleman said, it was the bravest thing ever."

"Please, constable, let us go. It's simply a case of drunk and disorderly, and you can prove it without us. Please!"

She looked up at him, and her lovely eyes won her case. He closed his notebook to salute her, standing to attention the while.

"I oughtn't to do it, miss, but I will. An' I'll never forget that minute as long as I live. God bless you, miss, wherever you go an' whatever you do. Now, ma'am"—he turned to the woman with the perambulator, "may I have your name an' address, please? 'Ere, somebody get 'er a glass o' water or somethin', an' 'old on to that pram! There's plenty of yer. George, you take 'im along to the station, an' I'll be along to charge 'im—drunk an' disorderly an' attemptin' to cause grievous bodily 'arm, as soon as I've got these names an' addresses down. Now, mister, don't you worry. You stopped that lorry like a hero, I know, but what's yer name an' where d'yer live? Miss, good night, an' God bless you! Take care of 'er, sir, an' I know I don't oughter let either 'er or you go, but since she asked it I will."

Christine's hand on Gees' arm urged him out from the crowd and away down the hill: some few of the onlookers followed them a little way, and an urgent Pressman pestered them until Gees threatened to hit him if he did not desist, after which he followed at a distance, saw Gees hail a taxicab at the bend of the street, and put the girl in it.

Of his own accord Gees took her hand and kissed it.

"My dear," he said gravely, "I wonder if you realise how wonderful you were? It was, as I said then, the bravest thing I have ever seen."

"If you are pleased with me, I am glad," she answered simply.

"Pleased?" he said, rather emotionally. "That child—" he paused, thinking of her as she made the crossing of the road with ugly death threatening her twice, and then soothed the child in the perambulator.

Then, as she looked out at him from the cab window, she spoilt it.

"Did you notice how that capitalist slave asked his God to bless me?" she asked. "The poor fool! And that child. I love all little children. They are the revolutionaries of to-morrow —we must save them all. As the Czarists killed my father, so I hope that child will be taught to kill capitalists. Good night, Grigori—I shall see you at Kestwell, after you come back from Sunderland to-morrow."

He stood back, bareheaded, and motioned the driver to go on—he had already given Oddenino's as her destination. Then he too went on, marvelling at the miracle of such a woman, such a contradiction.

"Revolutionaries of to-morrow. The capitalist slave asked his God. Taught to kill capitalists . . ."

In a way, he could understand her. She was crazed by the shooting of her father, as Lenin had been crazed by his brother's death, a fanatic, and utterly implacable. There were wrongs on both sides, and these people sought to cure the ills from which the whole world suffered by killing off all who disagreed with them and reducing the underlings to a far worse state than that in which they lived at present. Wrongs on both sides, yes, but mass executions and the utter extinction of a class were new ideas, born of an exaggerated and perverted sense of wrong: no brotherhood of mankind could ever be achieved by class warfare: evolution, not revolution, was the solution.

Why the devil should one stand a man like Tony Briggs against a wall and shoot him? It was so damned silly! Tony was a good sport, and those Trinidad limes of his—

Gees went into the South-Western hotel by the station and had a long whisky and soda before catching his train. They had no Trinidad limes, so it was the next best thing. And he drank success to Tott who had had him thrown out of the office, and ignored the wink of a tall girl who saw that he looked interested in something or other—perhaps in her. But no! She was far too like Christine, though not nearly so lovely.

# CHAPTER XI

## COLLATED FACTS—AND INFERENCE

WHEN, on the Tuesday morning, Detective-Sergeant Johns appeared before his superior officer in the latter's office to take his orders for the day, there was a gleam in Inspector Tott's eyes that betrayed the man's humanity: he was a fellow-human, as well as a police inspector, and in presence of Johns was not ashamed of it.

"Hullo, Johns. How's the wife?"

"Oh, blooming, sir, absolutely blooming."

"And the kid?"

"In the pink, sir. If I started to tell you—"

"Oh, no, you don't!" Tott interrupted. "Y'know, Johns, since you married that woman you've been altogether different. Spry at your job, up to all I ask of you—it looked as if you'd hit the bullseye when we made you that presentation and wished you all the luck there is, and by gum it still looks like it! But we'll cut out the home and family and get down to business. The Allen affair, now?"

Johns shook his head. "Nothing to report, sir," he said. "It's got to cook for a while. There's no doubt the earl is implicated, now, but I've got to get proof before I put the case before you."

"Quite right, Johns—quite right—we can't proceed without definite evidence. And what do you propose to do about it?"

"Well, sir, if I put to-day into it, I may get something. With people as cautious as they are, I have to be cautious too. But I don't think I shall lose out at the finish. It's a business of patience."

"Quite right, Johns—everything is. Now with regard to this affair of the gang that hang out at Kestwell. I got your report on Sunday afternoon's meeting, and don't worry about that fool Green having seen you. I don't know what he's playing at, and I don't care a damn. He's just another of those amateurs who think they can do our job. But he put out a word or two which may be the goods and again may not. This Allen business—how are you fixed?"

"Well, sir, I ought to put in all to-day on it, and maybe most of to-morrow. I've got to get something definite, you see."

"Of course you have, man. What about to-morrow afternoon, though, from four o'clock onward, say? Could you go to Kestwell then?"

"I think so, sir. Yes, I could, though it would mean delaying a report to you on the Allen affair till Thursday. It's just as you think best, sir. I'll go to Kestwell and write the report when I get back in the evening. You'd have it first thing Thursday morning, then, and I could put in a report on anything at Kestwell at the same time."

"We'll fix it so, then, Johns," Tott decided. "Now, I'll tell you exactly how things stand. That fool Green came to me yesterday afternoon with a tale of bombs being stored at Kestwell. Very dangerous bombs, according to him. I don't believe it—I don't believe a word the blighter tells me, since he did the dirty on you as you know, and on me as you don't know. Never mind about that, though. The point is that he's bragged about bombs being stored somewhere at Kestwell, and if there were anything at all in what he said, those bombs would amount to something. Now you'll have time to go down to Kestwell and investigate to-morrow afternoon, eh? Say between four and five o'clock?"

"Yes, sir. I could manage that all right," Johns agreed, with a thought of the young wife waiting, and himself missing the grand ceremony of putting the baby to bed. But business had to come first, he knew.

"Right you are, then. Carry on with the Allen business as far as it goes, and make Kestwell tomorrow afternoon and investigate this suggestion of bombs being stored somewhere about the place. One other thing, now I think of it. Did you hear what happened at Richmond last night—the woman Lenoir, I mean?"

Johns shook his head. "I was on the Allen business, sir," he said.

"Yes, of course. Well, she rescued a child that had been knocked into the road in front of an oncoming lorry. I had the story of it from Sparkes—one of his men was on hand and saw the whole thing, and let her go without taking her name and address—and Green was with her at the time! Sparkes told me his man was ready to go down on his knees to the woman—reckoned it the pluckiest thing he'd ever seen either man or woman do. Which merely proves what funny things people are, of course, and especially women. To me, the main point of it is that Green was with her, and that he's evidently fallen for her badly. Which is why I mistrust his tale of the bombs at Kestwell—he's got some ulterior reason for wanting me to nose round there, I feel sure. Still, you go and nose to-morrow afternoon."

"Righto, sir. Before I go off, now—was there anything on Schlatzenbaum that might be useful when they searched him?"

"Only the gun that gives us our chance to fire him out of the country, and a slip of paper with half a dozen names on it. They're six of the people he's contacted and bribed up north, and I had the names already, so it doesn't amount to anything."

"I see, sir. Well, he's one less to worry about."

"And a point for you to mark, Johns—none of the others will carry guns, now, so you needn't be afraid of being held up with one. They know they may get stopped on the same pretext, if they do, so they'll park their artillery for the present. But I'll have Smirilov next, when they hold their meeting in that Chelsea place next Saturday night. A pal of his is due over from Paris to-day, and I've given instructions that he is to be let through. His name is Conrad Barter, Polish subject, and he's bringing a bundle of really seditious pamphlets. Smirilov is to distribute them on Saturday night, and we'll put him inside for a dose of stone-breaking and then slant him out of the country."

"And Denghisovski, sir?" Johns asked.

"Oh, no, Johns! Let him run a while longer. He's one of the most useful bits of dirt we've ever had to watch. I don't think this man Barter amounts to anything—we'll see what use he is when he gets here, though. And the Lenoir woman—I think I'll push her back home in a week or two. Give her a hint that the country isn't healthy. You might do it, some time next week. I don't like the idea of running her in after the show she put up at Richmond last night. It might have been your kid that she saved, you know, and that sort of thing gives me a sneaking liking for her. Pity she's cracked on this business."

"She's a lovely thing, too," Johns reflected aloud.

"Which makes it all the worse. And that poor mutt Green had to go and fall for her! Well, maybe when we hoof her out he'll go too, and we'll be shut of him. Two birds with one stone, eh? I must get along, though, and so must you. Cardwell is keeping an eye on Denghisovski to-day, since you're busy on the Allen affair. Get in touch with him before you go to Kestwell to-morrow, and see if he has anything useful for you. That's all, I think. If you're not back in time for me to see you to-morrow night, let me have a report first thing on Thursday, and if Green wasn't lying we'll go down and collar the bombs."

He took his hat and stick, and bade Johns good-bye at the door, for they were going in different directions.

Having finished his breakfast that Tuesday morning, Gees took his daily paper into Miss Brandon's room and put it down on her desk, so folded as to display a quarter-column under the heading—"UNKNOWN WOMAN'S BRAVERY." He pointed to the heading.

"Have a look at that, Miss Brandon," he invited. "Wheresoever the accident is, there will the Pressmen be gathered together."

She read the account, and looked up at him.

"And she was—?" she asked, merely for confirmation of her surmise.

"Correct—our devil," Gees told her. "I was the mysterious man with her. Gosh, it really thrilled me! Made me like her, too, till she spoilt it all by doing a slight rave about the policeman being a capitalist slave or something of the sort. And she told me Tott's immobilised Schlatzenbaum— jugged him, that is—and I'm to take over his job up north. Initial visit to Sunderland to-day—you know about that, though. I shall be back to-night. Now get the good old book out and make marks. We'll bring the record up to date."

For nearly half an hour he dictated, and then pointed to the paper.

"You can cut that out and paste it in on your typescript," he directed. "One copy as usual, and destroy your notes. Cigarette? Yes. Miss Brandon, how would you like to have twelve thousand pounds?"

"Don't ask me," she retorted as she took a light from him. "Thank you, Mr. Green. I've got a sweep ticket for the Derby, of course, but it won't win anything. I never do win anything."

"Just as well. You'd give me notice if you did."

"No, I wouldn't. I swear I wouldn't. I'd invest it and—and go on working. I like working with you."

"Gee-whiz! Nice to hear you call it work. But I know where twelve thousand pounds is hanging in the wind—literally hanging in the wind, some of the time. I shall be sitting next it and Schroder sitting on it to-day. Miss Brandon, I want that money."

"But—but it will be confiscated when Inspector Tott arrests these people, surely?" she asked. "He knows they have it, doesn't he?"

"Not a doubt of it. But I've got to get in first, somehow. I lay awake for hours last night thinking about that package of notes, and trying to plan out a way of getting it. There *must* be some way!"

"It doesn't seem possible, to me," she remarked thoughtfully.

"Remember Bruce and the spider, Miss Brandon. Remember—Oh, remember any old thing you like! I've got to have that packet, or bust. What do we run this office for, if not to get money?"

"The vicar of Codderlewbar hasn't turned up again," she observed, rather irrelevantly. "Not that I thought he ever would."

"Probably the schoolmistress apologised—or he did, to his wife," Gees surmised. "In any case, he wouldn't have been worth twelve thousand pounds to us, if we had taken up his case. These people are."

"Not yet," she objected. "You haven't got it."

"Don't be so damned discouraging, Miss Brandon! I know quite well it's still hanging in the wind, but that doesn't mean I won't get it. Now let me see! Yes, here's the key of the safe. I'm off in a few minutes, so you can put that report in the safe with the others when you've finished it. Better put the lot in a stiff folder, and stand it up at the side. My twelve thousand pounds will take up nearly all the room in that safe, and we want to be able to get at our reports. The inference, you observe, is that I'm going to get it."

"When?" she inquired demurely.

"Oh, the sooner the better. If Tott finds those bombs at Kestwell, he'll probably shop all our nice friends and spoil my chance. I ought to bag it either to-day or to-morrow, really. You shall have a new fur coat out of it—a fifty-pound one, say."

"It's the wrong time of year," she objected.

"You would cold-water my idea, wouldn't you?" he said derisively. "Spend it on sweets, then, or get yourself a hat. I'm going to buy me a really nice shaving-brush out of it— mine is very nearly worn out. And I'm giving the rest to the poor, which is me. We can do a lot of display advertising, and make this business really hum."

"Then I shall have to work," she pointed out.

"No, because I shall be able to afford an assistant for you. This room would hold another desk, easily. And we'll pay off the whole of the furniture instalments, and the landlord can have his rent punctually on quarter-day. No more of his— 'Dear sir, unless—' letters. No more money worries—no more anything, Miss Brandon."

"I'll put the reports in a folder, and stand it up," she promised.

"If I hear any more sceptical remarks like that, you shan't have the fifty pounds," he threatened. "Haven't I got brains? Don't I know where the stuff is for me to lay hands on?"

"You know where it is," she assented. "I didn't mean to sound sceptical, Mr. Green. But—well, the hen hasn't laid, yet."

"That's just where you're wrong! All I have to do is collect the eggs before the nest gets turned over. And I don't like that silence of yours over my having brains. It sounds ominous."

"Can silence sound anything?" she inquired.

"Oh, you know what I mean! All right, then—I haven't got brains! Now look me out—no, I'll find it myself. One of these places where they let you hire cars and drive yourself. Which reminds me—ring up the Rolls place in Conduit Street some time to-day and ask how soon they can give delivery of a Rolls-Bentley drop-head coupe, slate-grey with black wings. Don't actually order it yet, but find out how soon I can have it, licensed to the end of the year. Then ask the Commercial Union Insurance people about insurance for it, and make a note of the total cost and put it on my desk. That will be all for to-day—I don't expect to get back in time to see you before you go this evening, so we'll carry on the report to-morrow morning."

"Very good, Mr. Green. But do you really mean that about the car?"

"Now look here! Do I look dafter than usual, or what's wrong with me? Do I really mean it? Would I go into details like that if I didn't mean it? Slate-grey with black wings, drop-head coupe, Rolls-Bentley. Commercial Union Insurance. Licensed to end of year—the car, not the insurance. And the reports stood up in a folder."

"Very good, Mr. Green."

"And put the safe key in the toe of my right dress shoe in my bedroom—wrap it in paper to prevent it from flopping about. If I bring the money back tonight, I don't want it to be lying round for the charwoman to see when she comes in to-morrow morning. Now I'll get along for Sunderland. Good-bye for to-day, Miss Brandon."

"Just one thing before you go, Mr. Green," she asked.

"Yes? Do you want a day off, or what is it?"

"No, not that. But if—if anything does happen so that the business grows, please don't get an assistant. That is, not till I find I can't do it all myself. I—I'd like to do it all, if I can."

"Bless you, child! All right, I won't without consulting you first. Oh, you'll find there's seventy-five quid in the safe, so take anything you want for petty cash. It'll be fifty, though —I shall have to leave a deposit on the car when I hire it to-day. Take what you want out of it, just the same. It's pure fat, and we shall never have to account for it, any more than we shall for the twelve thousand. Now I really must go—take care of yourself and don't overwork."

In his own room, he looked out the address of a car hire firm, and then, going to the bedroom across the corridor, took a fairly heavy coat and cap: the day was quite warm, but he was going flying.

"I hope that girl isn't getting to like me too much," he soliloquised as he went down the stairs. "It would be perfectly damnable if I asked her again about kissing and she said I might."

But, still reflecting over it as he went his way to hire a car, he decided that it might be not altogether damnable, as an experience. It would mean getting a new secretary, of course. He resolved that he would avoid trouble by not saying anything about it to Eve Madeleine.

She typed steadily after he had gone, and as she worked thought of the same possibility as occupied his mind. He was really very nice, and probably, if she let him, would kiss rather thrillingly. And she was quite sure one kiss would not content him: if she gave it, he would want others, and in a very little time it would be impossible to remain on here as his secretary.

She resolved that, when he asked her again, she would refuse as before. A post like this, with such an employer, was worth holding.

Christine, having taken an early train to Leatherhead, hired a car in the town and had herself driven out to Kestwell, where she dismissed the driver and told him to return for her in about two hours' time. She found Schroder alone with his aeroplane at the back of the copse: he had just finished filling his petrol tank from a store of cans in one of the outbuildings as she approached across the grass.

"A good day for flying, Comrade Ivan," she greeted him.

He looked up at the sky. "There will be pockets, comrade," he answered. "Otherwise—yes, good. And Comrade Green?"

"I have not seen him since last night. He will be here soon, I think. You need not start quite at once, need you?"

"No. Scadder will be waiting for us at two o'clock. I ought to get away before noon. I asked because I must warm up the engine, and do not want to start it too soon. When Comrade Green comes, I think."

"Yes. You have heard about Schlatzenbaum?"

Schroder nodded. "Comrade Leonid told me, last night," he said.

"Another comrade, Barter, will arrive from Paris to-day to replace him," she announced. "But Comrade Green must take over the north, now. You will take him to all the centres in turn, during the next fortnight, and introduce our agents to him. An Englishman is best for handling Englishmen, and we can find plenty of work in London for Barter. Has Comrade Leonid told you not to carry a pistol?"

He nodded. "It was for that he came to tell me about Schlatzenbaum," he answered. "Mine is under the board with his, and with the tea-things. Smirilov has hidden his too, but I do not know where."

"And Comrade Green has mine," she said. "He has a permit for one."

Schroder gave her a meaning look. "You trust him, comrade?" he asked. "I mean—not only with your pistol?"

"I trust him far more than I trusted Schlatzenbaum," she answered. "He is completely one of us. When I first met him, he betrayed that he has criminal instincts, and the police hate him. Yesterday Inspector Tott had him thrown out from the police station, so much do they hate him. It was when he went to make it safe for the bombs to be brought here by telling Tott we mean to make a college of Kestwell."

"It is better to be thrown out of a police station than into one," Schroder observed gravely. "And he told Tott that. I am glad you feel that he is to be trusted, comrade, for I like the man. He is clever, and quick of thought, also he is a flying man. I think criminal instincts are useful, too, if properly guided."

"In a good revolutionary, they are essential," she agreed. "Criminal, that is, from the capitalist point of view—the perverted view, not ours. A good criminal, like Comrade Green, will always be a good leader of the wage-slaves. And—I found him!"

There was intense self-congratulation in the last three words. Schroder nodded a grave assent, and gazed toward the house as if hopeful that the good criminal might soon put in an appearance.

"You will have him for your lover?" he asked, quite unenviously: his mistress was the thing standing not far away from him.

"When the revolution is complete—or rather, when the bombs have been used and it has begun—I shall have him as my lover," she assented. "Already he understands that I want him, and last night, over my saving a child from being run over, he let his eyes tell how much he wants me. And in the month or less that must pass before our plans for the revolution are complete, that want of his will grow to white heat, perhaps become stronger than mine. Love is a wonderful thing."

"So I have always heard," Schroder agreed thoughtfully. "As wonderful, perhaps, as hate. I know hate. That man Tott, for one."

"Comrade Leonid wishes to do the killing, in that case," she pointed out. "But there will be others. Sergeant Johns, for instance."

"I would like to kill Johns," Schroder said, rather wistfully.

"Patience, comrade. The time is not far off, now. Comrade Leonid will bring the first of the bombs here to-day—and then some one of you must be always here on guard. Barter, I think, most of the time."

Schroder took a sausage from his pocket, blew and brushed cigarette dust off it, and bit off a piece. "We need more men," he observed as he chewed, "and now those damned police have taken Schlatzenbaum! It is time there was a revolution in this country."

And, still gazing toward the house, he bit off another piece of sausage, and went on chewing.

# CHAPTER XII

# MIKE SCADDER

THE car was a Hillman Minx saloon, and by the time Gees came to Richmond in it he decided that the makers had different ideals from those of Mr. Hore-Belisha: one had to learn that the accelerator pedal was adjusted with almost desperate anxiety for the fulfilment of its purpose, and, having learned this, Gees slid nicely up past the Roebuck and Star and Garter home, and headed for the Kingston gate at the far end of the park. He was not risking travel on the by-pass road until he knew this car a little better: the straight stretches would be much too tempting, and the police might not like him.

Some two hundred yards or so short of the turning leading to the Ham gate, he drew into the side of the road and stopped. There were two or three other cars drawn up not far off, and a cyclist or two out for exercise, but, on the whole, it was a peaceful spot. Gees got out and sought the tool-box of the car: he found a pair of pliers, and, something equally necessary to his purpose, a bit of wash-leather. Also he took out an adjustable spanner, and with this kit got back to the driving seat and took Christine's automatic pistol out of his pocket. It was a neat, blued-steel weapon with vulcanite handle, of Continental make, and of .32 calibre. Rather heavy for a woman, but useful.

He withdrew the magazine, and pulled back the recoil mechanism: as he had anticipated, there was one cartridge in the chamber ready for firing, and it fell out on to his wash-leather. He emptied seven more live cartridges from the magazine, and put both pistol and magazine back in his pocket. Then he set to work on the cartridges.

Holding each one in turn between the jaws of the adjustable spanner, he wrapped the bullet in wash-leather, gripped it with the pliers, and withdrew it. Then he shook the powder out of each shell on to the wash-leather, and carefully scraped out each shell with the aid of the corkscrew in his pocket-knife. Next, he shook the wash-leather out of the window to get rid of the powder, and hoped no motor-cyclist would stop just there to light a cigarette until he himself was well out of the park. To conclude the operation, he had recourse to the wash-leather and pliers again, and fitted each bullet back into its brass socket. Eight apparently deadly but in reality quite harmless cartridges lay on his knees, and the wash-leather had prevented the pliers from marking the bullets: unless the cartridges were examined closely, which was unlikely, they would show no signs of having been rendered harmless. He took out the magazine, reloaded it with its seven useless charges, and put the eighth back in the chamber of the pistol. Then he put the magazine back in its place, pocketed the pistol again, and started the Minx engine. It was time to go on to Kestwell.

He knew quite well that neither Christine nor any of the others would fire a pistol except in a last extremity: that extremity, though, might eventuate at any time, and he knew now that if this pistol chanced to be pointed at his head, the formality of the trigger being pressed would not worry him, while, on the other hand, the person holding the pistol would probably be extremely worried.

At about half-past eleven he drove in at the gateway of Kestwell, left the car under the chestnut tree, and went round to the back: the house, he saw, was closed, and gave no sign of occupancy. He reached Christine and Schroder just as the latter put the last piece of sausage into his mouth, and, giving them cordial greeting, took out Christine's pistol and handed it to her.

"Best not to carry it, I think," he said. "Schlatzenbaum did."

"You are quite right, Grigori," she assented. "I will put it under the board with the others. Thank you for taking care of it."

But, he noted, she worked the recoil mechanism to assure herself that the weapon was loaded before putting it away. Since the action ejected the cartridge already in the chamber and thrust another into its place, she withdrew the magazine to replace the ejected cartridge in it, and Gees, observing her, knew that she suspected nothing.

"It will be ready when needed," she said. "I will put it under the board. And now"—Schroder had climbed into the driving seat and started his engine—"it is time for you to go, Grigori. I wish I were going with you, but—this evening?"

"I've got a car," he told her. "I'm leaving it round at the front till we get back. It will be safe there, eh?"

"Yes. I shall stay here till Comrade Leonid arrives with the bombs, and after that somebody must be here always."

Schroder got out again and joined them. "We ought to go," he declared. "She is fast, my Gnomon, but there is not much time."

So Gees clasped Christine's hand and gazed into her eyes for a moment, and then got aboard the monoplane with the little man and waved to her as the engine roared out and the plane began to move. Schroder had turned it directly away from the house for starting, and they went taxi-ing toward the big hawthorn hedge: for seconds Gees thought they would crash on the forest-like barrier, but the Gnomon lifted well in time. They went over, up, and Surrey appeared to caper drunkenly as Schroder banked to turn northward and go over London on his way.

He got his direction and straightened out, lifting all the time. Gees observed the controls, and saw that, as Schroder had said, the monoplane practically flew itself. There was a ratchet throttle control, and the pilot set it within two notches of full out: he set his steering, too, and then turned his head to grin at Gees.

"Is she not beautiful, my Gnomon?" he yelled.

Gees nodded for answer—talking was almost an impossibility. They rose and rose: the altimeter on the board showed two thousand five hundred metres by the time they passed over the Crystal Palace—something like eight thousand feet, Gees estimated. All the instruments and gauges, he noted, were calibrated on the metric system.

It was a perfect day, almost cloudless, and, looking down on London, Gees was just able to identify the Tower north of its bridge. With that glimpse of history in stone he forgot the man beside him, and, gazing out and down, knew that he was looking at history.

Highgate and the northern heights, flattened, at this distance. Barnet, where feudalism made its last stand and Montagu and Warwick, the hero brothers, died. Now came the crazy patchwork of open England with the railway threaded through it: Tring and the Chilterns away there to the left: Peterborough soon showing a little to the east—the Golden Borough that Hereward's Danish allies sacked not long after Saxon Harold had died. Farther eastward and very small, the twin towers of Ely, Hereward's isle that Norman William could not win from him until a woman had enslaved the hero. And there was the Wash, where shameful John came by his greatest shame, and Stamford where Harold Hardrada made his brave death, and York, taken and sacked and retaken in the wars of old time, and over to the east where the water glittered in the sun was Ravenscar where Edward the oath-breaker landed to the final ruin of the Lancastrian cause. Somewhere down there, too, was Marston Moor, scene of the battle that has never been fully told in any story, grim Cromwell's victory snatched from defeat.

History, all of it, the tale of a people conglomerate of many peoples, warring among themselves for centuries, yet each in his way striving toward peace. And for two hundred years, now, they had known peace in their land— this land like to no other on earth, loved as—with the possible exception of France—is no other on earth. And now mean things like this beside him, people not even English, wanted to impose a new slavery on the free people of England!

They wanted to impose that slavery on all the earth, to set up in every country their tyranny backed by a secret police, to enslave all they could and kill the rest, standing them in rows for mass executions. Men like Tony Briggs, men like Tott and Johns . . .

There were slag heaps like little mountains, tall chimneys belching darkness, the winding gears of colliery heads, and rows on rows of little houses all alike—and everything growing larger and then twisting and reeling about as Schroder sought his landing. They came down easily in a big meadow: Gees took careful note of the way in which the little man dropped and straightened out, and knew that, as Schroder had said, the Gnomon had a very low and safe landing speed. They were not quite at rest when a man came running from the side of the meadow, one as small as was Schroder, dingily clad in shabby black, with a flaming scarlet tie encircling a dirty india-rubber collar, and uncleaned shoes of glace kid on his splay feet. He put his hand under his checked tweed cap to scratch his head as he neared the monoplane, and Gees, observing the mean, sallow face of him, concluded that his head really needed scratching—and scrubbing as well.

Some five hundred yards away, a policeman with a bicycle leaned on the gate of the meadow and looked at the plane: others joined him to stand at gaze, but none approached. Schroder left his engine idling and got out, and Gees followed him. The man in black stared at him.

"Comrade," Schroder said cheerfully, "a new worker with us. Comrade Green, this is Comrade Mike Scadder, organiser of Communist cells among the workers here. He has been in jail twice."

The recommendation was enough, evidently, to put Scadder among the heroes of his cause. Gees shook hands, because he knew he must.

"I am honoured to meet you, comrade," he said.

"Comrade Green will take charge of our organisation up here," Schroder explained. "I am taking him round to introduce him."

"D'jer bring the money?" Mike Scadder inquired anxiously.

"Of course I brought the money," Schroder assured him. He unbuttoned his leather flying-coat, and took from an inner breast pocket a flat package, which he handed over. "Fifty, in pound notes," he explained. "That is ten each for Marks and Coleman, five each for Gannett and Barbury— Comrade Green will meet them the next time he comes, and by then he will be able to give you your final orders for the day. That is thirty, and the rest, comrade, is reward for what you have already done. The greater reward will follow the great work before you."

"Yer mean—blowin' 'em to hell?" Scadder suggested.

"I mean blowing certain things just there," Schroder assented.

"I got the gas works fixed," Scadder told him. "Had a dekko round, I did. Four o' them three-pounders you told me about—I'll want four, wi' three-minute fuses on 'em. Know where to plant 'em, I do. Marks is good for the big power station—he'll want three more, an' better have five minutes o' fuse on his. Thass seven. Then two more—nine altogether. Why ain't Schlatzy with you this time, comrade?"

"Comrade Green is taking his place," Schroder answered. "You will take orders from him as you took them from Schlatzenbaum, and he, too, comrade, has power to kill traitors. But we trust you."

"Blimey, I'd think so, arter all I done f'r the protelariat."

"Proletariat, comrade," Schroder corrected him. "Go on working for solidarity, for freedom, and for the destruction of the capitalist class. The day of your reward is not far off, now. Comrade Denghisovski will let you know when to expect us again—it will not be long."

"An' thass all f'r this time, is it?" Scadder asked.

"All for this time," Schroder assured him. "The money, and for us the certainty that you are working for the cause. It is enough."

"Thass all right—I'll work like hell," Scadder promised solemnly. "Now I'll git along an' hand over the dibs to them chaps, an' tell 'em they'll be seein' Comrade Green soon—sooner it was you instead o' Schlatzy, chum. I never really took to him."

"I am delighted to have your approval, comrade," Gees assured him.

"Thass all right, comrade. Gi's your mitt, an' then I'll git along. An' nine eggs, don't forgit, when it's time to plant 'em."

"Nine eggs it shall be," Gees assented. "Four with three-minute fuses, and five with five minutes on each, eh?"

"I c'n see you know the job, comrade. Thass it. So long f'r now."

Again they all shook hands, and Schroder turned toward the monoplane. Gees touched him on the shoulder.

"Comrade, will you let me fly her back?" he asked.

"You are sure you know her well enough?" Schroder asked doubtfully.

Gees smiled. "Watch the take-off—if you let me fly her."

"You shall fly her," Schroder promised, with sudden faith.

They got aboard, and Gees reflected that he was—almost certainly—sitting on that twelve thousand pounds when he saw the controls before him. He opened out and headed straight for the gateway of the meadow, and the policeman and other onlookers began hunting for shelter—one man threw himself flat on his face, possibly in prayer. But the Gnomon lifted a good two hundred yards away from them, for now the engine was properly warmed up. She went up and away: Gees found the line of railway running south— the way over which he had travelled with Christine so little time ago—and followed it.

He crossed the Thames and found Dartford under him, for on nearing London he had kept farther to the east than Schroder had steered on the northward run. Over the Westerham valley, circling, he saw and recognised the tower on Leith Hill, and bore due west, searching the country for Kestwell. As Schroder touched his shoulder to point, he himself saw the big hawthorn hedge, a heavy, white-starred line on the landscape before and beneath him. He banked steeply on a turn, went away to the south to get landing room, turned again, and came back five hundred feet or less above ground level. The Gnomon dropped beautifully, bumped on the turf, and came to rest within fifty yards of the copse behind the farmhouse, and Gees, climbing out, felt that a child could handle such a machine.

"Comrade," said Schroder beside him, "surely you were born in the air. I would trust her to you now in any weather."

"There was something about a stork," Gees replied reminiscently.

"A stork, comrade? But I do not comprehend."

"Cabbage stalk," Gees amended. "Never mind. Here's Comrade Leonid, and Comrade Lenoir—we're quite a nice little party. And too late for tea, by the look of things. It must be nearly six o'clock."

"All but fifteen minutes, Grigori." Christine, near enough to hear his estimate, checked it for him. "Comrade Leonid waited to see you. Our new ally, Comrade Barter, is in the house."

"And it's kept fine for him," Gees remarked casually.

"The weather is still lovely, but we are promised thunder to-morrow," she confirmed his surmise. "Yes, Comrade Ivan—what is it?"

"He—he flew the Gnomon back from Sunderland," Schroder said.

"We saw you land." There was a look of pride in her possession of Gees as Christine eyed him. "A perfect landing, *hein?*"

"Easy—plenty of room, here," he said. "An easy machine, too."

"It is well that we have two pilots," Denghisovski observed rather pompously. "Comrade Green, Comrade Lenoir and I have been talking, and it is evident you are not yet fully conversant with all our plans. She has not told you everything—I think you have other things to talk about, with her. So we have agreed that you shall come here at this time to-morrow, or a little later—say seven o'clock, to meet Smirilov and myself. We will post you fully with regard to the workers in the north, tell you about Clydeside and Elswick and all the rest, and then your journeys with Schroder will be simplified. Is it not so?"

"It is undoubtedly so," Gees agreed. "Seven tomorrow. Then I will keep the car I hired, and come here in it."

"And, Schroder," Denghisovski pursued, "I need five hundred pounds from the common store. You will get it for me?"

"I have it loose," Schroder answered. "There is no need to open the big package for it. A thousand, if you wish, comrade."

Gees felt an intense relief at hearing that the big package was not to be opened. He knew he could not get it to-night, but he would feel happier if it remained intact. Twelve thousand was such a nice round sum to put in the safe behind his wardrobe.

"Five hundred only, comrade," Denghisovski insisted. "We must not waste money. It will be fully three weeks before the revolution begins, and for some time after that the notes will still be useful."

If only Tott would come and find those bombs, Gees reflected, money would continue to be useful far longer than three weeks.

"You will come and meet Comrade Barter?" Denghisovski asked him.

"Comrade, not to-night." Christine negatived the suggestion in a way that implied she would have none of it, and that must be reason enough. "I have waited for Comrade Green to drive me back to London, and he can meet Barter when he comes here to-morrow." She gave Gees a glance, half-questioning, half-alluring, and he nodded assent.

"To-morrow will be time enough, Comrade Leonid," he said.

"If Comrade Lenoir orders, of course," Denghisovski said, rather sulkily. It was evident that he resented her interference.

"Comrade Lenoir commands, Comrade Leonid," she observed, with a silky sweetness in her tone that made the claws under the velvet even more apparent. "Grigori, take me to London, please."

"With pleasure, Christine," he answered. The chief pleasure consisted in getting away from Denghisovski, who, he felt, was ready to quarrel with him. And, though he was no weakling himself, he did not relish the idea of getting into trouble with a man who had arms and a chest like those of the panjandrum. Quite possibly that knob-headed fool would forget the little difference and be amiable again on the morrow: Gees meant to keep the appointment—meant to keep any appointments that might be suggested in the vicinity of the Gnomon, as long as the big package remained intact under the driving seat.

She took his arm—she had her hat and coat on in readiness for the journey—and they went together toward the left corner of the house: she guided him away from the back door, which stood open.

"There is no need to go through the house," she remarked. "You will meet Barter when you come here to-morrow."

"You won't be here, then?" he asked, inwardly reflecting that, in her absence, Denghisovski might try to bully him.

"Not by seven," she answered. "By eight, or perhaps a little before. Then, as to-night, you shall drive me back."

She looked up at him as if she had indicated a reward for his faithfulness to the cause. He handed her into the Minx, and, getting in himself, looked back and saw Denghisovski standing at the corner of the house, watching them. And, like a child in a paddy, the man was biting his nails

# CHAPTER XIII

## CROSS CURRENTS

LEAVING Leatherhead on his right, Gees drove into the main road, passed the gas works and went up over the railway bridge, and took the Hook road toward Kingston. Then, and not before, Christine spoke.

"Grigori, I do not wish you to be at Kestwell by seven to-morrow. I myself will be there by half-past seven, and will meet you then."

"Just as you like," he agreed, "but won't the pan—I mean, won't Denghisovski be a trifle peeved? He wants a heart-to-heart with me."

"Wants a—?" She gave him a puzzled look, but he was watching the road, and congratulating himself on the impossibility, or at least the prohibitive danger, of, kissing a girl and driving a car at the same time. He meant to keep on driving the car.

"Well, wants to impart information, then," he amended.

"He may, while I am there," she said significantly.

He glanced at her. "Are you anticipating trouble?" he asked.

"Difficulty," she answered thoughtfully. "The difficulty that must arise if any of our comrades are not single to their aim. First and above all, Grigori, the revolution. That alone, until the bombs are launched and it is successfully begun. Then, rewards."

"Go to the *guichet* and cash the betting slip," he suggested.

"You—you use strange allusions." She frowned slightly, he saw. "When we are masters, our rewards—and yours you know. Denghisovski knows it too, and there is the difficulty. He is beginning to hate you, because I want you and do not want him. You see?"

"Poor little feller," he remarked, and watched the road.

"Pity is inadmissible," she said calmly. "It is weakness— and there is no weakness in that man. He is a savage, civilised though he may be. Chosen to be chief of the revolution in this country, clever, unscrupulous enough, but now he begins to put a personal aim before the cause. I think, when his use ends, he must be removed."

"In a plain van," Gees commented, still watching the road.

"With a bullet," she said gravely. "For that passion for me, growing apparent now, is not only futile in itself, but will make the man a futility. Smirilov, Schroder, Barter, and others whom you will meet—all single-minded, devoted to the cause above all. It is strange that Denghisovski should appear the strongest of them all, and then should develop this weakness. There must be no pity for him."

"If I feel any, I'll conceal it," Gees promised gravely.

"You must not feel it!" she insisted earnestly.

"Very well, then—I won't. I suppose your government chose him for this job, before he saw how lovely you are."

"Government?" she echoed. "What government?"

"Why, the Russian Government, surely?"

"We own no government," she said. "We are world revolutionaries, destined to govern the world and destroy its capitalists and their system. Russia? Our forerunners captured Russia sixteen years and more ago, but already it is more than half lost through weakness—the government of to-day in that country is allying itself with capitalism. No. We world revolutionaries need such a stronghold as this country, developed, advanced fully in western civilisation, and then we can recapture Russia, destroy capitalism in France and all the Latin countries, and move as one great force against the United States and be masters of the world. I think Ulianov, whom you knew as Lenin—our greatest man, Grigori!—I think he saw before he died that while England remained capitalist our revolution would be in danger."

"Tragic, that," he observed. "It must have spoilt his sleep."

"He slept very little," she pointed out gravely. "But do not seek to identify our cause—your cause, too!—with the Russian government or any government that exists now. We will set up in this country the ideal form of government, and you shall show the world what a real secret police can be. If you need guidance, instruction, I shall be with you, and you can turn to me."

"That's a comfort, Christine. I might feel a bit lost, otherwise. But it seems to me there are very few to do all this."

"Wait till you go north again with Schroder," she counselled. "You see little here—it is in the industrial centres that our strength lies. Where there are many unemployed, many already discontented and ready to overthrow their tyrants. Here, in and about London it is nothing, and capitalism is still strong. A rotten strength, since it is pillared on the workers. *We* will lead them!"

"They'd crow with joy, if they knew," he remarked.

"The workers must never be told too much," she said. "They must see liberty and prosperity always as an ideal before them."

"Like the donkey and the carrot, eh?" he suggested.

"Like the—yes. You hold the carrot before the donkey, and he goes on—and the carrot is always before him. An ideal."

He drove for awhile in silence. Had she no sense of humour at all? He risked trying another one on her.

"Pleasing to think that you're my carrot, Christine."

"Ah, but you will have your carrot, when the revolution has begun," she pointed out. "I, too, shall have mine. Till then, the one aim."

The panjandrum, evidently, could whistle for a carrot—for the one he wanted, in any case. No wonder he was disgruntled.

"I think Denghisovski will try to make the others distrust you, Grigori," Christine said, evidently thinking of the panjandrum too. "That is why it will not be wise for you to go to Kestwell to-morrow before I do. Or only a very little while before. Then, if he tries to put them against you, I can turn them against him."

"You're sure of your power to that extent?" he asked.

"One word from me—they know it—one word from me can decree death for any one of them," she said, rather proudly. "I am here to assure that their work is done, and even Denghisovski dare not antagonise me. Perhaps, if you get there a quarter of an hour before me to-morrow, to let him declare himself fully—then I could take action. Denounce him to the others as working for himself rather than for the cause, and point out to them what they must do."

"You mean?" There was significance in: "What they must do."

"Would your police bestir themselves overmuch if Denghisovski were missing for a few days?" she asked in reply. "For a week or two, say. In three weeks, remember, we shall be masters, accountable to no police for the bodies we bury. But I think the threat will be enough for him."

"You don't think he'll try to wipe me out?" he inquired, a trifle anxiously. Arriving at Kestwell before her appeared likely to lead to unpleasantness, and the panjandrum was a tough handful.

"I shall see him in the morning, and warn him," she promised. "I shall tell him you will be there by half-past seven, and say nothing of my own arrival. But I shall be there soon after you. He may try to accuse you before the others, but no more than that."

Gees, having driven through Kingston, headed for and entered Richmond Park: for awhile Christine sat silent beside him.

"Do we dine at the Castle again?" he asked, glancing at her.

"Not to-night, Grigori," she answered. "There are things that I must do—and if we are together all the time, day after day, Tott will perhaps suspect you too much. It might mean harm for you. And not at any cost would I have you harmed by him or any man."

Just for a moment he felt a twinge of compunction over the part he was playing: it was only for a moment, though, for, as when she had saved the child, she added a remark to spoil the effect.

"Not that I would not kill you myself if I found you false to the cause, for that comes even before you. The death of capitalism."

He drove on to the Richmond Gate, and along by the terrace. Down to the left, the Thames appeared peaceful and lovely in the sunset.

"In the town, I will take a taxi," Christine said. "And to-morrow morning at about eleven, I want you to come to Keszca's. You will find the address in the telephone directory—Abram Keszca, furrier, in the Commercial Road. It is as well that you should know him."

"How do you spell him?" Gees asked.

She spelt the name out for him. "In the Commercial Road," she repeated. "If I am not there when you enter, ask for me by name."

"And what's the special reason?" he inquired. "Is he another comrade, or is this a meeting place for the rest of—us?" He had almost said—"For the rest of you," but changed it in time.

"Keszca is supplying the bombs," she explained. "If it becomes necessary to remove Denghisovski, you may have to take bombs to Kestwell for Schroder to distribute. So it is best for you to know him."

She got out from the car at the bend in the main street, and Gees saw her stop a taxi and enter it. He went on alone in the Minx.

"You're sure that's quite correct, Mr. Green?" Miss Brandon looked up from her notes as Gees relapsed to silence after dictating his report the next morning, and poised her pencil in anticipation of more.

"Of course it's correct," he insisted. "I spelt that name out."

"Not the name," she observed. "Didn't she want you to stop the car anywhere at all, on the way back from Kestwell?"

"If she did, she kept it dark," he answered. "Oh, yes, I get what you mean, but she's saving it all up for the revolution. I'm to hold shooting bees and make love to her between whiles for recreation."

"Meanwhile—" she glanced at the last page of the notes she had taken—"she'll kill you if she finds you out?"

"I believe she meant it," he assented. "It sounded real."

"Oh, they're all mad!" she exclaimed. "Killing—in this country!"

"Oh course they're all mad, Miss Brandon! But that same madness very nearly made bad trouble at the time of the big coal strike, not so very many years ago. I don't quite know how to feel about all this. I know Tott has them in hand—but does he realise just how mad they are, I wonder? When I talked to my friend Briggs about them, the whole thing sounded like a pork and pickles dream, or even like a bad joke. And then, when I went north yesterday with that little swipe Schroder and heard a supposed Britisher talk calmly of blowing up a gas works—and saw Schroder hand him fifty pounds too—it made me question whether Tott has them enough in hand. I know his policy of letting them cut their own throats, but are they going to cut any others as well? I'm partly amused, and partly uneasy over them."

She thought it over. "Did you bring the twelve thousand pounds back with you last night?" she inquired eventually.

He shook his head. "It's still under the pilot's seat of the Gnomon, as far as I know," he answered. "You'll find the key of the safe where you put it, when you want to store this last record away with the others. And if Tott has sense enough to take me seriously about the bombs, to-day is my last chance at that package."

He looked at his watch. "Gosh, I'm due at Keszca's place at eleven to meet our devil! I shall never make it."

"Taxi to Charing Cross underground, train to Aldgate East, and take a taxi on from there," she counselled. "And the rest of the day, Mr. Green? In the event of inquiries, when will you be back?"

"Oh, in time for lunch, probably. I'm due to look over Lots Road power station this afternoon, just to convince the gang that I'm hard at work for the cause. Then I'll come back here before sliding off to Kestwell—due there at seven-thirty. It's a hard life, but we're a hundred up, so far, and there's twelve thousand still hanging in the wind. Thank heaven our devil doesn't want me to make real love to her till after the revolution! I'll get away, Miss Brandon."

He followed her suggestions for the journey, and reached his destination in the Commercial Road only ten minutes late. It was a dingy-looking shop with a few ancient pelts in the window, and some of the white enamel letters announcing that Keszca repaired furs had fallen off the glass: over the top was the name and style of the proprietor, "ABRAM KESZCA, Manufacturing Furrier," and, as Gees entered, he saw a woman in nurse's uniform gazing at the specimens in the window. The interior was dusty and dingy—he reflected that everything about these people was dingy: the word belonged to them.

A tall, gaunt man advanced from the gloom at the back of the shop and faced Gees: his hair was black and lank, his face palely unhealthy.

"An appointment with Comrade Lenoir," Gees said.

"Ah! She is not yet arrive. Comrade Green?" There was a Frenchiness in the man's English. "I am Keszca." He held out his hand.

"And I am Green," Gees told him. "She said eleven o'clock."

"You wait—she will be here soon," Keszca promised.

Just a dozen doors beyond the point at which Gees' taxi had stopped, Christine was facing Denghisovski in an inner office of his establishment, a small apartment walled in with frosted glass from the larger general office in which his assistants transacted his import business. The little knob on the panjandrum's head was very pink indeed, and his expression, at that minute, fully justified Christine's description of him as a savage. But he managed to speak calmly.

"Through you, comrade," he said, "we have taken this man into our inner councils. Made him one of us. And what do we know of him?"

"Instinct is surer than knowledge." she retorted.

"Is it? A man of the capitalist class. A sneering man. You think he takes the cause seriously? I cannot think it."

"You may think what you will, comrade. He takes me seriously."

"I say you are blind. You have fallen in love with him, and—"

"You have fallen in love with me," she interrupted sharply.

"What if I have? Have I not more right to you than this interloper, this man you trust so blindly, without knowing—"

"What if you have?" Again she interrupted, contemptuously. "No man has a right to me unless I choose him. It is you who are blind, with jealousy, Comrade Leonid! Now hearken! You are chief of the revolution, and I am here to see that you play your part. I am here to give you to death if you do not play your part, and if I bring such a one as Grigori—as Comrade Green—into our councils, I will answer to the heads of the Left for what I do. You will answer to *me* for all you do! Which shall it be—obedience, or death, Comrade Leonid?"

"I only warn you," he said sullenly. "You know you can trust me."

"I know too that you want me—have known it since I landed here and saw you again. But I am not for you, comrade. You shall have your slow killings, and choose what women you will, when the day comes, but you will not have me either on that day or any day. And as you say you warn me, so I warn you—for the last time. Put the cause first as I put it first, drive from your mind all thought of me other than as one with power over you. I warn you for the last time."

The little knob on his head paled a trifle. Such words as the last she had spoken placed him very near the executioners who kill in cellars with revolvers, and the irony of it was that, if she were right about Comrade Green's loyalty, that same Green would soon be chief of those executioners, equal in power with the panjandrum himself.

"Have I given you cause to say that, comrade?" he asked.

"Had you done so," she retorted. "I should not give you this final warning. Even under capitalist rule in this country there are ways of removing those who fail us. Remember it, comrade."

She went out, then, and walked the little distance to Keszca's shop. Entering, she was in time to hear Keszca tell Gees that she would be here soon, and then, before she could speak, the woman in nurse's uniform whom he had seen looking into the window entered the shop. Keszca went to attend to her, and the other two waited.

"He will not be long," Christine said to Gees.

Looking at the other woman, he found something familiar about her: the face reminded him of something—somebody. He listened.

"I have a fox fur I want renovated," the woman said. "A necklet."

"But yes, madam," Keszca answered politely. "It is here—no?"

"I didn't bring it with me," she explained. "I thought perhaps you could tell me how much it would cost. The fur is rubbed in places—you know, the hairs don't all lie one way. As if some of them had got broken and tangled. It is a good fur."

"I cannot tell you how much it would cost unless I see the fur, madam," Keszca said. "If you will bring it—to-day, perhaps?"

"To-morrow," she demurred. "I couldn't, to-day."

"Vairy good, madam. Then you will bring it tomorrow."

"To-morrow, about this time," she assented.

"Thank you, madam. I do good work for you."

She turned toward the door. Christine signalled with her hand, and a stunted youth whom, up to that moment, Gees had not observed as present came forward: he must have been in hiding at the back.

"Percy," Christine ordered, "follow that woman and see where she goes. Come back here and tell me, or your father if I am gone, what becomes of her. I think she will go to a police station."

Percy disappeared, reappeared with a cap on his head, and went out. And, with his going, Gees knew why the woman had seemed familiar: she was the more sober of the two charwomen who had attended the meeting in the temple of the pentagram. Tott was missing nothing.

"We will go," Keszca said. "My wife will attend the shop."

He led the way through an untidy sitting-room and crossed a small, paved yard at the back of the premises. They entered a wooden shed about twelve feet by ten, and in it a man worked at a bench. He was not so tall as Keszca, but looked as if his food did him more good: there was even a little colour in his face as he turned to look at his visitors, and smiled when he saw Christine. His features proclaimed some close relationship with the furrier.

"My brother Peter, Comrade Green," Keszca introduced.

"Pleasetermeetcher, comrade," said Peter. "Me 'ands ain't none too clean. Take the will fer the deed, wontcher?"

"Gladly, comrade," Gees assented. "Consider it done."

"Peter fills the bombs," Christine explained.

There were a hundred or more iron spheres on the board flooring of the shed. In each was a circular aperture, and Gees saw on the bench a quantity of iron studs, screw-threaded, and evidently intended as stoppers for the apertures after the explosives had been loaded into the spheres. He took up an empty sphere, and found it surprisingly light. They had been described to him as three-pound bombs.

"Fired by fulminate?" he inquired.

Peter shook his head. "A better way," he answered. "With each goes a small battery, to be put on at the last possible moment. Then the length of fuse—three minutes, five minutes, what you will. The fuse burns to the battery, and there is a mechanism. On the studs are points like those on sparking plugs, and the battery makes one spark. Presto! It is done. One spark is enough."

He had utterly dropped his affectation of Cockney dialect, and spoke like an educated Englishman, Gees noted.

"And if dropped from an aeroplane, no spark is necessary," Gees suggested, and put the sphere down with its fellows.

"No spark is necessary, then," Peter agreed.

"He is a great chemist, our Peter," Christine said, almost affectionately. "Comrade Peter, it is just possible that Comrade Green will take some of the bombs to Kestwell for us, so I asked him to come here with me. If he comes for bombs, you will consider him as having taken Comrade Denghisovski's place, by my order."

"I will so consider him, Comrade Lenoir," Peter promised.

"Comrade Denghisovski will take twenty more in his car to-day," she proceeded to instruct him. "Whether he or Comrade Green will take another twenty tomorrow, I cannot yet tell you. But one of them will come to you for another load. You have plenty of cases?"

"Only for sixty more," Peter answered.

"That is for to-day, to-morrow, and the next day. I will see that cases for the rest are sent you. Remind me to-night, after we have finished at Kestwell, Comrade Green. There is much to think about."

"I won't forget," Gees promised.

"That is all, Peter," she said. "I wanted you to see Comrade Green and know that you may trust him without question. Now we will go." She gave Peter a nod and smile, and turned to go out from the shed. In the yard, she turned to Gees questioningly.

"Have you remembered Lots Road?" she asked.

"I am making the primary arrangements this afternoon," he answered.

"For another man, that is? You will be needed in the north."

"I shall see that other man this afternoon," he explained. "And the arrangements for Battersea are well advanced, now."

She pressed his arm momentarily. "I knew we could trust you," she said, possibly remembering the panjandrum's doubts.

The phrase was growing a trifle tiresome, Gees reflected. But, unless he were badly mistaken, that package was still waiting under the pilot's seat in the Gnomon. While it remained there, he could endure more than a tiresome phrase or two.

"And I shall see you at Kestwell this evening?" he queried.

"Yes. You had better go alone from here. So far, there is no watch kept on Keszca's shop, and we ought not to go out together."

"What about that woman you asked the boy to follow?" he asked.

"She was not watching the shop, but may have been following me."

But Gees felt that he knew better. Quite probably some member of Tott's staff had seen the panjandrum load cases on to his car here, and now Keszca was as much under observation as the rest of them.

The boy Percy was in time to board the tram for which the woman in nurse's uniform had waited, and they both travelled on it to Bishopsgate. Thence he followed her on to Liverpool Street station, and saw her go on to one of the main line platforms from which a train was due to leave in ten minutes. He noted that she showed a pass of some sort to the man at the barrier, and, having no ticket himself, could not follow her any further. She entered the train, and he kept watch to assure himself that she did not simply pass through a compartment and come back by way of the next platform.

She did nothing of the sort: he saw that she had a word with the guard when that functionary passed her compartment, leaning out of the window to speak to the man. Presently he blew his whistle, and she was still looking out from the window when the train went out.

Percy went and studied a time-table placarded on the booking-office wall. He ascertained that that particular train was a Norwich-Cromer express: the board at the entrance to the platform had told him as much, but the time-table assured him that the train did not stop between Liverpool Street and Norwich, and with that information he went back to Keszca's shop to reassure his father and Christine, who had not left when he returned. She dismissed the woman from her mind, then.

The express went out through the Bishopsgate arches, gathered way, and rolled smoothly on until it was near Romford. There the driver set his whistle screaming, but all in vain, for the signal at the far end of the platform would not drop, in spite of his screaming. He pulled the train to a standstill alongside the platform, and a woman in an ordinary light summer coat and beret got out, after which the signal dropped and the train went on.

The sometime charwoman had merely turned her coat inside out and put her nurse's headgear in her handbag. She caught a suburban train back to Liverpool Street, and went to Tott's office to report the meeting between Gees and Christine at the furrier's.

# CHAPTER XIV

# THE GAME GOES ON

AT A LITTLE AFTER TWELVE O'CLOCK, Gees entered a telephone call-box at the Mansion House tube station and got through to Tott's office: the usual guarded voice gave him back the number he had dialled.

"Can I speak to Detective-Inspector Tott?" he asked.

"Who is speaking, please?" the voice inquired.

"My name is Green. I want Inspector Tott."

"Sorry, sir. Inspector Tott is not in, just now."

"Detective-Sergeant Johns, then?"

"Sorry, sir. Detective-Sergeant Johns is not in either."

"When do you expect either of them to be back?"

"I couldn't tell you, sir."

Gees paused to reflect. He knew that breaking a way through the wall of official reserve was impossible, but he had already realised that, unless he were careful, Tott might get him over this case. He had to safeguard himself by proving that he was not in real collusion with the gang of revolutionaries.

"Can you take a message for Inspector Tott?" he asked at last.

"Yes, sir, certainly. I've got a pad and pencil in front of me."

"Good. Just take this down, please. *Re* bombs already reported as being stored at Kestwell. Place of origin of said bombs is a wooden shed in the backyard of the furrier's shop kept by Abram Keszca—" he gave the address—"and Peter Keszca, brother of Abram, is at the present time engaged in filling bombs ready for transport to Kestwell, whence they are to be distributed by Schroder, air pilot, in his machine. Information supplied by G. G. G. Green, ex-police constable. Please repeat that back, whoever you are."

The recipient of the message repeated it back in a slightly altered tone: he sounded impressed, as possibly he was.

"Now, how soon can you get that message to Inspector Tott?" Gees asked. "There is a certain urgency about it."

"Some time to-day, sir, but I can't tell you when."

Gees hung up after a brief good-bye. His chief anxiety was that Tott should get the message before taking any action against himself. He did not like that woman having seen him and Christine together again. It appeared probable that Tott was keeping close watch on Christine now, and might act against her at any time.

But—Gees remembered it suddenly—there was Tony Briggs. He went back to the telephone box, and managed to get Tony in his office.

"The pleasure of buying you a lunch, Tony. Don't refuse."

"As long as it's a good lunch. And the venue?" Tony inquired.

"How about Frascati's, at one-fifteen?"

Tony assented cheerfully, and Gees hung up again and went out. He saw a youth not unlike Percy in the booking-hall, and, cursing softly, went up to the street and took a taxi, instructing the driver to take him to Golders Green underground station. It was bad enough to be trailed by Tott's men and women, but the appearance of that youth was a hint that the panjandrum also might be suspicious of the new comrade's movements. So to Golders Green he went, and paid the fare with one of the notes the panjandrum had handed him. And on the platform was the same youth: it was plain that the panjandrum was having Gees trailed.

When a Tottenham Court Road train came in, he waited until the doors were about to close, and then made a dart at it: the youth made a dart at the next doorway. The doors closed on him, but not on Gees, who watched the train go out with the lad aboard and then returned to the station yard, where he took another taxi to Oxford Circus: it was expensive, but the panjandrum was paying.

A brisk walk along Oxford Street revealed Tony Briggs waiting at Frascati's. Gees took him straight to a table on the first floor, whence they could overlook the ground floor and main entrance. He accepted Tony's suggestions as to what to eat and drink, gave the necessary orders, and then, having assured himself that their conversation would not be overheard, proceeded to talk.

"I got you to come along, Tony, because I look like being in trouble shortly, unless I'm careful," he began.

"Sorry, but I never lend money," Tony responded cheerfully. "You never know, once you begin that sort of thing—"

"I don't want your blasted money," Gees assured him. "I wouldn't have brought you here if it had been that, with Lyons next door."

"Well, have you got to marry the girl, or is the husband after you?" Tony inquired. "Because I know a solicitor chap—"

"You would," Gees interrupted a second time. "Not that either, Tony. Remember our little talk last Sunday about a few unpleasant people you said Tott has his eye on?"

Tony nodded. "Stout feller, Tott," he observed.

"Stout or thin, he's got his eye on me too," Gees informed him. "You see, I mixed myself in with that crowd to get information, and at the same time I got on the wrong side of Tott. Tony lad, I'm afraid he doesn't take that gang seriously enough. They're building bombs by the hundred—I was in the factory this morning."

"Umph! Have you told Tott about it yet?"

"Left a message, but he wasn't in. He thinks I've fallen for the fair Christine, and doesn't believe a word I say. You know, thinks I'm in it up to the neck for luv's sweet sake, and only telling him things to mislead him up the garden and cloak the real activities of the gang. Told me he wouldn't trust me, and had me thrown out of his office most cheerfully when I asked to be thrown, in order to mislead the gang as to my real intentions in calling on him. There was an earnestness about that chuck-out that might have discouraged me if I hadn't been made of good, stout stuff. Tott doesn't like me, Tony."

"What do you want me to do about it?" Tony asked thoughtfully.

"For the present, nothing. I want you to be convinced that I wouldn't touch the revolution these people are planning with a barge sweep, and that I'm standing in with them to get all the information I can about their nefarious conspiracy—good phrase that, Tony!—because I've nothing else to do at my agency just for the present. As far as confidential inquiries go, the market is depressed, so it seemed to me I might as well do a little of this to keep my hand in. Also because it's interesting. I merely want you as an anchor to windward."

"I don't object to that, as long as you stand me a lunch like this occasionally," Tony said. "That is—what have you done, so far?"

"Taken a trip up north with Schroder and met a very dirty little man who took fifty pounds on account of blowing up a gas works and power station. Engaged to plant bombs at Battersea and Lots Road power stations on 'the day' and blow 'em both to hell—by proxy, since Christine means me to take charge of all the destruction in the north, and Denghisovski is going to give me full instructions about it this evening at Kestwell Farm, just beyond Leatherhead. I've told Tott they are storing their bombs there. Oh, and Denghisovski gave me a hundred pounds for working expenses.

This lunch is a working expense, and I lent a good chap I know twenty quid—another working expense."

"Are you joshing me?" Tony demanded incredulously.

"*Sach Khuda-ka,* sahib," Gees assured him. "Which as my revered parent told me, means the solemn truth and then some."

"Well, how the hell do they trust anyone like you?"

"Thanks for the compliment, old son. You see, Christine and I travelled down from Edinburgh last week. Tott knew it, by the way, and that was what put him agin me at the start. Then his man Johns watched Christine come to my office, and I led her out the back way and fooled Johns—and charged him two guineas for doing it. You can guess how Tott's hair stood on end over that. But it made these people believe I was dead against the police and out for crime, and now Christine has fallen for me good and strong. I'm to be chief of the secret police when the revolution gets going, and she and I are going to live in a garden of roses with a hedge of automatic pistols to keep the wind off us. It's all funnier than Laurel and Hardy in *Fra Diavolo,* and yet I've a feeling at the back of my mind that it isn't all funny. Has Tott got 'em taped, or hasn't he?"

"By what you say, he's got you taped," Tony averred solemnly. "I shall see him to-morrow, and then I'll ask him how he regards the gang—not mentioning you, of course— and whether he's heard anything about bombs. But some of them are always doing this sort of thing."

"In a small way, but these people have money. Hence your lunch."

"A very good lunch, too. Gees, since you say Denghisovski is paying, I want some strawberries. I see they're on at half-a-guinea a go, and I like strawberries. Especially early ones. I wouldn't worry about the gang, if I were you. Tott knows most things."

"But he doesn't know I'm honest," Gees protested.

"You can't expect a practical man like him to believe in miracles," Tony pointed out. "I take it that I'm to bail you out when he runs you in, and tell him you won't do it again. Is that it?"

"No, tell him I haven't done it at all. I'm telling you just what I have done, and why, because he won't believe me if I tell him."

"Umm-m! Did you fall for the fair Christine, Gees?"

"She won't let me. She talks blood and thunder stuff in a way that would revolt an octopus—capitalist slaves and all that muck. The woman is a fanatic of the Lenin type, incurably perverted to Communist extremism. Told me in one breath that she was in love with me—or implied it—and in the next said straight out that she'd kill me herself if I were not loyal to the cause. You can't fall for that. I'm being quite frank with you, Tony, and she leaves me stone cold."

"Yet she's got faith in you as a revolutionary, apparently?"

"My secretary explained that—she's got a full report of everything to hand to Tott when I think it's time. She said a woman in love believes what she wants to believe, or words to that effect."

"M'yes, it's probably true. Gees, you'll be in for a hot time when this gang find you out. And a hundred from Denghisovski, too."

"But don't you see, old son, I want to land 'em in a corner where Tott can bag the lot? Hence my informing him about the bombs, and keeping this daily report of my own activities. There's a private war between Christine and Denghisovski over me already. He wants her to step into his little rose garden, and doesn't like her regarding me as her Romeo. I am the beetle in his marmalade, in fact."

"Well, I'll have a liqueur brandy with the coffee. And don't think you can push Tott into bagging the lot just to suit your convenience, for he won't. That report of yours may be useful to him, since Christine appears to have put you on the inside of their movements. Could you let me have a copy of it some time? To-morrow, say?"

"I'll get my secretary on to making you one tomorrow— she'll be glad of something to keep her busy. Reading gets monotonous after a time, and we've nothing on hand except this business, for the moment. My talk with Denghisovski this evening should be illuminating, and ought to be included, since he's to give me full instructions about superintending bombing operations in the northern industrial centres."

"Yes, put that in, and include as many names as possible. Tott may find a new one or two among them. You're a low hound, Gees."

"That's what Denghisovski thinks. Unfortunately, Tott has similar ideas about me. But now you know the facts, I shall feel happier, and heaven send that Denghisovski chooses the right gun if he wants to shoot me! Y'know, Tony, Christine asked me to take care of her gun, and I took the bullets out of all the cartridges, picked the powder out, and put the bullets back. Now they're hiding all their guns in a hole in the floor at Kestwell, and hers is the top one. So if he takes it out and shoots me to save fumbling underneath for his own, I shall still be able to stand you lunches. As long as his money lasts, I mean. After that, you'll have to stand me lunches."

They talked for a while longer, and then Gees called for the bill. After he had paid it, they went out together—and on the far side of the street, near the Tube entrance, stood the youth whom Gees had lost or thought he had lost at Golders Green, now apparently engrossed in an inspection of a shop window and its contents. Gees and Tony shook hands and parted, and the youth followed Tony into the Tube station.

"Which has about ripped it," Gees told himself as he watched.

He had no idea how the youth had traced him here, for certainly Golders Green had made a break in the trail. But, somehow, the youngster had picked it up again, and now, Gees concluded, he would trail Tony to the Foreign Office, possibly ascertain his identity, and then hare off to Denghisovski with the information that the new comrade was imparting the revolutionary plans to a Foreign Office official. It was perfectly damnable—and that twelve thousand pounds was still intact under the pilot's seat in the Gnomon!

But Gees was an optimist of the incurable variety, and, let Denghisovski think what he liked, Christine would take a lot of convincing over her chosen mate's duplicity. All was not lost yet, especially if he told her that he had had to see Tony in order to get into Lots Road power station: she might believe that too because she wanted to believe in him, and in any case it was worth trying on her.

And the name of that man old Reggie had mentioned as the one to whom he would write at Lots Road? Gees had not put it down, and now, rather than ring up Reggie and ask him, he racked his own brains. Thomson's *City of Dreadful Night;* no, Young's *Night Thoughts*—that was it. Something to do with Young's *Night Thoughts!* Yes, Dodgson, of course! Gees took another taxi, and hoped some minion of Denghisovski was hot on his trail as he was driven through the park, down to Chelsea, and deposited outside the power station, where he asked for Mr. Dodgson after paying off his driver—with Denghisovski's money.

Reggie had kept his promise, and Dodgson welcomed this sight-seer and gave him an interesting hour among the big dynamos. And, emerging to the street again after rendering thanks for his tour, Gees could have fallen with gratitude on the neck of the youth whom Denghisovski had put to trailing him, for here he was again, conspicuously inconspicuous, and ready to go and report this visit as well as the lunch at Frascati's. Gees concluded that there must have been two or more of them after him all the time, for this one could not have found him again so speedily after going off to track Tony Briggs back to work. However that might be, Denghisovski would learn that he, Gees, had gone straight from lunch with a Foreign Office man to the power station, and would be considerably puzzled thereat, while it would be easy to convince Christine that the first appointment was a necessity in connection with the second. Yes, all went well. Now for the office, to bring that report up to the very hour, and then get the Minx out and make for Kestwell. There was plenty of time, though.

Was it merely a ridiculous, childish game, or was it serious? The man Mike Scadder, beyond doubt, was a dangerous type—far more so, in Gees' opinion, than Denghisovski or Smirilov, for those two would merely sit back and pull strings, and bolt to cover if danger threatened them, while Scadder, for the sake of his fifty pounds and more to come if he earned it, would actually do the dirty work. And glory in it too, Gees felt sure: the players of the game moved pawns like him, and were careful to choose hungry, vengeful pawns, men with grudges against the established order: without such pawns to move, these players of the game would be negligible.

A big black cloud deposited big dark splashes on the pavement as Gees made his way past the World's End to the bus stop. As he entered a 22 bus to go to Piccadilly Circus, the rain came down with tropical violence, and a crash of thunder sounded over the noise of jarring gears as the bus driver started his vehicle. People ran for shelter: a misty spray rose from the rain-beaten, suddenly splashy pavements, and the storm surr-r-red on the bus windows. The fine weather of the past fortnight, had, as prophesied by the pundits, broken in thunderstorms. But it might clear in time for the drive to Kestwell.

For some part of that ride to Piccadilly Circus Gees deliberated over whether to go to Kestwell at all: he had an unpleasant premonition about it, a sense that he was playing rather lightly with something which might strike out at him as a cobra strikes, but without even the initial warning that the cobra always gives. That round button atop the panjandrum's head was an ugly thing, and the panjandrum himself was uglier—was, in fact, a deadly thing.

But, Gees believed, the big package was still intact under the aeroplane seat. Yes, he would go to Kestwell, panjandrum or no panjandrum. Christine had said that she would be there, and his premonition was probably only the sense of awe induced by standing under those mighty dynamos and feeling what a small thing he was by comparison.

"Anything doing, Miss Brandon?" She looked up and saw Gees' face protruded round the edge of her door.

"A woman rang up and asked for you," she said. "She wouldn't give her name, but said she would ring again."

"What sort of voice?" he inquired. "Refined or raffeened?"

"The former—quite a nice voice. It might have been—"

"Our devil," he completed. "Probably it was. Well, I'm going to dress for a party, so if she rings up again, tell her to hold on and call me. I won't be many minutes changing, and then I'll come back and dictate a few small items for the report."

He went to his bedroom and got out a suit of dark grey flannel and a pair of rubber-soled brown shoes, which he donned in place of the clothes and shoes he had been wearing. He had in mind the fact that Kestwell, being an unfurnished house, gave away any searcher in ordinary leather-soled shoes, and he wanted to find out where those bombs were being stored, if possible. The dark grey would render him inconspicuous—if the sky remained overcast as it was now—and he might be able to make discoveries without the panjandrum's knowledge. And, as he changed, he questioned why Christine had rung him up. Was there some alteration in her plan for going to Kestwell, or had the panjandrum contacted her and told her of that lunch with a Foreign Office man? He kept one ear lifting for the sound of the telephone bell, but it did not ring again, and eventually he went back to Miss Brandon's room, seated himself on her desk, and lighted a cigarette.

For nearly a quarter of an hour he dictated steadily: each time that he added to this record, he realised more fully the necessity of providing a full statement of all his actions and movements, in case Tott should see fit to change from passive watching to active hostility. Even then, with Tott in his present vindictive mood, things might be difficult. There was Tony Briggs as a sheet anchor, of course: Tony would do his best, Gees knew, and it might be enough.

"And that's all, Miss Brandon. Four forty-five already— you won't have time to transcribe it to-night. Never mind— take the notebook home with you. Or lock it in the safe, to save the trouble of carrying it. If anyone breaks in here, I don't want 'em to know anything about this record. Put the safe key back in the toe of my shoe as before, and hie off home. I'll wait a while in case that woman rings again, and we'll meet at the usual time in the morning."

"If—is there any danger in this, Mr. Green?" she asked.

"Extreme danger, I'd say—for the panjandrum and his friends," he answered. "They look like getting anything up to ten years apiece, if there's as much virtue in those bombs as they claim.

There's also a danger of my going in for two years hard or thereabouts if our report on the case isn't convincing enough for the great Tott. But we should worry. I've never done any hard labour yet."

"Which is not exactly a safeguard for the future," she observed.

"You mean you have hopes for me," he suggested. "Well, real optimism like that is a fine thing, but I'll do my damndest to disappoint you. If I don't, you'll get no salary while I'm inside, remember."

"I might take charge of the twelve thousand pounds," she said.

"Which reminds me. Let me have your home address, please. No, though, I won't lodge it there in case of need— Tott might connect up and get a search warrant to overhaul your abode. It's got to go—let me see, though. I'll think it out—don't worry about it, Miss Brandon. You can get away, now, and I'll hang on for this call."

He went to his own room, dragged the telephone instrument to the near edge of his desk, and sat down to wait. The caller, he felt certain, had been Christine, and there was some change in her plans that had caused her to ring him. Had she heard anything from the panjandrum to render her suspicious, she would not have rung at all. He sat brooding over possibilities, smoking cigarette after cigarette, but no call came through. And now came back the question: should he go to Kestwell, or give it all up? He had made a hundred pounds out of it all, money that the panjandrum could not possibly reclaim.

The premonition he had felt as he left the Lots Road power station recurred as he sat waiting: this was no game, but dangerous earnest, and why should he run risks over it when it was not his business at all—when Tott resented his interference and hated him already? The trailing to which he had been subjected to-day both by Tott and the panjandrum was proof that neither side trusted him, both suspected him—abruptly he got up from his chair and went to the window, where he had a good view of the street below—and of the panjandrum's youthful spy blatantly and unconcealedly on guard.

The sight decided him: in cold fury against the panjandrum he determined to go to Kestwell. Barnes and his men would be working in the wine cellars until six o'clock, and he could go out that way and fool this youth as he had fooled Johns, leave him on watch here over the empty flat. He went to his bedroom and switched on the light there, so that the youth should see it as soon as darkness began to grow, and conclude from it that the flat was still occupied. Then he went down the stairs to the basement, knocked on the iron door, and entered the wine cellars to find Barnes and his men bottling as before.

"Looking us up again, sir," Barnes greeted him. "Maybe you'd like to try this stuff—a sherry you don't often taste."

"It sounds good to me," Gees admitted. "I'm just off to a merry little party, and a spot for the road wouldn't come amiss."

Barnes reached for a tin cup, filled it at one of his bottling pipes, and handed it over. "And going out the back way to get there, sir, by the look of it," he observed. "That is, I guess you want the street again, the same as you did the other day with the lady. Try that stuff, sir, and see if velvet is any softer."

Gees tested it, and nodded approval. "Any for sale?" he asked.

"There'll be about twenty dozen, sir," Barnes answered.

"Well, if everything goes well at my party this evening, I'll have ten dozen for my father's cellar. He'll appreciate a sherry like this. But that's not a firm order yet, though. Now, as you say, I want the street, and I haven't been here, any more than last time."

"Right you are, sir, leave it to me."

One of Denghisovski's pound-notes changed ownership: one of the two boys conducted Gees to the lift and worked it, and he stepped out into the street. The afternoon sun was shining again, though there were more black clouds rising in the west. That sherry had been wonderfully heartening, and Gees went on to the garage at which he had left the Minx, and drove off thence for Kestwell.

In Little Oakfield Street, Denghisovski's spy went on watching an empty flat: he did not know of the back entrance through the cellars.

# CHAPTER XV

## JOHNS

RAIN-WASHED, the air was limpidly clear as Gees went through Richmond in the Minx and took the hill into the park. He halted to gaze at the rhododendron groves, and to inhale the mixed fragrance of hawthorn blossom, lime trees, and new-moistened earth—the annual miracle of spring in England. Although he had waited long in the hope of another telephone call from Christine, there was still plenty of time in which to get to Kestwell by half-past seven, and, remembering how the panjandrum had had him trailed that day, he was distinctly averse to an early arrival. Not that he was in any sense a fearful man, but he knew that there were pistols under the floor at Kestwell, and men who might use them at a pinch: he knew, too, that in any muscular contest he would be no match for the panjandrum, though he could tackle an ordinary man with justifiable confidence. As things were, he wanted to be only a little ahead of Christine.

Since the incident of her courage in saving the child, he had felt a kindness for her—no more than that. She was, as he had told Tony Briggs, far too perverted in her outlook for any deeper feeling to develop in him: the feeling he had was a blend of pity, contempt, and unwilling admiration. There was so much in her that might have been fine, had it not been for the insensate hatred of a class that warped her vision. She was, and evidently would remain, a might-have-been.

He drove on, through Kingston, and on to the Hook road. At the crest of the hill that overlooks Pachesham he saw such a storm as had nearly flooded Chelsea streets earlier in the afternoon, far off to the east, hiding not more than a quarter of the sky between horizon and zenith. All about him the world was brilliantly clear under the westering sun. His dashboard clock registered a quarter past seven as he passed the gas works outside Leatherhead, and he turned off from the main road and headed for Kestwell, going easily.

Turning into the lane, he drove slowly, and noted the gateway in which Johns had made a Sunday picnic with his young wife and child. A little way beyond it was the Kestwell gateway, and, swinging the car on to the ridged drive, he saw the big American saloon under the chestnut tree again: the panjandrum was there, awaiting his arrival. But abruptly he jammed on his brakes, put in reverse, and backed out, turning the car toward the exit from the lane. The premonition that had already troubled him twice returned a third time, stronger than ever, and he wanted to bolt, to give up this game altogether.

He had the impulse under control by the time he reached the gateway on the other side of the lane, and, as Johns had done, he pulled the car close in to the gate, well off the road, and stopped it there. As he got out he realised that, if the panjandrum had seen this hasty retreat, he would think it odd. But, having overcome the impulse to flight, Gees determined to go back to the house and let the panjandrum think what he liked. Christine would be here soon, too.

He walked along the drive and saw the front door of the house standing open as on the Sunday afternoon, and, as then, there was no sign of occupancy, unless the saloon car might count as such. He looked into both front rooms and found them empty: into the two behind them, also untenanted. Entering the scullery, he heard the rumble of the Gnomon's engine running idle out at the back, and, guessing that whoever had arrived was out there with Schroder, made for the back staircase and went up to the room overlooking the back premises, the one into which Christine had taken him on the Sunday. There he saw Schroder standing beside the monoplane, which had been swung round to face toward the big hawthorn hedge, as if in readiness for a flight. But Schroder was not in flying kit, and he stood in an idle, negligent attitude with his hands in his trousers pockets, gazing at his machine. Midway between the copse and the back of the house stood the panjandrum and Smirilov, deep in argument over something: Smirilov was gesticulating with both hands as he talked. Then they came on toward the house, and Gees hurried to get down the staircase before they could enter. But then, noting his own soundless progress in his rubber-soled shoes, and remembering that his car was out of sight from any of the windows, he paused, so far back from the bend of the stairs as to be invisible from the ground floor. He heard the panjandrum and Smirilov talking, apparently halted in the scullery, and, fortunately from Gees' point of view, they were speaking English.

"One of us must go." It was the panjandrum's voice.

"Comrade, it is your car," said Smirilov.

"That may be," the panjandrum rejoined, a trifle irritably, "but you can drive. And we know that there are no implements in the place."

"But one who buys a spade may be suspected," Smirilov objected.

(What could they want with a spade? Were they burying the bombs?)

"Why more than one who buys a hatchet, or any other garden tool, comrade? It is the spring, and men dig in their gardens."

"We might leave it," Smirilov objected again weakly, in the tone of one who knows that his objection will be overborne.

"For Schroder to find?" the panjandrum queried, as if such a thing were unthinkable. "Comrade, Schroder must not know. He would take fright if he did. No, but you will take the car to Leatherhead and buy a spade, quickly, while I go out again and make certain that Schroder does not go near the shrubbery—ask him to go and watch in the lane for Comrade Green, if he stops his engine and leaves the machine. For he knows nothing, not even that Green will not come here now."

"Then you think he will not come, now?" Smirilov asked. Gees gathered that he was gaining time over this business of fetching a spade, a matter which the panjandrum's last remark made ominous.

"Of course he will not come now!" The panjandrum sounded impatient over it, as well as certain. "Having sent that other, he will know what will happen to him if he comes himself. But you waste time, comrade. We must have the spade and get it done to-night."

"I will go now," Smirilov promised, reluctantly.

"It is no more than twenty minutes, with the car," the panjandrum said. "There are shops in Leatherhead. A strong spade, mind, for we must dig among the roots, and deeply, too."

"I will go now," Smirilov repeated, and Gees heard him enter the central passage of the house and go along it. Heard, too, that the panjandrum went out again at the back, probably to make certain, as he had said, that Schroder did not go near the shrubbery. But why must Schroder not go near the shrubbery? What was hidden in it?

The grinding of the self-starter on the saloon preceded the car's departure. Gees went back into the first floor room, then, and looked out: he saw Schroder beside the monoplane, the panjandrum halted where he had paused before with Smirilov, between the shrubbery and the house, and the propeller blade of the machine still turning. And he asked himself with chill apprehension what other they thought he had sent here, and what had happened to that other, since they wanted a spade. His thoughts, suddenly racing, went to the Minx in the lane: would Smirilov deduce his presence here from it, and return to warn the panjandrum that he had arrived? But Smirilov had not seen him with the car, and they had sounded certain—the panjandrum, at least, had appeared convinced—that he would not come to Kestwell now. What was it that he was supposed to know would happen to him if he came here after having sent that other? *What was hidden in the shrubbery?*

The panjandrum went on, passed the shrubbery, and joined Schroder beside the aeroplane, where they stood talking together. At that, letting curiosity outrun discretion, Gees hurried down the stair and out at the back: the thick growth of the shrubbery masked him from sight of the other two, but he had scarcely emerged from the yard before the Gnomon engine ceased to sound. At that he turned and raced back to his upstair retreat, and saw from the window that he had been only just in time, for the pair were coming toward the house, and would have seen him before he could get hiding in the shrubbery undergrowth, if he had not hurried back here. He stood well back from the window until certain that they would enter the house: then he went to his listening post on the stair, and waited. If only they would go through to the front, into one of the rooms there, he could get to the shrubbery and search it before Smirilov returned with the spade.

They halted in the passage, near the foot of the stair.

"Comrade Green has not yet arrived," Schroder observed questioningly. "I thought he was to have been here half an hour ago."

"Comrade Green has not yet arrived," the panjandrum echoed tonelessly. "He was to have been here half an hour ago—and more, now."

"You do not like Comrade Green, comrade?" Schroder asked.

"In the cause, there are comrades and enemies," the panjandrum said darkly. "There is neither like nor dislike, only the cause."

"Yet I like Comrade Green," Schroder said rather dubiously.

"But if he were false to the cause, comrade—if he betrayed us? What then?" the panjandrum asked, with silky, deadly menace.

"Then, of course, I should hate him," Schroder answered promptly. "But he is loyal to us." Again he made it half a question.

"Comrade Lenoir thinks he is loyal," the panjandrum said.

"And we all must obey Comrade Lenoir, *hein?*"

"While we know that she too is loyal," the panjandrum answered, still more darkly. He sounded like a schoolmaster instructing a backward pupil, patient with him, and leading him on step by step to the solution of a problem that to himself was no problem at all.

"But—but she is sent by the heads of the Left!" Schroder protested, evidently aghast at the imputation. "She has but to say the word, and any one of us may be removed. Even here, at need."

"It may not be always so," the panjandrum told him. "I will have that woman—" But on that he checked himself abruptly, and Gees knew that he had let his Slav savagery betray his real grievance against Christine. They were dallying here in the passage instead of going on to the front rooms, and every minute brought Smirilov nearer the end of his quest for a spade, rendered search of the shrubbery more nearly impossible. Schroder gave a little, apologetic cough.

"As for me, I know I must do as she bids," he said. "The Left is all-powerful, surely, and even after the revolution will be so."

"Comrade—" there was a grating determination in the panjandrum's tone—"after the revolution *we* may be the Left, masters of those who are now our masters. But let be—there is yet much to do. And still Comrade Green is not here! I will watch for him from the window, and you may go back to your monoplane, if you will. We may need it again soon, and if so I will come and tell you."

"Do you mean it may be needed to-night?" Schroder asked.

"I do not know myself. Comrade Barter should be here soon with news for me—I shall know then. You may go back, comrade."

On that, their footsteps sounded up to Gees. The panjandrum, presumably, went along the passage to one of the front rooms, while Schroder returned from the house to his Gnomon. For awhile there was silence, and Gees stood hesitant. Then he heard the panjandrum pacing heavily back and forth on the bare boards of one of the rooms, and on that went up and looked out from the first floor window. There was Schroder, with a box of tools or something of the sort beside his plane: it should be possible to get out to the shrubbery, now.

But Smirilov would soon be back with the spade, surely, and then he and the panjandrum would come out—Gees had guessed by this time the use for which that spade was designed. He looked at his watch and saw that it was already eight o'clock: Christine should have been here before this. He wished now that he had waited longer for her telephone call, for now he had no doubt that she had changed her plans for some reason, and had meant to advise him either that she would reach Kestwell at a later hour, or else would not come at all.

Schroder, out there, was kneeling beside his box, engrossed in whatever he was doing. Then voices sounded from the front of the house, and Gees stole down the stairs to listen again. He heard the deep rumble of the panjandrum's voice, and then another that he did not recognise: it was a thin, high-pitched voice, but it was not that of Smirilov. Probably Barter, whom Gees had not seen, had arrived.

"There was a car there on Sunday," the panjandrum said. "It is probably nothing. Was there anyone near it when you passed, comrade?"

"Dere vas nopotty," said the other voice. "Nopotty ad all."

At that—an irrelevant conclusion in this evening's happenings—Gees realised why they had considered Barter hardly the man to take charge of the work Schlatzenbaum had begun in the north. His accent would be against him: all the others spoke good English.

"They have got over the hedge into the field to make love," the panjandrum decided, but sounded rather doubtful over it. "Was it a small car, placed quite in the gateway, did you see?"

"*Ja*, a leetle gar, comrade."

"The same that was there on Sunday, probably," the panjandrum concluded. "We will wait, comrade. Comrade Smirilov will be back soon. He has gone to Leatherhead to get food for you. We shall go back and leave you here for the night, with Schroder."

Nothing about the spade, evidently. This man, like Schroder, was to be kept in ignorance of the need for one. Probably either the panjandrum or Smirilov would keep the other two entertained, and so leave either free to dig in the shrubbery undisturbed.

"Dere is a bed?" the other man asked, rather timidly.

"I have rugs in the car, when Smirilov comes back," the panjandrum answered. "But he is gone a long time, for so short a distance."

"Ve may go to der road, undt look-zee," the other suggested.

"No. It is not well that the people with the small car should see us here. Let us wait, Comrade Barter. Surely Smirilov will not be much longer. It is only a little way to Leatherhead."

Abruptly Gees realised why Smirilov was so long away. It was early-closing day in Leatherhead, of course. Quite probably he had gone on to Epsom in quest of the implement, and in any case, since these two appeared likely to remain in the front room until he returned, it would be worth while to investigate the shrubbery at once.

Rubber-soled and noiseless, Gees gained the passage and stole toward the scullery, keeping near the wall to prevent boards from creaking until he gained the brick floor of the scullery itself. He heard the murmur of the two voices in the front room: he had been right in his conjecture, for the panjandrum's last clearly-heard words had proved that the man with him was Barter. Now, gaining the open stretch between the back of the house and the shrubbery, he looked round for a possible line of retreat at need. Yes, by keeping well away to the left of the house he could reach that thin place in the hedge, and would only put himself in an acute angle of vision from the front windows. Unless the two in the front room chanced to be looking in that direction, they would not see him passing through the hedge into the lane, and he estimated the thin place as not more than a score yards from the gateway in which he had left the Minx. When he had ascertained exactly what was hidden in the shrubbery, he could get out to his car without going near the house again, and drive away.

Drive away, and leave that twelve thousand pounds under the seat of the Gnomon? Heedless of the passage of time and the imminence of Smirilov's return, he stood deliberating over it. Yet Schroder was out there by the Gnomon, and if he, Gees, stayed to get the money after making a mess of Schroder—which would have to be done before he could lay hands on the package—he might not get away at all.

The two in the house were still talking: their voices reached him as a faint murmur that alternated between bass and high tenor. As far as the money was concerned, he determined to be guided by circumstance; if he saw a good chance, he would out Schroder and annex it before making a bolt for the Minx, but, whatever he did, he had to take care not to come within reach of the panjandrum's long arms. Even twelve thousand pounds in easily negotiable form was not enough to justify him in taking that risk, for the panjandrum had hinted fairly plainly to Smirilov what he would do if he caught Comrade Green here.

All the west was dark with cloud, now. It was not yet the sunset hour, but the untended, thickly-grown shrubbery— there may have been half an acre of it—looked gloomy and forbidding. Advancing toward it, Gees was careful to keep it between himself and the aeroplane, so that Schroder might know nothing of his presence. A faint, tinkling noise told that the pilot was hammering at something, and, absorbed in whatever he was doing, would not notice so small a rustle as Gees would make among the undergrowth. There was a rumble of very distant thunder: another of the day's storms was gathering in the west. So much the better, for if those two in the house heard it they were more likely to stay inside, in order to keep themselves dry.

Gees took a survey of the bushy tract as he advanced toward it. If Smirilov got back before he, Gees, had finished his exploration, it should be possible to work a way through to the left side, and get away unseen, for one digging in there would not be able to see him, and the other, intent on keeping both Schroder and Barter from knowledge of what the shrubbery concealed, would lead either or both of them well away from it—into the house, probably, under pretext of sheltering from the storm that appeared to be rising.

Country-born as he was, and used to woodlands, in childhood and early youth, Gees soon espied a point where twigs had been broken as if by careless, hurried entry from the open grass land to hiding among the dense, mixed growth under the trees. He glanced back, but there was no sign of anyone in or at the back of the house. Then he made for the point where pendent twigs dangled, and forced a way in, holding his hands up before him to protect his face from back-springing boughs. He saw a muddled confusion of tracks in the leaf mould, leading to a little clearing between two laurel bushes, and there he stood utterly aghast, knowing that the panjandrum and Smirilov had great and instant need of a spade.

The body that he saw lay sprawled in the clearing. A terrible gash in the throat proved it no more than a body, and the gushing blood from the severed carotid had spouted and splashed the dead brown laurel leaves near it. There was a horror in the staring eyes which indicated that the living man had seen his death approach: the panjandrum, perhaps, had held him with those terrible long arms while Smirilov had cut his throat. Murder—murder foul and terrible!

Gees backed from the sight, half-dazed by it, though he had expected something of the sort here, and so had risked delay to explore the shrubbery. He pushed a way over to the left, to avoid the house and gain the thin place in the hedge unseen from the windows: the aeroplane would screen him to some extent from Schroder's view.

He whispered his horror of what he had seen.

"My God! Johns!"

# CHAPTER XVI

## A MESSAGE FOR TOTT

A HAPPY young wife, holding a chubby body aloft as she sat with the afternoon sunlight falling on her: the child gurgling with delight as it looked down at its mother, and Johns, packing the tea-basket they had brought out for their picnic, only three days ago! The picture, first connected thought to form in Gees' mind after he had turned away from that sprawled body between the laurels, was vividly distinct, and then, superimposed on it, came a picture of the young wife knowing herself widowed, her child fatherless. In bleak rage against these hellish plotters he pushed a way through the bushes and came out in the open, to the left of the shrubbery as he faced toward the house, and as near as could be to the thin place in the hedge.

And there was Schroder, going toward the house, not half a dozen yards distant. Discovery by him meant discovery by the panjandrum—

"Aha!" Schroder remarked cheerfully. "You are here, comrade."

"I am here," Gees said, approaching him.

The sudden panic in his eyes proved that he realised this as no comrade, but an enemy—too late. For as he tried to turn Gees' great fist made contact with his body in the region of the solar plexus, and with a winded grunt he would have dropped on the grass, but Gees stayed his fall, and with a grip on each of his arms dragged him back into the shelter of the shrubbery.

And there, rage-blinded as he remembered the young widow and her child, Gees went mad for a time. This man had had no hand in the murder, but he was one of them, thirsting to destroy the order that such men as Johns protected and held to the ways of law. Gees got him by the throat with both hands and crashed his skull against a tree trunk, not caring, then, if he killed the man. When Schroder collapsed limply at the foot of the tree, Gees battered at the expressionless, jaw-dropped face with his hammy fists, and then took an arm and twisted it till he heard something between a click and a crack. The sound sobered him, and he stood erect to look down at the mess he had made of a man, a little ashamed of himself, yet knowing that, brutal though it might be, he had done the most sensible thing: Schroder had discovered him: Schroder, if he lived, would not regain consciousness for hours, after that bang of his skull against the tree-trunk. Gees stooped again, felt at the unconscious man's heart, and found that it was still beating.

He dragged the body to where two laurels grew close together, and thrust it in between them: then he went to the other side of the bushes, reached in, and pulled Schroder farther in by the hair. When he had finished, nothing was visible of the unconscious figure, and he smoothed out the track left by dragging such a weight over the dead leaves and mould. It was unlikely that the panjandrum would find his man, for darkness would be over the shrubbery before he thought to make a thorough search: besides, he would not think to find Schroder in here. Much more would he think that the little man had found Johns' body, and had fled the place altogether in fear of consequences.

Back at the left edge of the shrubbery, Gees looked out cautiously from behind an evergreen on which spring had laid emerald fingers at the tips of dark-green boughs. This time, the way to the hedge and car in the lane beyond appeared clear, though at any moment the panjandrum might come out from the back of the house, or round the corner from the front: but the risk must be taken, and he strode out and across the open, not looking back, and not hurrying greatly, for haste would serve him but little if he were seen. He gained the hedge, forced a way through, and from beyond the screen of foliage looked back, parting a couple of boughs enough to permit of clear sight of the house. Had they seen him? For, if they had, they might take to flight in fear of his having discovered Johns' body in the shrubbery.

But there was no sign of life about the house. No face showed at either front window, and it was only from the front that he could have been seen as he crossed from the shrubbery—unless one or other of the two in there had gone up to a first-floor window at the back, which was very unlikely. As when he had arrived, the front door stood open, but the grass-grown gravel in front of it was vacant— Smirilov had not yet returned with the spade. Had he perhaps fled altogether in fear, or merely gone on from Leatherhead to Ashstead or Epsom on his errand, and found difficulty there too? Gees pictured him, fearful of asking for such a thing because of its implications, a foreigner unused to country ironmongers' shops, regarding the simplest question concerning his requirement with suspicion and fear. On an ordinary afternoon he would have had no difficulty, but the shop-assistants' Sabbath, early closing day, was defeating him.

Gees turned toward the Minx, less than a score yards distant on the other side of the road, and then paused. Smirilov had not come back with the spade, and until he did come back those other two would stay in the house, for the panjandrum wanted Barter to remain ignorant of what the shrubbery concealed—he would not take the man out there. Beyond the shrubbery stood the Volodskanya Gnomon, its engine warmed up ready for flight, its tail swung round toward the house so that one had only to start up and open out for the take-off. And the big package, almost certainly, was still under the seat behind the controls! And Schroder would not regain consciousness for hours!

It was altogether too tempting for resistance, but, first, he must assure punishment for these murderers. He went and climbed over the gate behind the Minx to ensure that Smirilov should not see him if the saloon came back, and there, seated on damp grass with the hedge concealing him from the road, he took a notebook and pencil from his pocket and wrote as plainly as he could, putting Detective-Inspector Tott's name and telephone number at the head of the message. At first he thought of informing the Leatherhead police of the murder, but decided against it. Tott would act more quickly, would grasp the situation and break all records between here and London to avenge his man on receipt of this message, and the distance was so small that, with his greater facilities, he would get here almost as soon as Leatherhead men could arrive if the message were sent to them.

It was concisely informative, and Gees risked calling himself "Detective Green" in order to impress the messenger he meant to find:

"Body of Detective-Sergeant Johns discovered in copse behind Kestwell farmhouse at about 8 p.m. to-day. Johns has been murdered by Denghisovski and Smirilov. Schroder is lying unconscious in copse and knows nothing of the murder. The two murderers are in the house with another man, Barter. Care is necessary in approaching, as they have arms in the house.

DETECTIVE GREEN."

He tore out the page with the message on it, and got over the gate again. His watch told him it was nearly half past eight—Smirilov would get no spade at this time, unless by a lucky chance. He himself went along the lane until he came to its junction with the road, and then, turning to the left, walked a hundred yards or so away from Leatherhead, letting two cars going in that direction pass him, since he did not want to be recognised if Smirilov returned with the saloon before he himself could get back to the Gnomon and its contents.

A third car came along toward Leatherhead, and he hailed it, but the driver would not stop. When the next appeared, Gees stepped out into the middle of the road and held up his hand with the message paper in it, for he could not afford delay: Smirilov might appear at any moment, now, and after his return getting to the Gnomon would be out of the question. The car, a chauffeur-driven Daimler, came to a standstill, and the man at the wheel said: " 'Ere, what's the game?" in a distinctly hostile tone. He had an elderly man and his wife in the separately-enclosed body of the car behind him, and they peered at the tall, lank figure of Gees approaching with his paper.

"Police," Gees explained in a word to the chauffeur. He had no time for more than the one word, for the man broke out angrily.

"Police or no police, you've got no right to stop me like this! And how do I know you're police at all? Where's your warrant card?"

Abreast of the driving seat by that time, Gees thrust his paper before the chauffeur's eyes. "Read that!" he commanded sharply. "You'll find it warrant enough for stopping you. I demand your assistance in the name of the law! Read it—read it aloud before you go!"

By that time the male passenger had his head out of the driving side window. He looked old and tottery, but did not sound so.

"What is all this?" he demanded. "Who are you, and what do you want, my man? You've no right to stop me like this, you know."

"I represent the law, sir, and in a case of urgency have the right to stop anyone and demand assistance," Gees answered. He withdrew his paper from before the chauffeur's eyes, which had begun to goggle, and offered it to the old man. "Murder has been committed near here, and I want this message transmitted to the man whose telephone number is at the top there—telephoned to him as quickly as possible. If you will be so good as to read the message, you will realise its urgency. Can I rely on you to telephone it on for me?"

The old man felt for a pair of pince-nez at the end of a silken cord, adjusted them fumblingly on his nose, and reached for the paper, which he took and held closely before his myopic eyes.

"Why not send it yourself?" he asked.

"Because I am here alone," Gees answered. "Read it, please."

The old man read, slowly, and Gees could have cursed him for the delay, but knew the folly of over-urging with such a one.

"Murder? But these names, officer. How is one to—?" He broke off, and looked at Gees in a way that proved he was impressed.

"Denghisovski—Smirilov—Schroder," Gees said slowly and distinctly. "You can spell them out, if you like. Inspector Tott will recognise them. He knows the men—Communist plotters."

"Ah, Communists!" As if it explained everything. "You should have said that at first. Now you want me to send this for you?"

"I'm immensely grateful to you, sir. I want you to stop at the first public telephone you see, and get this through to the number at the top, and ask for Inspector Tott. You may not get him, but a subordinate officer. In that case, tell the man to take the message for Inspector Tott, give it him, and that's all I ask of you. He'll do the rest, quickly enough. Now can I leave this paper with you and be sure the message will get to its destination?"

"You may rely on me, officer," the old man said crisply. "This Communism is a curse, a terrible curse! I will transmit the message myself, and lose no time over it. And that is all you require?"

"All, except secrecy," Gees answered.

"You shall have that too, I promise you. Harold"—he spoke to the chauffeur—"stop at the first public telephone you see, and be careful not to miss one. Good night, officer—you may rely on me."

"One moment, sir," Gees asked, with a notebook and pencil out. "May I have your name, please?"

"Jitterbury—Sir John Jitterbury, of Guildford."

"Thank you very much, Sir John," and Gees stood back from the car and signed to the chauffeur to go on. He took the registration number and letters from the back number plate, and inscribed them with the name in his book, being well aware that he might need all the evidence he could get about his own activities, before long.

He had even a doubt about going back to Kestwell, although, as nearly as he could tell, Smirilov had not returned. It was possible, of course, that another road from Leatherhead connected with the far end of the lane, and the saloon had come in from that direction, but against that was the fact that all wheel tracks turning into Kestwell driveway from the lane showed as coming from the direction of this road. Almost certainly, Smirilov was still hunting for that spade.

In addition, it made no difference whether he, Gees, went back or no, now, as far as Tott was concerned. By sending that message, he had connected himself up with the murder of Johns, and, if Tott chose to run him in as an accessory, he might as well have the twelve thousand pounds to use in establishing and conducting the best possible defence that could be obtained. He went back, entered the lane, and at sound of a car coming along the road jumped for the shelter of the Minx. The car turned into the lane as Gees had feared it would, and, peering through the windows of the Minx as the other vehicle passed, Gees saw Smirilov alone at the driving wheel, looking worried as he frowned at the way ahead of him. He swung the wheel and made a bad turn into the ridged drive of Kestwell, and as the saloon disappeared Gees came out from behind the Minx and went to the thin place in the hedge. Could he reach the Gnomon, or would Smirilov or the panjandrum go out at the back with the spade and cut him off? With three of them there, he must not be caught, he knew: men who had killed Johns would not hesitate over killing him.

He saw Smirilov get out from the saloon and the panjandrum come out from the front doorway of the house to greet him. As nearly as could be seen, the quest of a spade had been a failure. The two stood talking for a minute or so, and Smirilov used both hands to emphasise what he said: then they turned and entered the house, and at that Gees went through the hedge and scuttled beyond sight from the front windows of the house. He had got beyond the end of the sidewall when he heard the panjandrum's deep voice booming from somewhere near the back door in a loud and apparently rather angry call:

"Schroder? Comrade Schroder? Where are you?" There was a small, isolated shed only a few yards from Gees when he heard the call. He made for it, since its doorway was invisible from the back door of the house, and got inside. The black dust on the floor proclaimed that it had been used as a coal shed, and there was a single pane of glass occupying the place of a couple of bricks in the back wall, a dusty, dirty pane, yielding a modified view of the back of the house. Gees ventured to clean an eyehole on the glass with the ball of his thumb, and peered through.

He saw the panjandrum come out from the backyard and stand gazing toward the shrubbery. Then Smirilov came out, and the panjandrum called to Schroder again, at which Gees prayed to all his gods that he had banged the pilot's head hard enough against the tree trunk, for if Schroder wakened and answered it would be very inconvenient indeed. But no voice answered the call: Smirilov and the panjandrum moved to get a view of the Gnomon beyond the shrubbery, and so came quite near the shed in which Gees had concealed himself. He heard them as they talked, anxiously, and the panjandrum irritably: he saw, too, that the panjandrum's coat cuff was stained dark brown—with Johns' blood, almost certainly—while there were blood splashes on Smirilov's right sleeve, too. If only Tott would get here and take them with that evidence on them! But Tott would be a full hour, yet, allowing for the time it would take for Sir John Jitterbury to telephone him.

"He is not there!" the panjandrum exclaimed angrily.

"He is not there," Smirilov assented, rather meekly. "Comrade, have you told Barter anything about—about that in the shrubbery?"

"Am I a fool?" the panjandrum retorted, still more angrily. "He must not know, as Schroder must not know. Comrade, now Barter is not here, what did the boy tell you? I could not ask in Barter's presence."

"His brother Peter is keeping watch on the flat. Green is still in it. There is a light in one window, and Peter has watched the door all the time. It is as you said, comrade. Having sent that man Johns to spy on us, he will not come here himself. Yet I thought him loyal to the cause. He seemed loyal, to me."

"Bah! If you thought him loyal, you are the only one, except for Comrade Lenoir. I am glad he is not. Our own people must rule these English. Theirs would be squeamish over the killings, and with them in power we should never extirpate the capitalists. Green loyal?" A bitterly ironic flavour characterised the last two words.

"Schroder liked him," Smirilov said, and Gees remembered how he had handled Schroder, and felt a little twinge of remorse over it.

"Schroder?" the panjandrum echoed. "No more than a fool, that man, though a good pilot. Comrade, he is not there with the monoplane. I think he found what we left in the shrubbery after we had finished with it, and fled away from this place altogether. Else, why does he not answer or come here when I call him? No, he has gone."

He shouted again, and again there was no reply.

"You see?" he said. "He is not there—he is not anywhere within our hearing. He is afraid, that Schroder—but he will come back to the monoplane. It is a wonder that he did not go in it."

"The money?" Smirilov asked. "Is it still there?"

At that, to Gees utter dismay, the panjandrum suddenly set off toward the Gnomon, and Smirilov followed him. The coal shed window would not give a view of their movements, and the doorway was no better, for in order to see them from that side Gees would have had to put his head out and betray his presence. He waited awhile, and the pair came back. To his relief, neither of them was carrying the package.

"It will be safe there," were the first words he caught. "Nobody will know the seat lifts up, so nobody will look for it."

"Barter will miss us, soon," Smirilov observed, standing quite close to the back window of the shed. "And Green may come here, yet."

"Being guilty of treachery, he will not come here," the panjandrum averred confidently, and Gees, listening, treasured the sentence in his mind, in case he might have need of it yet. "And let Barter wait. I told him to watch the gateway. Is there no place where we can find a spade, comrade? I do not like leaving that thing lying there."

"It will be safe till to-morrow," Smirilov said. "I tried, but—this cursed country! One man was in his home at his shop, but he said he dared not sell me one, because of the law. The law!"

"The capitalist law," the panjandrum observed. "There will be few holidays for the workers under our law, when we have made the revolution. Except for the long holiday we will give to those who do not obey our laws. Half days in the week—Bah! Petted fools!"

"Petted or otherwise, always fools," Smirilov observed reflectively. "But stubborn, these people. We must kill very many of them."

"That one—Johns—it took all my strength to hold him while you used the knife," the panjandrum said, far less irritably. "But it was a good killing. Just so I will kill that Tott—the knife for me, with him. We will tie him, and you shall hold his head, if you wish."

"And you think Schroder has gone?" Smirilov asked.

"Gone, but he will recover his nerve and return," the panjandrum prophesied. "If he had not gone, he would not have kept hidden when I called. We will tell him to say nothing of what he saw, and, comrade, no word to Barter of it. No hint, even, that Johns has been here. By to-morrow night we must have the body buried deep, and all the bombs taken away—we cannot use this place, now. For Tott will know Johns has been here, and may send other men to search for him. We must wait awhile with Barter as if we expected Schroder to return to-night, and after it is dark the two of us can go.

Then, if Tott should send to search this place to-night, he may catch Barter, but he will not catch us, and we are the chiefs of the revolution. Barter is too visionary, a man in the clouds, as they say in this country. We need men like ourselves—men who can kill, not visionaries."

"It is true, Comrade Leonid. Weakness would be fatal for us."

"Let us go in, comrade. In an hour it will be dark, and we can leave Barter here and go. He will not find what is in the shrubbery in the dark, and I will come here early in the morning."

Through his peephole Gees saw the pair go toward the house, and as they gained the entrance to the yard he turned and made for the door of the shed. Now, while they went to talk to Barter, was his chance. The engine of the Gnomon would not be cold, yet, and the package for which he had risked return to this place was still intact under the seat. And in less than an hour Tott would be here with his men, if all went well: that package must be taken away now, or never.

# CHAPTER XVII

## DIVIDED COUNSELS

NEITHER then nor at any time was Gees to know whether the panjandrum had suspected his presence in the coal shed: possibly the peep-hole he had rubbed on the dirty glass had looked suspicious, but however it may have been, he heard the panjandrum call when he was not more than ten yards beyond the end of the shed on his way to the Gnomon: the tone of the call was smoothly detestable.

"Comrade Green? You are late, surely? And we are here in the house—there is nobody out there now."

For a fraction of a second Gees made mental measurement of his distances, and knew he could not gain the driving seat of the monoplane and get away, even though the engine was still warm: neither could he get back to the Minx and make his escape in it. His only chance consisted in temporising—if that were possible—until Tott and his men got here. It was on the cards that they would find his corpse with that of Johns, and that either the panjandrum or Smirilov would hold his head while the other dug the knife into his throat. He had made this gamble for the sake of the package under the seat of the Gnomon, and had lost. He faced toward the panjandrum.

"Nobody there?" he said. "I thought I might find Schroder."

"But you were coming to consult with me," the panjandrum said, as smoothly as before. "Over an hour ago, was it not?"

"Sorry to be late—I was detained at Lots Road," Gees told him.

"Come inside, and let us talk," the panjandrum invited. "Comrade Barter is there, and you have yet to meet him. Let us talk, about Lots Road and other things, comrade. Many other things."

The menace in the suggestion was plainly evident. Gees, facing the man, saw that the little round button atop was very pink indeed: he meditated one good kick in the panjandrum's stomach as prelude to making a bolt for safety, but possibly his expression betrayed the intent. The panjandrum kept a safe distance, and motioned him toward the back door, while Smirilov watched him cautiously.

"Many other things, eh?" Gees remarked. "Well—you go first, comrade. I have no right to precede you, you know."

"No, you go first," the panjandrum dissented, and made it a command. "We will not keep you very long for it is growing late."

The menace was even plainer, now. But Tott would not be long—Gees went through the yard and in at the back door. He entered the passage, and the panjandrum, close behind him, spoke again.

"Straight through, comrade. Barter is in the front room on the right. We four can talk there—of many things."

So Gees went straight on. The door of the room on the right was open, and, entering, he saw a tall, melancholy-looking man who wore horn-rimmed glasses and looked like a university don—a dark-complexioned man with a Grecian nose and rather kindly eyes, who turned from gazing through the window at the sound of this entry. Then, without a word of threat or explanation, the panjandrum suddenly reached out his long arms and gripped Gees' wrists from behind, drawing his hands behind his back before he could stiffen himself to resistance.

"Comrade Smirilov, your silk tie will serve to bind his wrists," the panjandrum said quietly—Gees felt the grip as that of a pair of steel manacles holding his wrists against each other. "Tie while I hold him thus. Comrade Barter, this is a man named Green, who has tried to betray us and wreck the revolution. He fooled Comrade Lenoir, but I will be fooled by him no longer. This is the end."

"Zo?" said Barter, and stared interestedly, while Gees felt a bandage of some sort—Smirilov's silk tie, he guessed— wound round his wrists and pulled tight. When it had been tied, the panjandrum released his hold and stood back, considering that he had his man sufficiently helpless. Gees decided to try argument first, and, if it failed, to use his feet later—and possibly his head as well—if Tott did not arrive to resolve the situation for him. He remembered a sentence he had overheard while concealed in the coal shed.

"If I had wanted to betray you, should I have come here to-night?" he asked, turning and noting that the panjandrum kept safe distance from him, and that Smirilov too watched and was alert.

"We shall see," the panjandrum said. "You say you are late because of your visit to Lots Road, but I know the time at which you left Lots Road, as I know that before going there you lunched at Frascati's with a Foreign Office official. I know that you were in your rooms so late as to need a light in one room, when a storm darkened the sky, so how do you say you were detained at Lots Road? Lies, eh, my friend?"

"Why should I lie?" Gees retorted. "You are over-suspicious, comrade. I had to meet the Foreign Office man to gain admission to Lots Road, don't you see? And it was my visit there that detained me, for I had to go back to my office, and had many things to do there before coming here to see you. I submit to your tying without protest, for you may think there is reason to suspect me. But I demand to know the reason. What do you think I have done—what has happened to give you cause for suspicion since I saw you last, comrade?"

As he ceased speaking, he listened for some sign that Tott and his men were here—they should be here soon, he felt. But there was dead silence about the place until the panjandrum spoke again.

"As chief of the revolution, I need give no reasons," he said.

On that, Gees knew that Barter was not to know Johns had been here and had been murdered in the shrubbery. Only the panjandrum and Smirilov knew of it. Still hoping for Tott's arrival, he decided to keep his knowledge of the crime as a card to play if his position grew desperate. It might give him five or ten minutes' delay, and save him.

"But on mere suspicion, you can do nothing," he observed.

"Nothing, except kill you," the panjandrum answered indifferently.

Gees managed a smile. "That sort of thing is not done in this country," he said. "When the revolution is accomplished—yes, but you will ruin your cause if you do anything of the sort before."

"Our cause?" the panjandrum asked. "Not yours too?"

"While my hands are tied like this, I have no cause," Gees fired back. "I came here at your bidding to talk of work in the north—"

"Then why did you go out to look for Schroder at the back?" the panjandrum interrupted. "Why did you come here an hour late, and even then not attempt to come to me, after talking with a man from your Foreign Office? Do you think you can blind me utterly?"

Let him go on arguing, Gees felt—Tott would be here soon.

"Why should I wish to blind you? If I went to see Schroder, it was because I thought you might be out there too."

"Is it your car in the road outside this place?" the panjandrum demanded. "The one beside the gateway on the other side of the road?"

"Yes." Gees dared not lie, though he knew the significance of the admission. The panjandrum knew the car, and would trap him in a lie.

"Then you have been here some time," the panjandrum said, very ominously. "Spying for the Foreign Office man, eh?"

"He needs no spying from me," Gees retorted. "I came to the house, but there was nobody in it, and the saloon was not here—"

"The car was there when I drove away in the saloon," Smirilov interposed. "Comrade Leonid, he has been here a very long time."

"I didn't see the saloon," Gees put in before the panjandrum could speak. Let them go on arguing: every minute brought Tott nearer. And, though they were almost certain that he had been acting against them, they apprehended no danger to-night, evidently.

"Since you were here before Comrade Smirilov drove away, you must have seen the saloon," the panjandrum pointed out. "Where were you?"

"Changing a wheel after a puncture," Gees explained. "The saloon may have passed me while I was doing it—I didn't see it, I tell you."

"You tell us much," the panjandrum retorted significantly. "You steal away from your office so that you are not perceived. You come here to see me, but do not look for me. You try to convince us of your loyalty, but I know you now for a liar and traitor, and the penalty for treachery is death. So—you must die, traitor."

"Comrade Barter!" Gees fired out the demand, intending to reveal the fact that Johns had already been murdered, and then changed his mind: he would keep that back a little longer. "This Comrade Leonid," he went on, "is blinded by jealousy because Comrade Lenoir preferred me to him. He is accusing me of treachery to get me out of his way. It is he who is betraying the cause for his own personal ends, and you know as I know that he is subject to Comrade Lenoir, answerable to her for all that he does. I demand judgment by her on these accusations."

There was a silence. No sound of Tott arriving came into it, Gees noted. Then Barter spoke, doubtfully, looking first at the panjandrum and then at Smirilov beside him: he appealed to the latter.

"Vas dot drue, Comrade Smirilov?" he asked. "Vas it dot Comrade Leonid lof Comrade Lenoir, undt she lof dis man Green?"

"Let her speak for herself," Gees interposed before Smirilov could answer. "You, Comrade Barter, know that she is in command. What I say of Comrade Leonid's jealousy is true, and if you let him kill me she will see that you do not escape punishment. Kill me, and you ruin the revolution. Comrade Lenoir will see that you do not escape punishment for that, apart from what she may feel for me."

"How—ruin der revolution?" Barter asked, evidently puzzled.

"Because"—Gees had an inspiration—"she warned me that Comrade Leonid was jealous of me, warned me not to trust myself alone with him. So, before I came here to-night, I left instructions with my secretary. That light in one of my windows is not for me, but for her. She is waiting there for me to return, and if I am not back safely by eleven o'clock to-night, she takes a sealed envelope straight to Inspector Tott. All your names are in that envelope."

"Ahh-h-h!" It was a long, fearful breath from Barter.

"So he is traitor," the panjandrum said fiercely. "He confesses himself traitor. Shall such a one live? No! We will take him out."

"The envelope is sealed," Gees said sharply. "Nothing in it will be revealed unless I do not go back. If I go back, I shall destroy it."

"Zo-o-o!" said Barter, with intense relief. "It vas brecaution. I dink you do not kill dis time, Comrade Leonid. Undt as he say, dis is not der gountry vor killings, till der revolution is gomplete."

"What will you do with him, then?" the panjandrum demanded contemptuously. "After what he has told us, you cannot let him go?"

"What have I told you?" Gees demanded in turn. "That *you* are a traitor, putting your own interests before the revolution! You plot to remove me because I stand between you and Comrade Lenoir. Leonid Denghisovski, I will denounce you to her for this night's work!"

"Being dead, you will not denounce anyone," the panjandrum retorted. "Comrade Smirilov, let us take him out—"

"Take Comrade Barter too!" Gees interrupted, and backed a step as Smirilov advanced and paused again. "He has heard me, and he is loyal to the revolution. He will denounce you—and you too, Smirilov—to Comrade Lenoir if you let him live. Now take me out!"

The gleam of fear in the panjandrum's eyes prompted him to make the challenge. Then, after the fear, came bestial ferocity, and the panjandrum's fingers twitched as if with longing to be at the throat of the man who thus defied him. He was getting near the end of his patience—and still there was no sign of Tott's arrival!

"You gannot take him out," Barter said stolidly. "Comrade Lenoir must first hear of all dis, bevore you kill. Undt it maybe dot you will not kill, Comrade Leonid. I do not know, but Comrade Lenoir must first know. Eltz, she will blame me for der killing."

Another silence. The room darkened with perceptible swiftness, and a muttering of distant thunder sounded from the west. Another of the day's storms was rising, perhaps to pass to the south as had the last, and perhaps to break on the farmstead. Smirilov spoke.

"I say, he must not go away from here. What can we do?"

"Take him out!" The panjandrum's voice was hoarse with evil desire. "We must not have blood in here. Take him out."

"I vill not haf him taken out," said Barter. "Eltz, if she is in lof with him, she will blame me too. She must first know."

Silence again, unbroken by Tott or by anything outside. Gees felt that he might hold them yet awhile, for Barter was against killing, Smirilov undecided though inclined to side with the panjandrum, and the panjandrum himself fiercely eager to get to work with his knife. Another ten minutes at the most, Gees estimated, would bring Tott to the house, and surely he could hold them for that time. If not, he must use his feet and head and begin on the panjandrum.

"You were here a long while before you looked for me," the panjandrum said abruptly. "Your car was there when Comrade Smirilov went away with the saloon. Where were you—what were you doing?"

"Why did Comrade Smirilov go away with the saloon?" Gees retorted.

"Why did you not drive your car in here—why did you leave it outside?" the panjandrum demanded fiercely—and Gees saw that his question about the saloon had brought a shadow of fear into the man's face: nobody might know about that quest for a spade, evidently.

"Comrade Lenoir warned me against you," he said quietly. "She told me you might be dangerous. In fact, she said that you might have to be removed, unless you left her alone and behaved yourself."

"She said dot?" Barter asked, and his tone showed that he was impressed by the statement. "Comrade, did she say dot?"

"To me, this morning, when I went to see Peter Keszca," Gees told him frankly. "She took me to see Peter Keszca because I am to bring bombs here if she finds it necessary to remove Comrade Leonid."

"Lies—all lies!" the panjandrum stormed. "Comrade Barter, why listen to him? He is mad—he has told us he will ruin the revolution! How shall such a one live? Comrade Smirilov, let us take him out."

"Until Comrade Lenoir has judged, you shall not dake him oudt," Barter declared. "Eltz, I mineself vill tell Comrade Lenoir apoud it."

"Comrade"—the panjandrum appealed, smoothly—"you do not know this country—the ways of this country. The revolution is very near, now, and if we let this man go he will betray us and ruin it—has he not told us himself that his secretary will go—"

"You damned liar!" Gees broke in. "I told you I left a sealed envelope with my secretary—sealed! While I live to get back to my office by eleven, you need have no fear from that envelope or what is inside it. On what Comrade Lenoir told me, I protected myself."

"Hear him, comrades!" The panjandrum appealed triumphantly to both Barter and Smirilov, and especially to Barter. "Hear him put his own safety before the revolution, and so confess himself a traitor. For it is not only that he may be delayed here, but anything on the road may delay him. The car may break down—anything —and whatever it is that may happen so that he does not return by eleven o'clock, if he is not there his secretary goes to Detective-Inspector Tott and we are all ruined—the revolution is lost. Is he a traitor or no? For my part, I say a traitor, worthy to die. You, Smirilov?"

Vindictive intensity made a bark of the question, and he glared at Smirilov as if defying him to utter an acquittal.

"Traitor," Smirilov answered unhesitatingly. "Let us take him—"

"Undt den der letter vill go to der police," Barter interrupted.

"But he will betray us in any case," the panjandrum protested.

A louder rumble of thunder followed on the statement. Barter gazed hard at Gees, at the panjandrum, and lastly at Smirilov. The room darkened still more: the sun had set, now, and the approaching storm added to the gloom of deepening twilight.

"Vat vill you do, den, mitout Comrade Lenoir?" Barter asked.

"Kill him," the panjandrum growled, in unison with the thunder.

"Undt if you are wrong, she vill kill you," Barter prophesied.

"I am not wrong—he is a traitor," the panjandrum declared.

"Undt she vill kill me too," Barter surmised, "if you are wrong."

Let them keep at it, Gees felt: Tott must arrive soon. He put in a statement to keep the argument alive, and felt almost hopeful.

"Comrade Leonid," he said, "you have not put forward one single fact to prove me a traitor. You are blindly jealous of me over Comrade Lenoir, and want to kill me so as to have her to yourself. You say I lunched with a Foreign Office official. It is true. I have had lunch with an engineer of the Battersea power station, because we want Battersea to be destroyed on the day. That too you know is true. What else have I done—why are my hands tied behind me? You have said nothing more than that I am a traitor. Prove it before you try to kill me, or else do not hope to escape the vengeance of Comrade Lenoir, who told me what you are and warned me not to trust myself to you in her absence. I trusted you in spite of her, and here I am!"

Specious though it was, the argument impressed Barter. He shook his head gravely at the panjandrum, and spoke just as gravely.

"You gannot kill dis man, comrade," he said. "Eltz, if vat he say is drue, Comrade Lenoir vill not only kill you, but me too."

"He put the police on us, Comrade Barter," the panjandrum accused.

*"Hein?"* Barter started and looked uneasy. "Comrade, do you say dot he vill put der police on us, or dot he did put der police on us?"

"He has put them on us," the panjandrum asserted, and looked at Smirilov, who shook his head as if he did not like this at all.

"Then where are they?" Gees challenged boldly. "If that were true, Comrade Barter, do you think you would be free and here? You know as I know of the bombs Peter Keszca is making, the bombs Comrade Leonid is bringing here. If I had meant to put the police on you, I should have told them about the bombs. If I had told them about the bombs, they would be here, arresting you. Where are these police?"

*"Ja.* Vhere are dey, Comrade Leonid?" Barter appeared to second Gees' triumphant assertion of innocence as he put the question.

"I say, he has put the police on us," the panjandrum insisted stubbornly—and, as Gees knew, with plenty of reason for the statement. "Comrade Smirilov here knows it—is it not so, comrade?"

"It is so," Smirilov assented solemnly. "So, it is time to kill."

"Wait, you fools!" Gees snapped out. "I've told you what will happen to you if you kill. By to-morrow your revolution will be smashed, and you all on a capitalist trial for murder."

But the final argument did not impress either of the pair, as he saw. If Johns' visit were due to betrayal, and not just a chance, they were in danger of trial for murder whether they killed another man or no. And the panjandrum's expression indicated that he was tired of argument, and determined on killing—and still Tott did not appear! How long was it since Sir John Jitterbury had promised to telephone that message through? The panjandrum spoke.

"Comrade Barter, I take command—you may go, so that you know nothing of what we do. Return in half an hour, for Comrade Smirilov will go back with me in the car. I *know* this man is guilty of treachery to the cause, and he must die. That story of his secretary waiting with a letter for the police is all a lie told to frighten us. You know nothing of what I have decided—you may go."

After a moment of irresolution Barter moved toward the door, but Gees, with a sudden movement, placed himself before the man.

"You are doomed if you consent to this, Barter," he said sharply—and then the panjandrum, reaching out from behind him, caught hold of his bound hands and dragged him aside with a force that sent him staggering toward the window and spun him half-round as he progressed. And, in the gathering gloom of approaching storm added to the coming of night, he caught sight of a single figure about to enter the house from the front, one that none of them, in their preoccupation, had seen approach along the drive. It was the faintest of momentary glimpses, and Gees questioned inwardly for an instant whether Tott had been such a fool as to send one man or come alone himself, and then realised that, on receipt of such a warning as Sir John had transmitted, the inspector would divide his forces and surround the house before entering or sending men in.

"Doomed, I tell you!" he repeated, raising his voice to prevent the others from hearing footsteps in the passage. "Wait, Barter! These two men have cut a detective's throat, and his body is lying out among the shrubs at the back. The police will be on you—"

A dazzling flash of lightning, illumining the room and revealing all their faces distinctly to each other, brought him to an amazed stop in his declamation. For it showed, not Tott nor any of his men, but Christine standing in the doorway, with parted lips and horror in her eyes at the accusation she had heard.

# CHAPTER XVIII

## CONDEMNATION

HALF-BLINDED BY THE GLARE as darkness came again, deeper for the contrast, Gees heard Barter's sharp, frightened—"Ach!" and heard, too, Christine's incisive demand—"Comrade Leonid, is this true?" Then heaven's artillery crashed, and if the panjandrum made any reply it was blotted out in the roar that seemed to shake the house.

"True? Of course it is true, Christine!" Gees barked out, and made his voice distinct above the echoes of thunder still pealing down the sky. "Sergeant Johns' body is out in the shrubbery at the back—Smirilov and Denghisovski killed him. They tied my hands behind me, or I'd strike a match and show you Johns' blood on them."

Not till that moment had he understood why she, a woman, was ranked above Denghisovski and all the rest, but now, as she took command with cool, deliberate grasp of the whole situation on no more than his statement, he saw that she was fit to be set over such as these.

"Untie his hands at once, Comrade Leonid," she bade quietly. "Comrade Barter, go to the door and keep watch there, and return here instantly to warn us if anyone approaches. In that event, we must all go out by the back door. Untie those hands instantly, Leonid!"

For the panjandrum had hesitated over obeying her, though Barter moved out at once as he heard her command. Gees felt hands fumbling with the knot on his wrists, and presently his hands were free.

"Thank you, Christine," he said. "Comrade Leonid was about to kill me as well as the detective. You were just in time."

"What is this of killing a detective?" she asked. "Who killed the man, and why? Was it you, Comrade Leonid, as he said?"

"He came here to-day and found the bombs," the panjandrum answered sullenly. "After that, we had to kill him. We could not let him go away when he knew the bombs were here. Smirilov and I killed him."

"You fools!" Her voice was bitter, wrathful, yet quiet and restrained. "You utter, dastard fools! You have killed the revolution!"

"But what could we do?" Smirilov almost whined. "He had found the bombs, and if he had got away after that—"

"Had he found you?" she demanded sharply.

"No." The panjandrum made the confession. "We came on him—"

"Fools, cowardly fools!" she interrupted. "Was Schroder here?"

"He was out at the back, with his machine," the panjandrum answered sullenly. "But what of it? Johns had found the—"

"Oh, the Left shall know of this!" she interrupted again. "The heads of the Left shall hear of it and judge you! Why, you might have hidden yourselves, sacrificed Schroder as guilty of bringing bombs here, and been none the worse. Schroder is loyal—he would not have betrayed any of us, and Grigori here could have taken his place as pilot, for the aeroplane is wanted mostly for work in the north. And there I meant Grigori to work for us, as you know. Leonid, your mad lust for blood at any cost has betrayed the revolution!"

She was incisively, terribly quiet in her denunciation. Gaining sight again after the effects of the blinding flash, Gees saw her plainly now, clad all in dark grey, and with a dark grey hat fitting closely to her little head. He moved to place himself beside her, and again listened for Tott's approach. But Barter would give warning of that, he realised, possibly in time to get her away. For, as she had saved him, so he meant to save her if he could, and he thought he perceived a way of doing it when they all had to take to flight.

"You are unjust, Comrade Lenoir," the panjandrum protested. "This infatuation of yours for the man Green blinds you to his treachery to the cause. To-day he was with a man of the English Foreign Office—"

"I have already explained that, Christine," Gees interrupted sharply. "That man's infatuation for you blinds him to everything else. He wants me out of the way, wants to have you himself, and for that he would have killed me if you had not come in—very late." He added the last words almost reproachfully.

"I telephoned you to tell you I should be late, Grigori," she said, "but you were not there, and I would not leave a message. When I rang again, there was no reply, and I knew you had come here. Leonid, I know what he says is true—you are blinded by that passion of yours, and can see only that because of him you may not have me. But I tell you, if I had been too late and you had killed him, then I would have had you killed without waiting for the heads of the Left to condemn you! And now, being fool beyond belief, you have killed yourself."

"I? Killed myself?" the panjandrum almost gasped.

"Grigori, did I not say they were fools?" she asked gibingly. "Why, you accursed fools, do you think you can kill a detective in this country and escape punishment? By to-morrow, it will be known to his chief—to the man Tott— that he is missing, and he will have left word that he was coming here. And Tott knows that you come here, knows that his man's failure to return will be due to you. By noon to-morrow every port will be watched, and even if you do escape from the country before the watch is set, do you think you will escape the vengeance of the heads of the Left after having wrecked the revolution? Wrecked it by your blood-lust! You could not wait till killing became your work, but must risk and bring ruin on us all for the killing of this one man! And now all the work must be begun again!"

It was unanswerable logic. Neither the panjandrum nor Smirilov attempted to answer. Rain beat suddenly on the window, and another lightning flash showed the four to each other in the bare room. The thunder crashed and rolled along the sky again, and Gees looked at the luminous hands of his watch after the flash. He could not see them distinctly, but made it out as about nine o'clock. He began to think that his message had miscarried, and Tott would not come at all to-night. But Christine had stated how the murderers had trapped themselves: even if they succeeded in escaping from Tott, the vengeance of their own chiefs would fall on them.

Gees laid his hand on Christine's arm, and felt her start at his touch. She peered up at him in the gloom, anxiety in her eyes.

"*Are* you loyal?" she demanded whisperingly.

With the question put in such a way, just after—as he knew well enough—she had saved his life, he could not lie.

"I am thinking of you, and for you, Christine," he answered. "I want to talk to you, alone. Will you trust me for that?"

"Leonid—and you, Smirilov," she answered indirectly, "Comrade Barter is on watch. Unless he gives an alarm, you will remain here while I talk to Comrade Grigori—Comrade Green. Grigori—" she turned to Gees again, but the panjandrum made a protest.

"The man is not to be trusted, Comrade Lenoir," he said. "Do not go—do not do anything he asks. You are blind, I tell you."

"It is you who are blind, you fool!" she retorted cuttingly. "Let us go to some other room, Grigori—to that one at the back we know, if you wish, and you shall tell me what you have thought for me."

She preceded him out, and the other two made no move. He followed her along the passage toward the back of the house, but when she would have turned to go up the staircase, he put his hand on her shoulder to restrain her, and, paused, she tried to see his face in the darkness of the passage, and suddenly grasped his arm.

"Where, then?" she asked, with the first trace of fear he had heard from her since, in the train, she had asked if he still belonged to the police. "What is it, Grigori? Where must we go?"

"Through the scullery—out," he answered. "Out from the house."

"But it is raining," she objected.

"There are worse things than rain," he told her grimly.

She went through the scullery and out to the yard at the back. There was light enough left, here under the sky, to show Gees her face clearly as she looked up at him, heedless of the raindrops beating down on her, and he saw that her eyes were wet with other than rain. She was very lovely, and although he knew what had saddened her—no regret for death, but for herself and her cause!—yet he pitied her.

"Worse things than rain." She echoed his words. "Grigori, they are such fools, such fools! I came to this country seeing a vision of what might be, and they have broken it all, spoiled it all. There is no hope, no escape. I know the English, and those two are doomed."

"You know you saved me?" he asked sombrely. "Know they would have killed me too, if you had not come in then —when you did?"

"I know." She almost whispered it. "I came to the door and heard your voice, Grigori. And then I saw you, framed in living light, and knew I loved you. Even as I love my cause. If what they said had been true—if you were traitor to my cause, still I love you."

"Because of that, Christine," he said, "and because of a certain small child, I am going to save you as you saved me. Out—this way." He pointed toward the meadow land. "There may not be much time."

Since she did not move, but stood staring at him wonderingly, he went on through the yard, and at that she hurried to get beside and keep pace with him, and hung on to his arm as if to restrain him. But he went on resolutely, dragging her forward with him.

"Grigori, what is it?" she asked. "What do you mean?"

"I will tell you when we get to the Gnomon," he answered. "Only, Christine, you are in as great danger as I was when you saved me. It is my turn, now, to save you—to cancel the debt."

She ceased to hold back, and kept evenly beside him. "Where there is love like mine for you," she said, "there can be no debt."

He led on in silence until they stood beside the machine. Then he turned and faced her: no sound came from the house—there was time to explain. He held both her hands and gazed down at her.

"In some measure, Christine, Denghisovski is right," he said, and felt her sudden start. "In that your love has blinded you, he is right. Above all things I love this country of mine, and I love little children. Do you understand that?"

"Yes." She spoke chokingly, and with evident difficulty.

"I saw you save one little child's life—the bravest deed I have ever seen," he went on. "You saved my life too. Now, because there is great danger in remaining here, we will go together, you and I. For so only can I save you—and I want to save you, Christine."

"You—you mean—?" She did not end it, but gazed up at him.

"In the Gnomon," he said. "Will you trust me?"

"I said"—her voice was tremulously uncertain—"I said, Grigori, that we—do you remember it—that we should not always travel separately? So little time ago—do you remember it?"

"I thought of it before you reminded me," he answered.

"And the cause is lost—they have ruined it, I know. With you, Grigori, where you will. Anywhere, if you are with me!"

He placed his hands under her arms and lifted her into the monoplane, and then climbed in beside her. Schroder had shown him the controls—Schroder who now lay senseless between the laurel bushes, but Gees had no pity for him— and he switched on the ignition and pressed the button of the two-stage starter. The engine, not yet quite cold, picked up after a few seconds, and from behind him Gees heard a shouting that beat up over the noise of the exhaust. He looked back and saw dark figures running: then he jerked at the ratchet throttle control, the engine roared up, and the Gnomon began to move. It taxied out toward the big hawthorn hedge, lifted in time, and away in the west, under the storm cloud, there showed a line of quietly pale sunset sky. Roaring full out, Gees drove the plane southward.

Since, owing to limitations of finance, the detective force is not altogether omniscient, such people as Inspector Tott had put on to watch Denghisovski had missed the transport of the first load of bombs from Keszca's place in the Commercial Road, and Denghisovski had not started with his second consignment when Gees telephoned in his report of Keszca's activities to Tott's office in the inspector's absence. But, all the same, Tott had seen enough of the brothers Keszca to decide that they were in the revolutionary game, and when, late in that Wednesday afternoon, he came back to his office and read the message Gees had left for him, he determined to take a chance. If Gees were leading him up the garden over this business of bombs, the arrest of a couple of naturalised aliens on a charge that could not be proved would not make much trouble: if, on the other hand, the information were correct, the capture of the Keszcas might prove a distinct scoop. It was worth while to take a chance, for once.

The raid, made in two police cars and a tender, proved a wonderful scoop. Tott raked in the two brothers Keszca and took the boy Percy as a makeweight, though he knew Percy would get off during the police court proceedings before the actual trial. He scooped up over a hundred unfilled bomb-cases, some forty bombs filled and ready for transport, and enough electrical firing gear for over fifty of the deadly things. He loaded the whole lot aboard the tender while day grew old and embryo night clamoured thunderously toward birth—but the trams in the Commercial Road played havoc with the thunder—and took his captives to the nearest police station to charge them and land them safely in cells for the night. For it was not his policy to identify proceedings of this sort with his own office. A far better way was that of making them ordinary criminal charges, for then the political significance of his work remained unnoted by the general public, among whom were a number of pale pink Communists who might protest. So far, Tott had evaded protests. He meant to go on evading them.

The business of charging the prisoners took time, during which Tott came to the conclusion that Gees was not such a dirty dog—perhaps!—as he had at first appeared to be. He might have fallen badly for Christine, but his giving the Keszcas away indicated that he was far from falling for Communism of the ranker sort as a principle of life. If only the man would give up that dam fool mumps and murder office of his, the inspector reflected, he might turn out quite decent.

It was past eight o'clock when, having disposed of the two Keszcas and Percy for the time being, he had a brief chat with a brother inspector, and the man who had taken Gees' message from Sir John Jitterbury rang through in the hope of finding his chief.

Having found him, the man relayed the message on as he had received it; Tott asked for a repetition, and got it. His complacency over the Keszca haul vanished: like Gees, he thought first of Johns' wife and child, and cursed himself for having sent a good man into that hornets' nest alone. But even then he had begun to act: his two car loads of men and the tender were waiting outside the East End police station, but they had not long to wait after Tott had hung up the telephone receiver.

Including his drivers, he had fifteen men with him, and he took them all for this quest of Johns' murderers, for, after rounding up the Keszca brothers, he regarded this second message from Gees as genuine and reliable—though the chap had no right to call himself a detective, damn him! Tott's orders to his drivers were concise:

"Leatherhead first. The quickest way, and for this run you can forget that there ever was such a person as Hore-Belisha."

They forgot very thoroughly, honking and blaring a way through the traffic from east to west in good road-hog style. But even so their progress was comparatively slow at first, for London streets are clogged to a far later hour than that at which the cars started. At Leatherhead Tott picked up a constable who could locate Kestwell Farm for him, and they went on, pulling up on the main road at the entrance to the lane in which Gees had left the Minx. Tott investigated it, but, naturally, found nothing of interest in or about it.

The local man showed them the thin place in the hedge that Gees had used, and Tott, after explaining to his men what he wanted of them, was first to go through into the meadow. His men followed silently, all but the one who had been left in charge of the cars. Ten went off first to guard the back and any other exit there might be, and then Tott himself, with the remaining four, advanced until in line with the frontage of the house, after which they moved toward it, out of sight from the front windows. Gees had said that the men inside were armed, and Tott wanted to make a surprise rush on them, if possible.

He very nearly succeeded, for after Gees and Christine had gone out the panjandrum went to the doorway to convince Barter that the detective whom Smirilov and himself had murdered had been quite alone, and in all probability the fact that he was missing would not be known until the morrow. The two were talking just inside the front doorway, and Smirilov was leaning against the lintel of the front room, when silence gave place to the sound of a rush of feet, and Tott's electric torch shone in from the rainy darkness.

The roar of the Gnomon's opened-out engine sounded simultaneously with the panjandrum's shout of alarm. He bolted into the house as Tott gained the doorstep, and, cannoning against Smirilov, who had started out into the passage, was deflected into the front room in which they had deliberated over killing Gees. Three of Tott's men went straight down the passage after Barter and Smirilov, who rushed out into the firm but not fond embraces of the police stationed at the back: Tott himself and the remaining one, a sergeant, went after the panjandrum, but not in time to prevent him from lifting the board in the floor and snatching out an automatic pistol. He raised it as Tott rushed him, and pulled the trigger with the muzzle not more than six feet away from the inspector's face. The weapon made a noise that was between a whine and a groan after the crack of the percussion cap: it was Christine's pistol, the one of which Gees had doctored the ammunition. Almost before the panjandrum could realise that it was useless the two men were on him, and the three of them fought it out silently in the darkness, a savage, mad struggle.

It was two to one, but, although the two were trained men for this sort of work, the panjandrum's giant strength almost overcame them both. It was not until, rolling on the floor with the other two, Tott felt and grasped the pistol the panjandrum had dropped as useless that he was able to end it. He managed to miss the sergeant and get in a crashing blow on the panjandrum's head with the pistol, and presently they had their dazed prisoner handcuffed, while Tott slipped the pistol in his pocket as evidence of attempted murder. By that time other of his men came in with Smirilov and Barter, and, soon after, another sergeant of the party came to report the discovery of Johns' body in the shrubbery, on which Tott formally charged all three of his prisoners, and went out to see their work.

Bareheaded in the rain, he looked down at his dead sergeant, the best man he had ever had working under him, and the tears streamed down his face as he thought of the young widow and her child, although the electric torches showed his emotion clearly to his men.

"There should be another of them somewhere among these bushes, according to the message I got," he said after a brief silence. "Two of you go and get the stretcher out of the tender, and the rest search through here. Did anyone see that aeroplane go?"

"I did, sir," a voice answered, "but it was too dark to see how many were in it. I think there were two, but there may have been more."

"Was one a woman, could you tell?"

"I think so, sir, but I'm not sure. It was too dark to tell."

"Right. Get busy searching with the rest. Sergeant Cardwell, get a driver and take one of the cars back to Leatherhead at once. Description of the woman Lenoir and the man Green to all stations south, with orders to hold if found and report to my office at once. Get my office and inform them there, and tell them to get the press in on it and hand out Lenoir's photograph. We've got to get her."

"Very good, sir. And Green's photograph?"

"No. Not for the present. Give the woman to the press, but hold him back for the present. I'm not at all sure about him."

Cardwell went off. Presently Schroder was reported found, unconscious, fearfully battered, and breathing heavily— just as Gees had left him, in fact. They loaded him aboard the tender carefully and set off for Leatherhead, where a doctor pronounced his unconsciousness due to severe concussion: it was severe, too, for three days elapsed before he was able to speak again. The tender went back to Kestwell, for Tott and his men were still searching the place, and there was not room enough in the two cars for Johns' body and all the men, to say nothing of the three prisoners.

"It'll be Surrey assizes," Tott reflected grimly, "and three nice new ropes at least. Four, perhaps, or even five."

The discovery of two cases containing bombs, twenty in each, and one smaller case of electrical firing gear for the whole forty, was reported to him by two men who had searched a stable at the back of the house. The search went on, and they found the box of tools Schroder had had out from the Gnomon before Gees disabled him. It was near on eleven o'clock when, leaving two men in charge of the place, Tott loaded the rest of his force and his prisoners on the cars and tender, and set off for the return journey.

He lodged and charged the prisoners at Kingston, where he would apply for a remand for them after formal evidence of arrest on the morrow, and, taking Sergeant Cardwell with him and dismissing the rest of his force for the night, he went on to Little Oakfield Street. The light Gees had left was puzzling, for the man could not be in two places at once, and it looked as if he were at home.

"Come on up, Cardwell," Tott ordered. "I'll chance it."

They went up, for the outer door of the building was open until midnight. Tott rang twice, and then leaned against the bell push for quite long time—vainly, of course.

"If he hadn't been in the force, I'd get in there somehow," he declared at last. "But he knows too much, damn him, and I haven't got a search warrant. An English policeman's home is still his castle, even if he's left the service. All right, Cardwell—you go off home, and I'll hang around for an hour or two. If he's in, he'll put that light out before morning, and then I'll get something and jam that bell push in till he opens the door to stop it. If he's not at home, he'll come back because of that secretary of his, and I'll have him then."

He composed himself to wait, confident that Gees would return if the light had been left on in his absence, and that it would be put out soon if he were in the flat.

# CHAPTER XIX

## THE GNOMON PUTS OUT TO SEA

WHEN Leith Hill, no more than five hundred feet below, went sliding to merge in the rest of the misty darkness beneath the Gnomon, the rain ceased, and Gees drove out to clarity, though of the middle twilight. The thundercloud overhead thinned, and he made out Capel without difficulty, saw the Warnham lake that Shelley knew in his day shining palely in the last of the afterglow, and Horsham Carfax a bulge of roadways among the streets of the town. Picts' Hill, and ahead loomed Chanctonbury, a dot on the downland— he kept the Gnomon low, searching for a landing. Back there at Kestwell men were searching, keen to avenge the murder of one of their kind: had the panjandrum been caught? Had he snatched at the first pistol and found that it betrayed him as Gees himself had betrayed him? Though the pistol could not feel the savage joy Gees felt in knowing that Tott had got his message, believed it, and come to catch Johns' murderers.

West Grinstead crossroads showed transiently—Gees was following the Worthing road, because he knew it. Here came Dial Post, and Washington was no more than minutes after, sliding, changing momently, with the ridge of the downs banked beyond it— Chanctonbury away there on the left, symbol of the days of the flint men, the first shepherds of the downs. Gees thought of them, and spared a glance at the woman beside him in this last triumph of twentieth century achievement, an aeroplane, and then sought again for a landing. There was Findon, and beyond it the loathsome villainy and bungalescence that has soiled and spoiled one of Old England's oldest habitations, the slope of Cissbury Hill. Car headlights along the Worthing road showed like twin fireflies, winking as they dipped to each other: in front were the lights of Worthing, and in the very last remnant of light from the dead day the sea lay white and flat beyond.

Still searching for his landing place, he banked steeply to the east just beyond Findon and on the turn the slant of the Gnomon gave him a good view of Cissbury. All along the coast between Worthing and Shoreham he saw lights, and farther east Brighton showed, a big, misshapen tract of light-points, merging into each other at this distance—the piers were mere glow-worms halted in crawling seaward. He kept on the turn until the plane pointed north again, questing for level on Cissbury: though he knew the roads of this district well, he was not familiar with the contours of the downs.

Back to the north-east of the rows and huddles of new monstrosities which men had made and in which they lived, close to the road, he saw a tract that looked level and open enough for his purpose. He went on, turned almost directly over Chanctonbury to head south again, and dropped to no more than two hundred feet to pass behind Findon. There came the level tract he had seen, rising toward him as he swooped: the landing wheels made contact: the Gnomon swayed heavily and jerkily among rabbit burrows, and came to rest, still pointed seaward. Then Gees got out, beckoned to Christine, and gave her a hand down. She was shivering, for though the flight had lasted minutes only the air had been cold, and Gees himself felt chilled.

"But why here?" she asked. "You said—" She did not end it.

"Here, because we travel separately again, soon," he answered.

She peered up at him, intently. "Are you afraid, then?" she asked. "Why not there?" She pointed toward the sea. "Over it—over France, and on. You said you wanted to save me."

"If I did that—even if we escaped by doing it—they would take it as evidence of guilt," he explained. "I could never come back."

"And I"—her voice was dropped to a whispering breath—"I did not know until to-night—I would give my very life for you!"

"Christine," he answered, very steadily, "above all things I love this country of mine, and I love little children. Because of one small child, just as much as over what you did for me to-night, I wanted to save you from Kestwell—to give you your chance of escape."

"This chance?" she asked, wonderingly.

"This chance," he echoed.

"Alone?" Piteously.

"Alone," he echoed again.

"I—I do not think I want it, Grigori," she said slowly. "It is not my fault that the revolution is ruined, but it is ruined, I know. By Denghisovski's folly—madness. Smirilov, too. I thought, since you took me away from Kestwell, that I had you left. And now—and now it seems that I have nothing. Nothing!"

"You have life, courage, and great beauty," he told her.

"Grigori"—she peered up at him again—"was what he said about you—what Denghisovski said—was it true, then?"

"Quite true. I hate this madness that seems to hold you all, this lust for destruction of an order and setting up of a new slavery with murders as common incidents in it. God, Christine! If only you would see what utter evil it is, what a woman you might be!"

"You—you lied all the time?" She took no notice of his exclamation as she put the question. "With intent to betray?"

"To betray them—not you, after what I saw you do at Richmond. But to betray the men who would betray England—ruin it. Their betrayal was my aim—and Denghisovski paid me to accomplish it, when he thought he was paying me to do his work!"

"And you have broken me—this is the end!"

"Make it a new beginning," he urged gently. "Christine, I'm not one little bit religious, and sometimes not even moral, so I've no right to preach. But just this. Get back belief in God, get back belief in the good there is in all men, all classes of men, and put your heart and mind into upholding the good that is, instead of trying to destroy anything because of what may be. That's all, for as I say, I have no right to preach. And we mustn't stay here."

"The good there is in all men," she repeated slowly, not heeding his final admonition. "Even when—when they break one as you have broken me. And still I love you. Oh, I love you, Grigori!"

"Yet after to-night," he reminded her inflexibly, "we travel separately. And as I said, we must not stay here."

"Where will you go?" she asked tremulously.

"Back to London, when I have finished with this." He pointed at the Gnomon. "You—I think Newhaven would be best. They'll be looking for you to-morrow. Have you your passport with you?"

"Two, always." She held up her handbag. "But—"

"I must give you some money," he reflected.

She started back from him as if she had been stung, and stared, and stared. "Grigori!" It was a cry of passionate reproach. "Am I then that to you? I would have given life—"

On that she turned her back to him, and set off toward the road with its lighted houses, taking a course that would bring her out by the Cissbury garage. She did not know of the existence of the garage, but Gees knew it, and knew she might hire a car there to take her to Newhaven—if she wished.

She went stumblingly, and with her head bowed, at first, but he saw or imagined that after she had gone a little way she lifted her head and went proudly, defiantly. He knew and resisted an impulse to call her back, even to run after her and tell her that he had offered money because he wanted her to escape. If he did that, she would misunderstand it, would think . . . No, let her go!

When she was an indistinct figure in the gloom—the sky was clear overhead, though a thunderstorm was in progress out over the sea—he climbed back into the Gnomon, started the engine again, and got out with the big package he found under the driving seat. It was a clumsy oblong, brown-paper wrapped and tied with stout string, but not over-heavy, he found. He carried it away from the monoplane, beyond the sweep of the tail-plane, and, putting it down for the time, returned and climbed up the side of the Gnomon. Leaning in, he found that he could just reach the controls: the engine was ticking easily, and he set the ailerons and rudder to give more than a normal lift: like the throttle control, they were designed to stay put, and he adjusted them to a nicety to give a dangerous angle of climb.

Then, still leaning in, he thrust the ratchet throttle control over to full, straightened himself, and leaped backward as the Gnomon began to move. Empty, but guided by the controls as he had set them, it bumped forward, and he just managed to get clear of the tail-plane as it passed. There were people approaching his landing place by this time, but when the machine went off they paused and stood at gaze, baulked, as they thought, of a sensation.

The Gnomon lifted, and as its speed increased the angle of its ascent grew steeper. It went roaring over Worthing, climbed by that time to two thousand feet and more. Gees, flat among tufts of grass to escape observation by the would-be sightseers, and with his package close beside him, watched the flight of the empty machine. He saw it, lost it, and saw it again, white and shining against the bank of black cloud in a lightning flash out at sea. It vanished with the flash, but he went on watching. Presently came another jagged chasm of light across the cloud, and in it he saw the Gnomon, a vertical white streak rushing down, down—and darkness came again.

He took up his package and set a course across the grass that would bring him to Findon: when he passed within a few yards of a couple of watchers who were busy telling each other that the aeroplane had fallen into the sea and everyone in it must be drowned, he made a mental note that for once the uninstructed were correct in their conclusions. They, of course, took him for one as curious as themselves.

A rustic, standing in meditation by the bus stop in Findon, wakened sufficiently from his somnolence when questioned by Gees to yield the information that he didn't know nuthin' about no sharry-bangs, but thought there wouldn't be no more reg'lar ones to-night. But he rackoned the Korsham bus would be along presently, an' it wur a fine night arter the rain, it wur. On receipt of this information Gees up-ended his package and sat on it for five minutes or thereabouts, after which the Horsham bus appeared. He climbed aboard with the unsuspected twelve thousand pounds, went up on the top deck because he wanted to smoke, and with the package beside him yielded to meditation while the bus rumbled on its way, up the long grade from Findon, down the hill into Washington. Stop, start again. Stop, start again—while all cloud vanished from the night sky and the stars shone clearly.

"I did not know until to-night—I would give my very life for you!"

"You have broken me—this is the end!"

"And still I love you. Oh, I love you, Grigori!" The name by which he had bidden her call him because he had hated it, but he could no more hate it now than he could hate her. A lessening, dimming figure that walked stumblingly and with bowed head, to merge at last into the night and be lost. Lost! Where? The bus rumbled down Picts Hill, and into Horsham. Gees got out at the Carfax and lugged his package to the station. He was hungry and tired, and, after ascertaining that there was a train at eleven-twenty for Victoria, arriving at twelve-forty, he went across the road to the station hotel—there was plenty of time—and found that cold beef with pickles was a feasible proposition. Then he went back, took a first-class single ticket, and got into an empty compartment when the train came in.

At first he put his package on the rack and sat facing it, looking up at it: after Three Bridges he put it on the seat beside himself and leaned an elbow on it: just beyond Redhill he put it down on the floor and put his feet on it, and by the time the train reached Purley he had the package up on the seat again and sat on it. A little later he got off, opened up his treasure and examined it to make certain that it was treasure indeed. He found new one-pound notes, banded in five hundreds, and there were twenty-four of the banded packets. He re-wrapped them in the brown paper, tied the package again securely, and sat on it till the train came to rest at the Victoria platform. There he rebuffed three porters in succession, carried the package out himself, and took a taxi, instructing the driver to head for the Kings' Road, Chelsea, and stop just beyond Markham Square. There he got out and paid the man off.

The road was emptily quiet. A vagrom policeman ceased flashing his belt lamp at doors for a few seconds while he eyed this inoffensive citizen with the bundle and the big feet, and then returned to his task of decent curiosity regarding other people's doors. Gees turned down by the Commercial and went to a house a few doors down the side street, where he leaned against the bell-push as, a little earlier, Inspector Tott had leaned against the button outside the flat in Little Oakfield Street—but with more success than had attended Tott's patient efforts. For a window on the top floor went up, and a head appeared, at which Gees released the bell-push.

"Stop that row!" said a voice. "Who is it?"

"Gees, George. Come down. I want you."

"The party was last night. There isn't a spot of whisky left," George responded, and slammed the window down again.

Gees leaned against the push-button again for quite a while, and a light showed eventually in the transom. Then George opened the door and revealed himself in dressing-gown over pyjamas, looking fierce.

"Damn you, Gees! You wait till Dorothy gets her hands on you!"

"I can't, to-night," Gees answered. "George, be a good sport and take care of this bundle for me till I call for it, will you?"

"What's inside? Will it blow up?"

"No, it's only papers. Rather important periodicals in connection with a case I happen to be handling, and I want to leave them where the other parties in the case can't possibly find them. My flat might get broken into and searched, and I thought you wouldn't mind."

"Right you are, Gees." George took the parcel. "Now buzz off. I have to get up in the morning. I'll guard it for you. Good night."

Gees went back to the Kings' Road and hailed another taxi, directing the driver to Tony Briggs' flat. He had an idea that Tott might be looking for him at Little Oakfield Street, knowing as he did something about that astute man's methods, and felt that he needed a spot of moral support. Tony was in a position to provide it.

Tony, magnificent in full evening kit, opened the door.

"Soup and fish—and the bird somewhere in the offing," Gees observed, gazing at the white vest. "S'pose the good old tuxedo is round at the cleaners', what?" He advanced past his friend into the sitting-room in which they had talked on Sunday. "Gosh, you've had a char-woman in or something! This room's very nearly decent."

"That's the difference between it and you," Tony responded. "Always making rude comments on people and their belongings, damn you! I've just got back from a small and early at Lady Benderneck's, and wish I'd never gone. Will you have a drink?"

"Will a cork float!" Gees responded, and seated himself on the chair arm he had occupied during his last visit here. "Make it fifty-fifty, and plenty of soda. Tony, old lad, I want help."

"Uh-huh!" Busy with a whisky decanter, syphon, and glasses, Tony did not look round. "Financial, or spiritual? You can have the latter!"

"Did you know Detective-Sergeant Johns?" Gees asked.

"Did I? I do, man. An excellent scout, Johns. Not exactly born in the purple, as you might say, but Tott gambles on him."

"Not any more, Tony. Johns was murdered at Kestwell to-day."

"Wha-at?" Tony spun round with the two filled glasses in his hands.

"Careful, man—don't spill good stuff," Gees urged. "And not all thy piety nor wit can lure it back to cancel half a line. Johns was murdered by Denghisovski and Smirilov, and I put Tott on to it. I believe he's got 'em, but I'm not sure—I had to leave at the end of the first act—no, the second, though. I'm talking like this because it's broken me up a bit—I saw Johns on Sunday with his wife and baby, and now—Oh, damn them all! People like those blasted Communist wreckers, I mean. And now I'm immorally certain Tott is waiting to arrest me as an accessory when I get to my flat, or else he's got some of his men there, and I want you to come along and tell him he mustn't. You're his spiritual guide and all that, I know."

"But you say you put him on to the murder?" Tony protested.

"Yes, and on to where they made their bombs, and I tried to get him to see I wasn't agin him, but I'd got him wrong at the start, and he reckoned I was playing double for Christine Lenoir's sake. He hates me like poison, Tony, and once he arrests me the game is up, even if I do swing clear at the trial. All I want is a chance to explain before he says the fatal words, and you can get it for me."

"But how did they manage to get Johns?"

"Oh, does it matter? They got him because Tott thought he was swatting mosquitoes instead of handling scorpions. I told him he'd find a store of bombs at Kestwell, and he sent Johns there alone to investigate. Denghisovski and Smirilov caught the man, and one held him while the other cut his throat—Smirilov used the knife. I hid in a coal shed and heard them gloat over it. If Tott caught them as I hope he did, on the message I managed to send him, you may be able to stop him from arresting me, Tony. If they got away, he'll arrest me in spite of you, and I shall have to think what to do next. But it'd break my father's heart, whatever I did. Finish that drink and come along with me, old son—I'm dog tired, for one thing."

"Let me get a coat. You're a damned nuisance, Gees."

"The panjandrum and Smirilov would back that statement heartily," Gees remarked. "I knew I could rely on you, Tony, and if ever you happen to be in trouble, especially financial, come straight along to me. I'll see you through."

"Financial?" Tony echoed, pausing on his way to the door. "How did you acquire wealth?"

"Father's going to kill the fatted elephant, and I'm going to live virtuously after this," Gees told him. "And he's not exactly on the dole, you know, while I'm all the son he's got, officially. Hurry up, Tony. It's a shame to keep Tott waiting for me like this."

# CHAPTER XX

## LET OFF WITH A CAUTION

"THERE he is!" Gees exclaimed softly, as with Tony he entered Little Oakfield Street from the Haymarket end. "Two outsize rozzers with him, too! I knew it!"

"I always think the man who says—'I told you so' is in the last stage of intellectual destitution," Tony observed. "But soft, we are observed! Now I'll spiel. Don't butt in too soon."

He threw away a half-smoked cigarette as they approached the doorway of number 37. Just outside it stood Tott, and across the street two very large, uniformed policemen stood as if in friendly converse, but Gees knew that was not the purpose for which Tott had summoned them. Apart from the actors in this scene, the street was deserted, for it was then near on two o'clock in the morning.

Tott moved a couple of steps forward as Gees and Tony came within speaking distance, and made a gesture to his men, who moved across the street to him with the easy haste that a policeman can use at need.

"George Gordon Green—" he began, but Tony interrupted sharply.

"Don't say it, Inspector! I want a word with you, first."

Recognising him then, Tott touched his hat respectfully. "I'm sorry, sir," he said, "but I've been waiting here some time to make this arrest, and though he may be an acquaintance of yours—"

"Rather more than an acquaintance," Tony interrupted again. "Just send these men of yours away, please, and then we can talk. Up in Mr. Green's flat, I think. An explanation is due to you, and you shall have it. Until then, let there be no more talk of an arrest."

All his careless insouciance had vanished: he was the curt official, speaking with authority to one whom he had a right to command. But still Tott hesitated, for he was sore and bitter over having lost Johns, and he had set his heart on getting Gees. Tony turned to the two policemen, waiting in case Gees should attempt to resist arrest.

"You men can go," he said sharply.

"Yes." Tott gave in, realising that no other course was open to him. "You can go. Report to your own station that I dismissed you."

Gees rang the bell of the outer door of 37, for the place was closed for the night, and he had not brought his key. Some minutes of waiting ended with the appearance of the sulky caretaker from the basement in which he lived, and the three men ascended the stairs, Gees leading. He took the other two into his sitting-room, and turned to Tott, pointing him to an armchair.

"Do sit down, Inspector," he invited. "Have a whisky-soda?"

"No, thanks," Tott grunted, and remained standing.

"Cigarette, then." The case came out. "No? You, then, Tony."

Tony took a cigarette and a light, and seated himself on the edge of the small dining-table. He regarded his cigarette thoughtfully.

"Better get that report you told me about, I think, Gees," he said. "It may help to clear your part in all this—and clear you."

"Just a minute," Gees objected. "Inspector, did you get Denghisovski and Smirilov, and find Schroder in the shrubbery?"

"And got Barter as well—though you've no right to ask," Tott said.

"I want to ask one thing more. Did anyone pull a gun on you?"

"Yes, Denghisovski did. If it hadn't missed fire when he pulled the trigger I shouldn't be here now. He was a bare two yards away."

"Ah, good!" Gees sounded very satisfied. "Have you the gun on you? You'd keep it for evidence, surely, I mean."

"Yes, I still have it on me," Tott admitted. "But look here, Mr. Briggs. Thanks to you, I'm answering this man's questions instead—"

"Because this man, as you call me, saved your life to-night, Inspector," Gees interrupted him. "Take that pistol out of your pocket, and you'll find it's a short .32 automatic, made in Ghent. Take out the magazine and examine the cartridges—pull the bullet out of each shell, and you'll find they come out easily, because I wrapped each one in wash-leather in Richmond Park to pull it out and get all the powder out of the shell before I put the bullet back. You see, Christine Lenoir entrusted that pistol to me after you arrested Schlatzenbaum for carrying one, and I doctored it like that before I handed it back to her. I think you found three under the board at Kestwell—or rather, you found two in addition to this. The others are deadly, because I had no chance to doctor them. Have a look at it. I know you don't trust my word, so try the cartridges."

"Phee-o-w!" From Tony Briggs. "Have a look at the cartridges, Inspector. It sounds as if he did save your life, you know."

Rather sheepishly, Tott took the pistol from his pocket, withdrew the magazine, and pushed out the seven cartridges. The bullets slid easily from their brass casings when he pulled at them, and he looked into the empty shells, and then at Gees, without a word.

"Now will you have a whisky, Inspector?" Gees asked triumphantly.

"Yes, I will, thanks." Tott gave in, finely. "I'm about all in after the day I've had. And—and when you've mixed it, Mr. Green, I'd like to shake hands. But"—he suddenly remembered—"you saved my life, it's true, but I've got to do my duty. The woman Lenoir."

"Gone," Gees told him. "She was not there when the murder was committed. Gone in the monoplane—from Kestwell."

"Where did that monoplane go, do you know?"

"It's at the bottom of the sea, some few miles off Worthing," Gees answered. "I expect they put out with the lifeboat when it fell, and you'll hear to-morrow that no bodies were recovered."

Tott sat thinking it over. Gees lifted an inquiring eyebrow at Tony, who nodded in response. Then Gees went to his sideboard, mixed three stiff drinks, and returned, handing Tott his first.

"A toast, Inspector," he said. "Here's to the woman who risked her life to save a little child, and saved my life to-night as surely as I saved yours. Christine Lenoir!" He lifted his glass and drank.

"I see," Tott said slowly, and did not drink. "Have you any idea where she was going after you'd said goodbye to her?"

"Not one in Hades," Gees answered. "But I'll tell you this. Not only is she absolutely innocent of any complicity in the murder of Johns, but she was as sore over it as you are, though for an entirely different reason. She saw what those two fiends couldn't see, that it meant ruin to all their plans, and she damned and blasted them in my hearing for a pair of fools. Oh, and that was when she saved me! Denghisovski had just persuaded the other two that I had to be killed too—he'd got me there with my hands tied behind me—when she came in and put a stop to it, made him turn me loose and I took her out at the back and went off with her in the monoplane. That must have been just as you made your raid, for I heard your men shouting when we went away. She'd saved me—I couldn't leave her to be caught."

"Well"—Tott thought it over again for a few seconds —"you're a pretty pair of angels, you and she, but I'm damned if I'll subscribe to a wedding present. If you hadn't fooled Johns that day—"

"Ain't going to be no wedding, Inspector," Gees interrupted. "We parted without even a kiss on the brow—in fact, she was distinctly angry with me when she left for gawdknowswhere. And as for my fooling Johns, what about your sending him to Kestwell alone—?"

"Ah, don't remind me!" Tott interrupted in turn, with sudden, bitter fierceness. "I shall never forgive myself for that. If I'd believed you altogether instead of only half—but I couldn't."

"My fault, I know." Gees took a step forward and held out his hand. "Drown the hatchet, Inspector, and shake," he offered. "Drink to the memory of a good man who died at his duty, if you don't like the other toast. May God be good to his widow and little child."

"Gosh, but he was proud of them!" Tott said rather huskily, as he shook hands. "Yes, God be good to her, poor girl, and we will, too." He sat down in the chair Gees had first indicated. "And now that report that Mr. Briggs mentioned, Mr. Green—what is it?"

"A complete record of all my dealings with this gang since you saw me at King's Cross with Miss Lenoir," Gees told him. "You've got a duplicate of part of it already. And I estimate, on the evidence I can give at the trial, you'll get a summing-up against Denghisovski and Smirilov that will leave the jury no option, and Schroder and Barter should be good for anything up to fifteen years apiece. They're both innocent of complicity in the murder."

"You're sure of that?" Tott asked.

"Dead sure. The other two didn't want anyone to know they'd killed Johns. I heard their talks, before they found out I was there. I think they realised what fools they'd been, and knew what Christine—what Miss Lenoir would say about it if she found out."

"We ought to have her, though," Tott reflected.

"Why?" Gees demanded sharply. "If you do get her, you can't pin a criminal charge on her. She's been the travelling inspector, the watcher to see that nothing went wrong, but she's been very careful to do nothing herself. And when you weigh this up, you'll see that with Johns dead mine is the most valuable evidence you have."

"You mean it won't tell against her," Tott suggested.

"I'll take damned good care it doesn't, if you do get her," Gees declared. "No, Tony, I'm not in love with her, but I can see how splendid she might be if it weren't for this—this mental aberration that comes of having seen her father shot when she was a child."

"That was the cause, was it?" Tony asked.

"It warped her—it might warp any one of us, if it had happened to us. 'There, but for the grace of God—' But don't let us get sentimental at nearly three in the morning."

"So it is!" Tott exclaimed, and rose to his feet. He put his empty glass down on the table. "And I've got to be at Kingston this morning to charge that gang—the Keszcas and their boy must wait till I get back for their dose of remand in custody. You'll get the usual warning to attend as witness, Mr. Green. I'll say good night, gentlemen."

He went out. Tony took up his hat and got off the table.

"Quite sure you're not in love with her, Gees?" he asked.

"Quite," Gees answered firmly.

"I'm not."

Then he too said good night, and departed.

Christine risked it.

She knew a description of herself and warning to arrest on sight might be out before she could make her escape, but she hired a car from the Cisswell garage to take her to Newhaven as Gees had advised, and arrived some ten minutes ahead of the boat train from Victoria. She was careful to take a return ticket, second class, and made anxious inquiries from the booking clerk about the possibility of getting a reduced rate, as she did not expect to be in Paris more than a couple of days. But he had no comfort for her over it.

The passport she showed declared her as Adeline Carisbrook, British subject, and was valid as from June of the preceding year for all European countries, including the U.S.S.R. It had been bought in Hamburg, where such things are easily procurable by those who know where to look for them, and bore stamps of Calais, Le Havre, St. Malo, and Lisbon: all had been imprinted in Hamburg, for the passport forgers do their business thoroughly.

Having obtained her ticket, she retired to the ladies' waiting room until the boat train came in. A pencil, skilfully used in that seclusion, spoilt and thickened her eyebrows: a lip-stick lavishly applied did like service with her lips, and a pair of "plumpers," or shaped rubber bladders fitting between cheeks and upper jawbones, bulged and completely altered the shape of her face. Then a travelling rouge-pot came out from her handbag, and she applied the stuff in such a way as to make it evident that she rouged, though the final touches were put on a level coating which completely altered the tint of her face and neck. Finally, she was generous with the powder puff, and she emerged to fall in with the rest of the passengers from Victoria, and face the passport barrier, as not merely a lady of easy virtue, but one of no virtue at all.

She was one of the last to go through. After the official who examined her passport had passed her with the rest, he spoke to his fellow, nodding toward the retreating passengers.

"Did you see that one in grey, Jim?"

"Aye. Work of art, wasn't it?"

"Not art—science. Comes from Bayswater, where my aunt used to live. No wonder she moved to Chiswick! Lady's maid. Huh! If the lady's anything like the maid, thank God I'm a married man. We do find 'em here, don't we? She'd laid it on with a trowel, and it ought to be scraped off with a hoe. How they can do it I don't know!"

Aboard the boat, Christine found that she could not get a berth, but must get what sleep she could in a deck chair with a rug and pillows. She went quite aft and stood over the propellers, watching the boat cast off and gather way quickly: its increasing speed reminded her of the way in which the Gnomon had taken off from the meadow behind Kestwell, when she had not travelled separately—when she had believed that the man beside her meant to hold her, and had been quite happy in spite of the utter wreckage of the planned revolution by those two savage fools, Denghisovski and Smirilov. And now she had nothing left, save for a few spoken phrases, unforgettable words.

"I am going to save you as you saved me."

"Above all things I love this country of mine, and I love little children. . . . The bravest deed I have ever seen."

"You have life, courage, and great beauty."

Life and beauty, yes. Courage? Had she courage even to go on, now? The boil of water from the screws racing back from under her—they had passed out beyond the lights to open sea, and the ray from under Beachy Head was moving over the face of the waters. One plunge into the foaming turbulence down there: under it was peace.

"But just this. Get back belief in God, get back belief in the good there is in all men, all classes of men, and put your heart and mind into upholding the good that is, instead of trying to destroy anything because of what may be."

Big hands, big feet, and big heart. One who found cause for laughter in life in a way she could not understand. She had not met his like anywhere before: men had been as cheap to her as women are to some men, and, as Denghisovski had said, she might have chosen lovers where she would—but until she met Grigori she had chosen none: they were beings of a too blatant desire, as she had known them. This one man had balanced his life in some way that put desire in its right place: he would desire, but first he would love, almost in the way that he loved little children, but more intensely, more fully.

*"I must give you some money."*

But the intolerable sting of that coolly-spoken sentence was fading out. She was realising that he had not meant to buy her as other men had offered to buy her, but had thought her penniless, and wanted to make certain that she had enough to ensure her escape. He had been thinking for her, not of possessing her at a price, she knew now.

*He* had courage! When she had seen him, framed in living light in the bare room at Kestwell, there had been no fear in his eyes, though he must have known that Denghisovski meant to kill him, and could not have known that she would get there to save him. Then she thought of Denghisovski, brutal, lustful, a being of passions and instincts as ugly as the knob on his bare scalp. Of Smirilov, who told tales of what he had done to Czarist women in Odessa, when Lenin was trying to create a paradise by turning Russia into a hell for all but his own followers. And the first decree of all—

"We abolish God!"

*"Trying to destroy anything because of what may be!"*

Something must be, surely? Some driving force—was all the wonderful plan and order of the universe automatic, causeless, a blind driving on until, aeons and aeons hence, the mechanism should have run down? Had Lenin abolished God?

It appeared, rather, that God had abolished Lenin. Certainly, in spite of the crystal tomb in Moscow, Russia was forgetting him, leaguing with capitalists instead of persisting in the task of destroying capitalism. Some few remembered, people like herself, and Denghisovski, and Smirilov, and Schroder who yearned rather wistfully to kill.

"Grigori, I don't want to be like them any more! Can you hear me? Can I send my heart across to you, make you hear me? Still I love you. Oh, I love you, Grigori!"

Somewhere about that time, Gees had closed the door on Tony Briggs and, back in his sitting-room, was telling himself what a good pal old Tony was, while he took up the three empty glasses to put them on the sideboard for his charwoman to find and wash in the morning. He paused suddenly with the glasses in his hand, for it seemed to him that he could see Christine out there on Cissbury Hill, and hear her voice, intense and tremulous—

"Still I love you. Oh, I love you, Grigori!" But she had gone, and unless Tott caught her the episode was ended. Gees hoped Tott would not catch her, for, if he did, he would have to let her go in the end, and she might come to the office for another initial consultation about something.

And Gees felt that, if he saw too much of her, the final pronouncement Tony Briggs had made before saying good night might come true.

Three days later, Christine Lenoir had resumed her own name and taken abode for the time at a cheap *pension* in Montreux. She had also removed all her odious make-up and put the deflated "plumpers" back in her handbag, for there might be occasion to use them again, though she did not think there would. In mid-afternoon she sat out on the veranda of the *pension* with a small, elderly man who wore a little, pointed grey beard, a pair of spectacles behind which his eyes looked like veined pebbles ringed in different colours, and shabby, heavily worn clothes. He listened to the story she had to tell, and saw that she had beside her the latest available English *Times* and *Telegraph*.

"And so it is broken," she ended. "They are broken."

"You too are broken," he half-accused.

"I do not know," she said. "Fedor, I do not know. One is so certain, so confident, and then life steps in, teaching that all one has known is nothing—a little less than nothing."

"And the cause?" he asked, regarding her intently.

"A little child, groping in the dark," she went on, disregarding the query. "Or one unborn and striving toward birth. I saw primroses growing, and hawthorn in blossom, and the young green set against the older, darker fronds of last year on the evergreens. And apple trees in bloom, and young rabbits playing in the meadows, and I heard children laugh—as if it were the first time I had heard such a thing in all my days. The sea beating among rocks, so that spray glittered in the sun, and there were gulls wheeling over it. The white smoke over a train, people going somewhere, and there was an old grey church on a little hill. Things I saw, Fedor, beautiful things in a country like no other, and now I am like a little child groping in the dark."

"And the cause?" he insisted.

"Yes, the cause," she echoed. "Fedor, I begin to think we have not quite abolished God, after all."

He stood up, and his eyes were more than ever like veined, ringed pebbles. When he spoke his voice was harsh.

"You know I shall report this to the heads of the Left?"

"What of it?" she asked, almost carelessly. "They can no more than kill, and long ago it was said that we should not fear those who only kill the body. If I am worth killing."

"Who was the man? This Green who betrayed everything?" he demanded.

"He never spoke one word of love to me, Fedor. When at the end he saved me, it was because I had saved him, and he said it was payment of a debt. You may tell that to the heads of the Left."

"I do not think they will order your death," he said cuttingly. "They will do worse—merely ignore you on my report. It is evident that you are of no more use to them."

"I am merely indifferent to what they decide to do," she observed.

"There is no more to be said," he answered, and, turning, proved it by leaving her without another word.

She sat on, indifferent even to the manner of his going. Seated thus, she could see dark pines far off and a small green carpet on a hillside: high over them, sunlight on the everlasting snow of the alpine peaks made a silent symphony of many colours: higher still was the blue beauty of endless space.

# CRAPTER XXI

## RIS LORDSRIP SUMS UP

AFTER her lunch hour on Thursday, Miss Brandon returned to the offices of the confidential agency and entered her room, expecting to do nothing as usual for the rest of the day. Gees had dictated no more report that morning, but had appeared at about eleven o'clock instead of at his usual time, and had gone out without giving her any orders for the day or telling her when he would return.

She removed her coat and hat, and was about to settle at her desk with the novel for which she had changed a finished one at her library during the lunch hour, when she heard Gees calling. She went to her door and stated that she was there: he had never shouted for her before, but had either come to her room or summoned her by means of his desk buzzer. She felt rather annoyed over this form of summons.

"Yes, I guessed you were there," he called. "I'm here, in the bedroom. Would you mind coming along? About the safe."

She went along the corridor and entered the room. There was a lot of crumpled brown paper on the floor, and Gees had pulled his wardrobe aside and stood before the open safe, pointing her attention to it. She looked inside and saw the folder of reports lying flat.

"Didn't I tell you that folder was to be stood up, Miss Brandon?" he demanded. "Look at it. Why isn't it upright?"

"Easily remedied." She went to the safe and stood the folder up at the side. "Anything else, Mr. Green?"

"Yes—look at the bed," he bade.

She obeyed, and saw package on package of what were obviously one-pound notes, thrown in a heap on the eiderdown.

"Now, Miss Brandon," Gees questioned sternly, "have I got brains, or have I got brains?"

"It looks as if you've got the money," she answered judicially.

"We'd better have that folder out altogether," he remarked, not pressing his previous question. "I want to take it along to Tott, and probably he'll have finished remanding people all over England some time this afternoon, and got the detail work into shape. Give me a hand, and we'll stack this loot. Eleven thousand nine hundred and fifty to me, and fifty to you as arranged between us."

"It wasn't," she contradicted. "Mr. Green, I'd rather not, please."

"Orders is orders," he retorted. "Start stacking, and I'll break open the last package and hand you your fifty. Kindly understand that all this is fat, pure and unadulterated, and take your share."

"But I've done nothing to earn it," she protested.

"Neither have I," he pointed out. "We've got it—financiers and people like us never do earn what we get. We just get it, which is a far, far better thing. Damned sight easier than earning, too. I think if you put 'em in endways we're more likely to make the safe hold the lot. Here, you bring 'em to me, and I'll stack."

There was more of ostentation than necessity in getting her to help. He arranged twenty-three of the packages to a nicety in the safe, and surveyed the result while she waited with the last five hundred. Then he turned, but did not take it from her.

"Bust the band, Miss Brandon, and peel off your fifty. One more word about not wanting to take it, and you can have the sack instead. This firm has got to be run on business lines, and I won't have any insubordination. Now I've got to mix all this lot so that the numbers aren't consecutive, crumple some of them a bit—and I'll save some coffee from breakfast and spill drops on a few. Then open another banking account, give my present bank manager epilepsy by paying off the overdraft on the account I've already got, and gradually divide all this lot between the two accounts. It'll look like income from the work we're doing, what? You needn't count fifty—the numbers are consecutive. Besides, if you do get a few over, so much the better. That lot is just pocket money for the pair of us, and doesn't go in the safe. It's to be devoted to ribaldry. Five pounds worth of ribaldry, please, and you needn't send it, miss. I'll take it with me."

The girl laughed, but rather shakily. Gees, to prove his assertion closed and locked the safe, and slid the wardrobe back into its place.

"Now we'd better get out of this," he said, pocketing the safe key. "Take that folder and make a neat packet of it— I'm going to see Tott. Got your fifty separate? All right. Now peel off another fifty and put 'em in your desk for office expenses. You might want a new typewriter ribbon before the year is out. Oh, and that estimate you got out for me! Write an order for the Rolls-Bentley, and put it on my desk for signature when I come back from seeing Tott. I'll get the new shaving brush myself. I think that's all, Miss Brandon."

"Except—I haven't said a word of thanks, Mr. Green," she said.

"You can save it till I hand you the weekly wage—don't start now. We've got to be busy. Bring me in the four hundred when you've made a package of the folder and taken off the fifty for petty cash. Now let me see! I think, if I go off to see Tott in about twenty minutes, I can get back in time to sign that order for the Rolls-Bentley before five, and then you can post it on your way home. Let's *buzz.*"

They buzzed. Gees went into his own office room and sat down.

"I can find out from Tott whether she got clear away," he told himself. Then at a thought he got up and went to Miss Brandon's door. She paused from packing the folder when he looked into the room.

"Just to remark, Miss Brandon, that the business of this firm is inviolably private and confidential," he told her.

"I came to work here on that understanding, Mr. Green," she answered.

"The stipulation," he added, "applies especially to all financial transactions, and most particularly to all receipts of money and profits derived from the business."

"If either of us talks about this, it won't be me," she said.

"Won't be I, you mean," he reproved her. "It sounds awkward, I know, but it's the grammatical form. Thanks so much for the assurance. Bring me that folder as soon as you've packed it."

"I wonder"—she hesitated, and went on tying the package while he waited—"well, about our devil, Mr. Green."

"Isn't," he said promptly. "Not any more, after last night. One reason for my wanting to go and see Tott is to find out if Miss Lenoir got away safely. You see, she saved my life. I'll tell you about it, some time. You needn't tie that any more—I'll take it, and the four hundred notes." He advanced into the room. "I believe, now I come to think about it, I'm rather in a hurry."

By the middle of July, Miss Brandon had read many more novels, had discarded quite a lot of old *lingerie* and laid in a new stock, and was looking forward to a holiday in Iceland. Gees had promised her three weeks, and Iceland sounded cool and refreshing for August, though she believed there were mosquitoes, and knew she would have to get riding kit. But some of the fifty pounds was still available.

A day came when defending counsel in what was known as the Kestwell case—it was so termed because most people shirked pronouncing the panjandrum's name—sat down after making his final plea, and the court adjourned for lunch. After the interval, counsel for the Crown stood up to summarise the case:

"My lord and members of the jury—

"My learned friend appearing on behalf of the four persons whom you see in the dock has, I think, done his best over what must have been an odious task for him. He has, I may say, used every device that the procedure of criminal courts permits—and even some that it ought not to permit—in his efforts at mitigating the offences with which these men stand charged. Even he cannot deny that those offences have been committed.

"Conscious of the weakness of his case, he has attempted to cast doubts on the evidence adduced in the conduct of the case for the Crown. He has done his best to asperse the character and attribute a motive of self-interest to the principal witness for the prosecution, Mr. Gordon Green. I submit, members of the jury, that he has failed utterly in his attempts. Whether you approve or disapprove of the methods used by Mr. Green to unmask this hideous conspiracy, I say that it is your duty to commend him for the results he achieved—results, as you have heard in evidence, obtained at the risk of his own life. Counsel for the defence did his utmost to shake this evidence, but the prisoner Denghisovski, as you have heard, so far contradicted himself when put in the witness box as actually to confirm the evidence of Mr. Green and his secretary, Miss Brandon.

"In my opening speech to you, I gave you a full statement of the case as it would be presented in evidence. There is therefore no need for me to recapitulate the circumstances under which Detective-Sergeant Johns was so foully done to death. I will, for a little while, and with your lordship's permission, draw your attention to the evidence given by the principal witness for the Crown in this case, Mr. Gordon Green.

"I ask you to recall that Mr. Green, in the course of his evidence, told you that he had compiled a statement or report of his activities in this case, and had dictated it to his secretary, Miss Brandon. In his cross-examination, he was subjected to a series of questions by my learned friend, who tried to make you believe that Mr. Green had compiled the whole of this report *after* the murder of Detective-Sergeant Johns, because he feared to be charged as an accessory to the crime. Now, members of the jury, remember that Detective-Inspector Tott, in the course of his evidence, told you that a very important part of Mr. Green's report was in his hands *before* the murder—two whole days before it, in fact. You will see, then, that this allegation on the part of the defence is utterly ridiculous. Mr. Green is, as he has told you, a confidential agent, whatever that may be. He found business slack, and took up this case as a matter of interest, never dreaming at the time that it would end in a murder. When he discovered that the murder had been committed, he went so far as to risk his own life to ensure that the murderers should not escape.

"You have heard Sir John Jitterbury say how he received the message from Mr. Green, and telephoned it to Inspector Tott. You have seen the written message as an exhibit in the case. You have heard how, although he need not have done so, Mr. Green went back to Kestwell after assuring himself that his message was on its way to Inspector Tott, and how he was saved from a violent death at the hands of Sergeant Johns' murderers by the woman Lenoir—saved in the nick of time. It is one of the most dramatic stories ever related in a criminal court, but the point I wish to make is that Mr. Green's conduct entitles him to your highest commendation, and that the allegations regarding him which my learned friend has seen fit to make are not only entirely without foundation, but slanderously unjust, though the privilege of criminal court procedure renders them possible.

"I want to draw your attention to the evidence given by Mr. Green in regard to the two accused men, Schroder and Barter. He has told you that these two, although cognisant of the manufacture of bombs and of their storage at Kestwell, were utterly ignorant of the murder of Johns. Nobody is in a position to confirm or confute this evidence except the accused men Denghisovski and Smirilov. My learned friend saw fit to put Denghisovski in the witness box, as you have both seen and heard, but he made such a mess of his evidence on his own behalf that this point of the innocence or guilt of Schroder and Barter was never reached, and you may note that I did not cross-examine the man as witness at all, for he convicted himself and Smirilov without any effort on my part. Even now, I would direct you to guide yourselves by the summing-up of the case which his lordship will presently address to you, and will refrain from any direction or attempt at influencing you as far as Denghisovski and Smirilov are concerned. Anything I might say would be superfluous. The case is clear.

"But, regarding Schroder and Barter, you have to decide on the evidence—were they accessories, or were they ignorant that murder had been committed? The principal witness against them, Mr. Gordon Green, has told you that both were ignorant even of Johns having been at Kestwell on the day of the murder. Barter until Mr. Green himself stated the fact just before the woman Lenoir appeared and saved his life, and Schroder altogether ignorant, since Mr. Green had knocked him about so unmercifully that he knew nothing at all for the next three days. Brutal treatment, yes—but remember that Mr. Green was attempting to conceal his presence at Kestwell from all these conspirators. If he had not silenced Schroder, the man would have revealed the fact of his being there to Denghisovski—and he would never have been able to hide in the coal shed and hear how Denghisovski held Johns down while Smirilov cut his throat, a ghastly detail of the case which you may wish to bear in mind while you deliberate on your verdict.

"Is Schroder an accessory to the murder, or is he guilty only of the other charges brought against him? Is Barter an accessory to the murder, or is he guilty only of the other charges brought against him? Mr. Green has told you that both these men were entirely ignorant that a murder has been committed. I do not doubt one word that he has said in evidence here. I feel that he is the mainstay of the Crown case, and that without him we might have had great difficulty in bringing this awful crime home to its perpetrators, who are here before you, I know, to hear the measure of their punishment for the shedding of man's blood. Without fear or favour, members of the jury, do your duty. His lordship will tell you what that duty is."

He sat down, and for a time the judge was silent, consulting his notes. Then he spoke, his voice resonant with the dignity of age-old law, and of procedure more inflexibly just than any other in the world.

"Members of the jury—

"I deviate, possibly, from my task in making one comment on this case, and that in respect of the evidence extracted from the accused man Denghisovski by learned counsel for the defence. The creed enunciated by Denghisovski in the course of his evidence was well defined by one of the great English poets of last century as 'red ruin, and the breaking up of laws.' Only the latitude which I felt bound to grant to an alien in a strange country prevented me from putting a stop to the utterances of Denghisovski concerning his creed, which is a total negation of the laws under which we live.

"You have heard learned counsel for the defence, in his final address to you, cast grave doubt on the statement made by the witness Green, who told you that he compiled a daily report of all that he did in connection with the activities of these people. Learned counsel for the Crown has pointed out to you that a vital portion of this report was in Detective-Inspector Tott's hands before the murder was committed. Therefore, if you doubt the evidence of the witness Green on this point, you must also doubt that of Detective-Inspector Tott, and you must doubt, too, the evidence of Miss Brandon, to whom Green alleges that he dictated these reports, and who alleges that she took down his dictation.

"If, on the other hand, you believe the evidence of the witness Green on this one point, you are justified in believing all the rest of what he has told you. For he had no object in distorting facts as to what happened at Kestwell in connection with the actual murder. An instinct of self-preservation might have caused him to say that he had compiled a daily report when he had not done anything of the kind, but two other witnesses support his statements on this point. None support him as to what happened at Kestwell on the day of the murder, but he need exercise no instinct of self-preservation in his evidence regarding the sequence of events on that day. And, as far as Denghisovski and Smirilov are concerned, the human blood proved to be soaked into the coat sleeves of both these men is silent but eloquent testimony to the truth of Green's statements about them.

"But, when you come to the guilt or innocence of complicity in the death of Johns, on the part of the accused men Schroder and Barter, you are on different ground. You must ask yourselves—do we believe Green's evidence to the effect that these two men knew nothing about it? According to Green, Barter must have arrived at Kestwell some time after the murder had been committed, so it is possible that he was kept in ignorance of what had transpired, and if you decide that he was ignorant of it, you must acquit him of the charge of murder and either acquit or convict him in respect of the other offences with which he is charged in common with the other three accused men.

"Schroder is in a different position, as you will have realised from the evidence. He was at Kestwell, undoubtedly, when Johns was done to death. Is it possible that Johns made no outcry, that Schroder heard nothing, saw nothing, of what was being done? Members of the jury, you must decide this question for yourselves. It is possible that he had the engine of his aeroplane running at the time. Green has told you he heard it running when he arrived at Kestwell, and Schroder was beside it, apparently making adjustments to the mechanism. It may have been running when Johns was caught and done to death. You must decide on his guilt or innocence of complicity in that doing to death, and then on his guilt or innocence of the other charges, for yourselves.

"With regard to Denghisovski and Smirilov, I have only one direction to give you. Consider the evidence that has been put before you, and that alone. This, of course, applies to the verdict you will deliver in respect of all these four accused men—you must be guided solely by the evidence, and put from your minds all else that you may have heard. A trial of four men on common charges, such as this, places a very heavy responsibility on you, members of the jury. I charge you, do not let your minds be influenced by the creed that Denghisovski preached in the course of his evidence, either to the side of vengeance or of mercy to any one of these four men. Consider each offence of which they stand charged, and their responsibility in it, solely on the evidence you have heard here, and return your verdict in accordance with that evidence.

"You may now retire to consider your verdict."

# CRAPTER XXII

## "—IN RALF-REARD MINOR QUIVERING—"

THE SUN WAS LOW when Gees came out from the assize court, evaded or rebuffed such reporters as sought him, and made his way to a car park where stood a grey Rolls-Bentley coupe with black wings. He tipped the park attendant, unlocked and got into the car, and had got the engine running when a voice accosted him.

"Do you think you could give me a lift?"

"God bless my soul, Father! Climb aboard, by all means."

General Green seated himself beside his son, who moved off.

"Home, Father?" he asked, after a brief silence.

"Please, if it's not out of your way. Fine car, this, Gordon."

"Well, you see, I had to have a barrow of some sort, and the best is good enough for me. In a business like mine, a good appearance counts for a lot. Impresses clients, you know."

"I see. As much as—as that infernal advertising of yours, eh?"

"Oh, I'm dropping that now—no need to waste money. This case, you see—marvellous publicity! Old lady turned up even before the case opened—seen my name in connection with the police court proceedings, and wanted me to find her dog. She paid five pounds cheerfully for the one I got her from the dogs' home, and really believes it's the one she lost. I'm not so sure myself, but what would you?"

"Gordon, who is paying for this car?"

"Nobody, Father. I paid for it. If you like to drop in at my office some time, I'll get my secretary to show you the receipt. I know you think my agency is dud show, but if you saw either of my bank pass books you'd change your mind. Money rolling into both accounts every week—I keep two accounts, now, and I'm going to see the manager who used to be no nice about my overdraft about turning myself into a limited company. See if I can dodge a spot of super-tax somehow. How do you like the running of his car, Father?"

"It's a far better car than I can afford," the general said.

"Ah, but you see I don't keep up a big establishment. One perfectly virtuous secretary and a charwoman—also virtuous, because she can't help it, I think. I had an idea of taking on a chauffeur, but the garage does everything, and I like driving myself."

The general made no reply. Gees drove him to Dawgeley Square and halted very precisely in front of his door.

"Gordon, do you think you could let me have a shilling?"

"Gosh, Father, you don't mean it! I've got the very identical one. I was going to have it framed." He felt in his breast pocket, produced the coin, and held it up. The general took it from him.

"That makes us square again, I think," he observed calmly. "But I do wish you wouldn't use that expression 'Gosh!' Gordon. It's—it's so damned commonplace. Why, a waiter said it at my club the other day when he dropped a glass! A transatlantic disharmony."

"I'll do my damndest, Father," Gees said humbly. "Are you getting out here, or are you getting out here?"

"There! Another blasted Americanism!" The general opened the door on his side, and got out of the car. "Gordon, can you dine with me to-morrow night, or are you too busy?"

"I'll be delighted, Father. Tails, or tuxedo?"

"Will you cut out that blasted Yankee slang, damn you, boy? Ordinary dinner jacket for decency's sake, nothing formal. Just you and myself, for a quiet talk. I'm a little troubled about the Shropshire estate. Things are none too good there."

"Well, we'd better talk it over at home, then. I should rush you two guineas merely for the initial consultation if you came to my office about it. Seven-fifteen for seven-thirty, eh?"

"Yes. Time for a sherry before the soup."

"That reminds me. Barnes got me to taste a marvellous pale dry, some while ago, and told me he had twenty dozen left for sale after the bottling. A lovely wine, Father. I'll get them to send you in ten dozen to-morrow, and we can try it out before dinner."

"But the price, Gordon. I know what their old sherries are."

"Don't worry about it, Father. Consider it my apology for the advertisements. I know you'll like it."

The general reached his hand into the car. "God bless you, Gordon," he said. "I was proud of you today. But if ever I see another of those damned advertisements I'll come round to that office of yours with a horsewhip!"

"It'll cost you two guineas at least," Gees grinned as he shook hands. "But as I told you, there's no need to advertise now."

In mid-afternoon of the next day Gees, shown into Inspector Tott's office—he had made the appointment by telephone—nodded pleasantly.

"Afternoon, Inspector. Lovely weather, what?"

"Take a seat, Mr. Green. Also take the weather—for granted." Tott sounded rather glum, and nodded at a chair.

Gees seated himself, produced the inevitable case, and offered it. Tott took one, and lighted up. Gees also lighted up.

"Now what do you want?" Tott asked.

"I suppose, to begin the interview, I ought to apologise for stealing your thunder," Gees answered meditatively, regarding his cigarette.

"We're not strong on apologies, here," Tott responded. "I don't recall ever modifying a charge-sheet because of an apology. I asked you, what do you want?"

"Well, mainly about poor Johns' widow and child, if you must be purely businesslike. I suppose you're opening a subscription?"

"Closing it, shortly. None of my lads have one-way pockets, thank heaven! But they'll have a thin time, all the same."

"Inspector, I'm going to head that subscription list," Gees said gravely. "I've got on me an open bearer cheque for one thousand pounds made out to you—that's what I came to see you about. My name is not to go on the list. I want you to put it as from 'A lover of all small children.' Will you do that for me? I saw him with them, the Sunday before he died."

He produced the cheque and handed it over. Tott examined it.

"A lover of all small children," he said musingly. "Yes."

Gees stood up. "That's all, Inspector."

"One minute, Mr. Green." Tott did not stand up. "I couldn't make out what became of the balance of the fund that Denghisovski drew out for his campaign. Now, by the look of it—" He paused, significantly.

Gees smiled amusedly. "Slay that bee, Inspector," he urged, with gentle irony. "Over the fame that I acquired in this case—partly at the expense of your glory, I admit—my father has forgiven me for running my agency. I could have ten thousand from him tomorrow, if I wanted it. Why worry about Denghisovski's money, what?"

"What became of it, then?" Tott demanded.

"I suggest that you ask Miss Lenoir. She was the travelling inspector, as I testified at the trial, and therefore would probably audit the accounts. Put it to her."

"Oh, yeah?" Tott gibed. "And who's going to pay me for chasing all over Europe, with nothing to justify me in arresting her, let alone applying for extradition? Tell me that!"

"I can't, since this is a friendly talk," Gees answered. "But if you like to come round to my office and have a two guinea consultation—initial consultation—I'll see if I can suggest anyone."

"Blast your office! I hope, now you've made it up with General Green, you'll give up that infernal nonsense."

"Give it up?" Gees looked horrified. "With all the free publicity I've got out of this case? Inspector, you've got another hope coming. At least, I hope you have, because this one is off.'"

"D'you mean you mean to carry on?" Tott demanded very acidly.

"I mean I mean to mean something to people who mean to mean business when they come in—at two guineas a time," Gees assured him. "A long-felt want—you know the dope. Mumps to murder—Inspector, I hope that cheque means something to your fund, and I'm damned glad of what I did to land those two foul things for the rope."

"They should have hanged all four," Tott said. "I shall never get another man like Johns."

"I wouldn't care if they had," Gees agreed. "But I think the good old British stomach would have turned if they'd hanged four men for the death of one. And by the time Schroder has done his ten years and Barter his eight at penal servitude, they may feel inclined to revolve a bit more quietly. Revolute, I mean. You know, to themselves, as one might say. Well, Inspector, I won't waste any more of your time. I'm dining with my father to-night, to discuss the future of our Shropshire estate. If you do happen to discover what became of the balance of Denghisovski's funds, let me know. The government might hand out some sort of bonus to us who were in the show, and I'd hate to be left out. Can I rely on you to let me know if anything of the sort turns up?"

"You can, Mr. Green," Tott said with a sort of acrid solemnity. "But I'm perfectly certain I shall not discover anything whatever. You see, you had two years in the police force."

"Sorry I had to leave, Inspector. Too much discipline, you know. I'm naturally Bohemian—by instinct, as one might say. But that's got nothing to do with the balance of Denghisovski's fund."

"As far as that's concerned," Tott said shortly, "you know as well as I do that whatever there is would be confiscated if it were located, and neither you nor I nor anyone concerned would get a smell at it. That's a nice car you're running, by the way."

"Yes, my father admired my taste, yesterday. The best there is. It pays to keep in with one's father, I find—he'll dine me well, to-night. Pass that cheque on and keep my name out of it, please, Inspector. I'd rather get my notoriety out of my cases, if any. See you again soon, I hope."

"But not at your office," Tott responded darkly.

"As you like. It's only two guineas on the old expense account. I think I'll walk out, this time—you needn't call a man. Good afternoon, Inspector."

He walked out. Tott sat reflecting, and frowning. "Blast his nerve!" he said at last. But he knew that he could not do it.

On the grounds that the Rolls-Bentley wanted exercise, and he himself felt like a spot of west-country ribaldry, Gees went to Devonshire on the Saturday of that week, returning to London on the Monday. He walked in on Miss Brandon just after she had returned from lunch.

"Now, Miss Brandon, we've got to get to work. If we can find any to get to, that is. What have you at your end of the table?"

"There are over thirty inquiries addressed to the firm," she answered. "I've opened them, and am ready to go through them with you. And here is one letter addressed to you personally."

"Umph!" He took the letter, looked at the Swiss stamp and Montreux postmark, and then at the fine, neat handwriting. "That, I think, will be from Miss Lenoir. If she wants me to disgorge our ill-gotten gains, she's got another want coming."

He opened the envelope and took out the letter. But, when he had read only two or three lines, his expression changed.

"I'll just study this for a bit, Miss Brandon, and then come and deal with the others. It won't take me long."

He went back to his own room, and sat down at his desk to read: there was no address at the head of the letter, no date, and no preamble of the usual type:

You may think that I ought not to write as I mean to do, but you are responsible for so much. For having taken away the courage you told me I had, and then having given it back. The Left has disowned me, and regards me as of so little importance that no action will be taken against me. I have a post as companion-secretary to an old man here, an easy post.

Until I came to England this last time, the greatest thing in my life and the most terrible was my father's death. It gave me hate as a driving force. Now there is a greater thing, not terrible at all, and the driving force is the exact reverse of hate. I have so far changed as to wish to put that no more plainly. Do I make myself clear to you? I have never written a letter like this before. I shall never write one like it again.

I read the account of the trial, and so know all that you did. They—and I with them—would have changed the world with a stroke, but I see now that changing the world is not the work of any one man or body of men, nor must it be done by violence. It must be the work of all men, of all classes of men, working together for the good of all. Thus greatly am I changed.

I want to learn your way of living, to find out how it is that you find so much cause for laughter in life. Being a woman, I want too to keep the beauty you told me I had, and the little, baseless hope that some day I may have need of it. To keep it unsoiled by even the slightest touch, and to make it—if that be possible—a casket for something better than the Christine you knew.

We saw and knew each other only for a very little time. I know now that I did not really know you at all until after I had left you. These weeks of returning courage, of increasing sight, and even of—please believe it—prayer. Not for myself, except that I may have so much strength and courage as to ask nothing else. Bound by gold chains—perhaps you know the quotation.

One other quotation. I do not know who wrote it, nor where I heard or saw it first, but have known it a long time. I would have you see me as I stood alone on the veranda here yesterday evening and watched while the peaks glowed, many-coloured in the last of the sunlight on their snow, though down here was darkness. I said it then. Listen, but quite closely, or you will not hear:

> "This I know, thy memory will linger
> And echo through my days,
> Like some sweet song, in half-heard minor quivering
> Down old, forgotten ways."

I have never written a letter like this before. I shall never write one like it again. If forgiveness means forgetting, do not forgive me.

Some ten minutes or more after he had finished reading, Gees refolded the letter and put it in its envelope. He stood up, and placed the envelope in his pocket.

" '—in half-heard minor quivering—' " he repeated to himself, but so softly that one would have had to listen very closely to hear the words. Then he went back to Miss Brandon's room.

"Now we'll get busy," he told her. "Bring forth the correspondence, and we'll see how many two guineases we can swindle out of people."

"Four or five of the letters look interesting," she said, and took down the full tray, labelled "In."

"Cash is what we're after, Miss Brandon, far more than interest. That Swiss letter, by the way, was from Miss Lenoir."

"Yes?" She glanced at him, only momentarily. If he did ask again whether he might kiss her, she was quite certain she would say no. A most decided no. NO, in fact.

But he did not ask.

"Yes," he said. "She wrote to ask me not to forgive her. I won't. Pass out the top letter there, and we'll take 'em as they come."

THE END

Gees will return *in Nightmare Farm* (1937), *Grey Shapes* (1938), *The Ninth Life* (1939) *and The Glass Too Many* (1940), published by Ramble House.

# RAMBLE HOUSE's

## HARRY STEPHEN KEELER WEBWORK MYSTERIES

(RH) indicates the title is available ONLY in the RAMBLE HOUSE edition

The Ace of Spades Murder
The Affair of the Bottled Deuce (RH)
The Amazing Web
The Barking Clock
Behind That Mask
The Book with the Orange Leaves
The Bottle with the Green Wax Seal
The Box from Japan
The Case of the Canny Killer
The Case of the Crazy Corpse (RH)
The Case of the Flying Hands (RH)
The Case of the Ivory Arrow
The Case of the Jeweled Ragpicker
The Case of the Lavender Gripsack
The Case of the Mysterious Moll
The Case of the 16 Beans
The Case of the Transparent Nude (RH)
The Case of the Transposed Legs
The Case of the Two-Headed Idiot (RH)
The Case of the Two Strange Ladies
The Circus Stealers (RH)
Cleopatra's Tears
A Copy of Beowulf (RH)
The Crimson Cube (RH)
The Face of the Man From Saturn
Find the Clock
The Five Silver Buddhas
The 4th King
The Gallows Waits, My Lord! (RH)
The Green Jade Hand
Finger! Finger!
Hangman's Nights (RH)
I, Chameleon (RH)
I Killed Lincoln at 10:13! (RH)
The Iron Ring
The Man Who Changed His Skin (RH)
The Man with the Crimson Box
The Man with the Magic Eardrums
The Man with the Wooden Spectacles
The Marceau Case
The Matilda Hunter Murder
The Monocled Monster

The Murder of London Lew
The Murdered Mathematician
The Mysterious Card (RH)
The Mysterious Ivory Ball of Wong Shing Li (RH)
The Mystery of the Fiddling Cracksman
The Peacock Fan
The Photo of Lady X (RH)
The Portrait of Jirjohn Cobb
Report on Vanessa Hewstone (RH)
Riddle of the Travelling Skull
Riddle of the Wooden Parrakeet (RH)
The Scarlet Mummy (RH)
The Search for X-Y-Z
The Sharkskin Book
Sing Sing Nights
The Six From Nowhere (RH)
The Skull of the Waltzing Clown
The Spectacles of Mr. Cagliostro
Stand By—London Calling!
The Steeltown Strangler
The Stolen Gravestone (RH)
Strange Journey (RH)
The Strange Will
The Straw Hat Murders (RH)
The Street of 1000 Eyes (RH)
Thieves' Nights
Three Novellos (RH)
The Tiger Snake
The Trap (RH)
Vagabond Nights (Defrauded Yeggman)
Vagabond Nights 2 (10 Hours)
The Vanishing Gold Truck
The Voice of the Seven Sparrows
The Washington Square Enigma
When Thief Meets Thief
The White Circle (RH)
The Wonderful Scheme of Mr. Christopher Thorne
X. Jones—of Scotland Yard
Y. Cheung, Business Detective

## Keeler Related Works

**A To Izzard: A Harry Stephen Keeler Companion** by Fender Tucker — Articles and stories about Harry, by Harry, and in his style. Included is a compleat bibliography.

**Wild About Harry: Reviews of Keeler Novels** — Edited by Richard Polt & Fender Tucker — 22 reviews of works by Harry Stephen Keeler from *Keeler News*. A perfect introduction to the author.

**The Keeler Keyhole Collection:** Annotated newsletter rants from Harry Stephen Keeler, edited by Francis M. Nevins. Over 400 pages of incredibly personal Keeleriana.

**Fakealoo** — Pastiches of the style of Harry Stephen Keeler by selected demented members of the HSK Society. Updated every year with the new winner.

# RAMBLE HOUSE's OTHER LOONS

**The End of It All and Other Stories** — Ed Gorman's latest short story collection

**Four Dancing Tuatara Press Books** — *Beast or Man?* By Sean M'Guire; *The Whistling Ancestors* by Richard E. Goddard; *The Shadow on the House* and *Sorcerer's Chessmen* by Mark Hansom. With introductions by John Pelan

**The Dumpling** — Political murder from 1907 by Coulson Kernahan

**Victims & Villains** — Intriguing Sherlockiana from Derham Groves

**Evidence in Blue** — 1938 mystery by E. Charles Vivian

**The Case of the Little Green Men** — Mack Reynolds wrote this love song to sci-fi fans back in 1951 and it's now back in print.

**Hell Fire** — A new hard-boiled novel by Jack Moskovitz about an arsonist, an arson cop and a Nazi hooker. It isn't pretty.

**Researching American-Made Toy Soldiers** — A 276-page collection of a lifetime of articles by toy soldier expert Richard O'Brien

**Strands of the Web: Short Stories of Harry Stephen Keeler** — Edited and Introduced by Fred Cleaver

**The Sam McCain Novels** — Ed Gorman's terrific series includes *The Day the Music Died, Wake Up Little Susie* and *Will You Still Love Me Tomorrow?*

**A Shot Rang Out** — Three decades of reviews from Jon Breen

**Mysterious Martin, the Master of Murder** — Two versions of a strange 1912 novel by Tod Robbins about a man who writes books that can kill.

**Dago Red** — 22 tales of dark suspense by Bill Pronzini

**The Night Remembers** — A 1991 Jack Walsh mystery from Ed Gorman

**Rough Cut & New, Improved Murder** — Ed Gorman's first two novels

**Hollywood Dreams** — A novel of the Depression by Richard O'Brien

**Seven Gelett Burgess Novels** — *The Master of Mysteries, The White Cat, Two O'Clock Courage, Ladies in Boxes, Find the Woman, The Heart Line, The Picaroons*

**The Organ Reader** — A huge compilation of just about everything published in the 1971-1972 radical bay-area newspaper, THE ORGAN.

**A Clear Path to Cross** — Sharon Knowles short mystery stories by Ed Lynskey

**Old Times' Sake** — Short stories by James Reasoner from Mike Shayne Magazine

**Freaks and Fantasies** — Eerie tales by Tod Robbins, collaborator of Tod Browning on the film FREAKS.

**Seven Jim Harmon Double Novels** — *Vixen Hollow/Celluloid Scandal, The Man Who Made Maniacs/Silent Siren, Ape Rape/Wanton Witch, Sex Burns Like Fire/Twist Session, Sudden Lust/Passion Strip, Sin Unlimited/Harlot Master, Twilight Girls/Sex Institution.* Written in the early 60s.

**Marblehead: A Novel of H.P. Lovecraft** — A long-lost masterpiece from Richard A. Lupoff. Published for the first time!

**The Compleat Ova Hamlet** — Parodies of SF authors by Richard A. Lupoff – A brand new edition with more stories and more illustrations by Trina Robbins.

**The Secret Adventures of Sherlock Holmes** — Three Sherlockian pastiches by the Brooklyn author/publisher, Gary Lovisi.

**The Universal Holmes** — Richard A. Lupoff's 2007 collection of five Holmesian pastiches and a recipe for giant rat stew.

**Four Joel Townsley Rogers Novels** — By the author of *The Red Right Hand: Once In a Red Moon, Lady With the Dice, The Stopped Clock, Never Leave My Bed*

**Two Joel Townsley Rogers Story Collections** — Night of Horror and Killing Time

**Twenty Norman Berrow Novels** — *The Bishop's Sword, Ghost House, Don't Go Out After Dark, Claws of the Cougar, The Smokers of Hashish, The Secret Dancer, Don't Jump Mr. Boland!, The Footprints of Satan, Fingers for Ransom, The Three Tiers of Fantasy, The Spaniard's Thumb, The Eleventh Plague, Words Have Wings, One Thrilling Night, The Lady's in Danger, It Howls at Night, The Terror in the Fog, Oil Under the Window, Murder in the Melody, The Singing Room*

**The N. R. De Mexico Novels** — Robert Bragg presents *Marijuana Girl, Madman on a Drum, Private Chauffeur* in one volume.

**Four Chelsea Quinn Yarbro Novels featuring Charlie Moon** — *Ogilvie, Tallant and Moon, Music When the Sweet Voice Dies, Poisonous Fruit* and *Dead Mice*

**Five Walter S. Masterman Mysteries** — *The Green Toad, The Flying Beast, The Yellow Mistletoe, The Wrong Verdict* and *The Perjured Alibi.* Fantastic impossible plots.

**Two Hake Talbot Novels** — *Rim of the Pit, The Hangman's Handyman.* Classic locked room mysteries.

**Two Alexander Laing Novels** — *The Motives of Nicholas Holtz* and *Dr. Scarlett,* stories of medical mayhem and intrigue from the 30s.

**Four David Hume Novels** — *Corpses Never Argue, Cemetery First Stop, Make Way for the Mourners, Eternity Here I Come*, and more to come.

**Three Wade Wright Novels** — *Echo of Fear, Death At Nostalgia Street* and *It Leads to Murder*, with more to come!

**Eight Rupert Penny Novels** — *Policeman's Holiday, Policeman's Evidence, Lucky Policeman, Policeman in Armour, Sealed Room Murder, Sweet Poison, The Talkative Policeman, She had to Have Gas* and *Cut and Run* (by Martin Tanner.)

**Five Jack Mann Novels** — Strange murder in the English countryside. *Gees' First Case, Nightmare Farm, Grey Shapes, The Ninth Life, The Glass Too Many.*

**Seven Max Afford Novels** — *Owl of Darkness, Death's Mannikins, Blood on His Hands, The Dead Are Blind, The Sheep and the Wolves, Sinners in Paradise* and *Two Locked Room Mysteries and a Ripping Yarn* by one of Australia's finest novelists.

**Five Joseph Shallit Novels** — *The Case of the Billion Dollar Body, Lady Don't Die on My Doorstep, Kiss the Killer, Yell Bloody Murder, Take Your Last Look.* One of America's best 50's authors.

**Two Crimson Clown Novels** — By Johnston McCulley, author of the Zorro novels, *The Crimson Clown* and *The Crimson Clown Again.*

**The Best of 10-Story Book** — edited by Chris Mikul, over 35 stories from the literary magazine Harry Stephen Keeler edited.

**A Young Man's Heart** — A forgotten early classic by Cornell Woolrich

**The Anthony Boucher Chronicles** — edited by Francis M. Nevins
Book reviews by Anthony Boucher written for the *San Francisco Chronicle,* 1942 – 1947. Essential and fascinating reading.

**Muddled Mind:** Complete Works of Ed Wood, Jr. — David Hayes and Hayden Davis deconstruct the life and works of a mad genius.

**Gadsby** — A lipogram (a novel without the letter E). Ernest Vincent Wright's last work, published in 1939 right before his death.

**My First Time:** The One Experience You Never Forget — Michael Birchwood — 64 true first-person narratives of how they lost it.

**A Roland Daniel Double: The Signal and The Return of Wu** Fang — Classic thrillers from the 30s

**Murder in Shawnee** — Two novels of the Alleghenies by John Douglas: *Shawnee Alley Fire* and *Haunts.*

**Deep Space and other Stories** — A collection of SF gems by Richard A. Lupoff

**Blood Moon** — The first of the Robert Payne series by Ed Gorman

**The Time Armada** — Fox B. Holden's 1953 SF gem.

**Black River Falls** — Suspense from the master, Ed Gorman

**Sideslip** — 1968 SF masterpiece by Ted White and Dave Van Arnam

**The Triune Man** — Mindscrambling science fiction from Richard A. Lupoff

**Detective Duff Unravels It** — Episodic mysteries by Harvey O'Higgins

**Automaton** — Brilliant treatise on robotics: 1928-style! By H. Stafford Hatfield

**The Incredible Adventures of Rowland Hern** — Rousing 1928 impossible crimes by Nicholas Olde.

**Slammer Days** — Two full-length prison memoirs: *Men into Beasts* (1952) by George Sylvester Viereck and *Home Away From Home* (1962) by Jack Woodford

**Murder in Black and White** — 1931 classic tennis whodunit by Evelyn Elder

**Killer's Caress** — Cary Moran's 1936 hardboiled thriller

**The Golden Dagger** — 1951 Scotland Yard yarn by E. R. Punshon

**A Smell of Smoke** — 1951 English countryside thriller by Miles Burton

**Ruled By Radio** — 1925 futuristic novel by Robert L. Hadfield & Frank E. Farncombe

**Murder in Silk** — A 1937 Yellow Peril novel of the silk trade by Ralph Trevor

**The Case of the Withered Hand** — 1936 potboiler by John G. Brandon

**Finger-prints Never Lie** — A 1939 classic detective novel by John G. Brandon

**Inclination to Murder** — 1966 thriller by New Zealand's Harriet Hunter

**Invaders from the Dark** — Classic werewolf tale from Greye La Spina

**Fatal Accident** — Murder by automobile, a 1936 mystery by Cecil M. Wills

**The Devil Drives** — A prison and lost treasure novel by Virgil Markham

**Dr. Odin** — Douglas Newton's 1933 potboiler comes back to life.

**The Chinese Jar Mystery** — Murder in the manor by John Stephen Strange, 1934

**The Julius Caesar Murder Case** — A classic 1935 re-telling of the assassination by Wallace Irwin that's much more fun than the Shakespeare version

**West Texas War and Other Western Stories** — by Gary Lovisi

**The Contested Earth and Other SF Stories** — A never-before published space opera and seven short stories by Jim Harmon.

**Tales of the Macabre and Ordinary** — Modern twisted horror by Chris Mikul, author of the *Bizarrism* series.

**The Gold Star Line** — Seaboard adventure from L.T. Reade and Robert Eustace.

**The Werewolf vs the Vampire Woman** — Hard to believe ultraviolence by either Arthur M. Scarm or Arthur M. Scram.

**Black Hogan Strikes Again** — Australia's Peter Renwick pens a tale of the outback.

**Don Diablo: Book of a Lost Film** — Two-volume treatment of a western by Paul Landres, with diagrams. Intro by Francis M. Nevins.

**The Charlie Chaplin Murder Mystery** — Movie hijinks by Wes D. Gehring

**The Koky Comics** — A collection of all of the 1978-1981 Sunday and daily comic strips by Richard O'Brien and Mort Gerberg, in two volumes.

**Suzy** — Another collection of comic strips from Richard O'Brien and Bob Vojtko

**Dime Novels: Ramble House's 10-Cent Books** — *Knife in the Dark* by Robert Leslie Bellem, *Hot Lead* and *Song of Death* by Ed Earl Repp, *A Hashish House in New York* by H.H. Kane, and five more.

**Blood in a Snap** — The *Finnegan's Wake* of the 21st century, by Jim Weiler

**Stakeout on Millennium Drive** — Award-winning Indianapolis Noir — Ian Woollen.

**Dope Tales #1** — Two dope-riddled classics; *Dope Runners* by Gerald Grantham and *Death Takes the Joystick* by Phillip Condé.

**Dope Tales #2** — Two more narco-classics; *The Invisible Hand* by Rex Dark and *The Smokers of Hashish* by Norman Berrow.

**Dope Tales #3** — Two enchanting novels of opium by the master, Sax Rohmer. *Dope* and *The Yellow Claw.*

**Tenebrae** — Ernest G. Henham's 1898 horror tale brought back.

**The Singular Problem of the Stygian House-Boat** — Two classic tales by John Kendrick Bangs about the denizens of Hades.

**Tiresias** — Psychotic modern horror novel by Jonathan M. Sweet.

**The One After Snelling** — Kickass modern noir from Richard O'Brien.

**The Sign of the Scorpion** — 1935 Edmund Snell tale of oriental evil.

**The House of the Vampire** — 1907 poetic thriller by George S. Viereck.

**An Angel in the Street** — Modern hardboiled noir by Peter Genovese.

**The Devil's Mistress** — Scottish gothic tale by J. W. Brodie-Innes.

**The Lord of Terror** — 1925 mystery with master-criminal, Fantômas.

**The Lady of the Terraces** — 1925 adventure by E. Charles Vivian.

**My Deadly Angel** — 1955 Cold War drama by John Chelton.

**Prose Bowl** — Futuristic satire — Bill Pronzini & Barry N. Malzberg .

**Satan's Den Exposed** — True crime in Truth or Consequences New Mexico — Award-winning journalism by the *Desert Journal*.

**The Amorous Intrigues & Adventures of Aaron Burr** — by Anonymous — Hot historical action.

**I Stole $16,000,000** — A true story by cracksman Herbert E. Wilson.

**The Black Dark Murders** — Vintage 50s college murder yarn by Milt Ozaki, writing as Robert O. Saber.

**Sex Slave** — Potboiler of lust in the days of Cleopatra — Dion Leclerq.

**You'll Die Laughing** — Bruce Elliott's 1945 novel of murder at a practical joker's English countryside manor.

**The Private Journal & Diary of John H. Surratt** — The memoirs of the man who conspired to assassinate President Lincoln.

**Dead Man Talks Too Much** — Hollywood boozer by Weed Dickenson

**Red Light** — History of legal prostitution in Shreveport Louisiana by Eric Brock. Includes wonderful photos of the houses and the ladies.

**A Snark Selection** — Lewis Carroll's *The Hunting of the Snark* with two Snarkian chapters by Harry Stephen Keeler — Illustrated by Gavin L. O'Keefe.

**Ripped from the Headlines!** — The Jack the Ripper story as told in the newspaper articles in the *New York* and *London Times*.

**Geronimo** — S. M. Barrett's 1905 autobiography of a noble American.

**The White Peril in the Far East** — Sidney Lewis Gulick's 1905 indictment of the West and assurance that Japan would never attack the U.S.

**The Compleat Calhoon** — All of Fender Tucker's works: Includes *Totah Six-Pack, Weed, Women and Song* and *Tales from the Tower,* plus a CD of all of his songs.

**Totah Six-Pack** — Just Fender Tucker's six tales about Farmington in one sleek volume.

## RAMBLE HOUSE
Fender Tucker, Prop.
www.ramblehouse.com    fender@ramblehouse.com
228-826-1783   10329 Sheephead Drive, Vancleave MS 39565

Made in the USA
Monee, IL
10 December 2022

20560761R00125